A Hope Divided

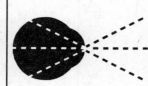

This Large Print Book carries the
Seal of Approval of N.A.V.H.

A HOPE DIVIDED

ALYSSA COLE

THORNDIKE PRESS
A part of Gale, a Cengage Company

GALE
A Cengage Company

Farmington Hills, Mich • San Francisco • New York • Waterville, Maine
Meriden, Conn • Mason, Ohio • Chicago

Thorndike Press® Large Print African-American.
The text of this Large Print edition is unabridged.
Other aspects of the book may vary from the original edition.
Set in 16 pt. Plantin.

LIBRARY OF CONGRESS CIP DATA ON FILE.
CATALOGUING IN PUBLICATION FOR THIS BOOK
IS AVAILABLE FROM THE LIBRARY OF CONGRESS

ISBN-13: 978-1-4328-4566-7 (hardcover)
ISBN-10: 1-4328-4566-7 (hardcover)

Published in 2018 by arrangement with Kensington Books, an imprint
of Kensington Publishing Corp.

Printed in the United States of America
1 2 3 4 5 6 7 22 21 20 19 18

*Dedicated to all those who hope
when it seems only a fool would dare to.
Be foolish.*

PROLOGUE

Western North Carolina, 1853

Marlie sat too close to her mother on the bench seat of their dilapidated buggy as it jumped along the rocky dirt road. There wasn't a chill in the spring air, but she snaked her arm through her mother's and settled closer to her. She glanced up at her, feeling the mix of awe and envy that had always been inseparable from her love for the woman. Vivienne sat straight-backed and regal with the reins draped loosely over her palms. Her long braids were bound by a length of white fabric, and her smooth, dark skin was radiant in the late afternoon sun.

Her mother sighed and leaned into the embrace, and Marlie felt an unbidden press of tears behind her eyes. She blinked them away. She was too old for such behavior — almost thirteen — but she'd been unsettled all morning. The strange dream she'd had the previous night had draped over her like

7

a thin caul of sorrow, slowing her down as she got the water from the well, gathered the eggs from the henhouse, and performed the rest of her morning tasks. She'd waited for her maman to ask her about her dream, as she did most every morning, but Vivienne had been tight-lipped and broody when Marlie pulled aside the curtain and walked into the portion of their cabin that served as her mother's mixing room. Marlie hadn't pushed for a divination but had sat silently at her mother's side, passing her the dried plants, grinding stone, and other implements she needed to ply her craft.

Their craft.

They'd gone about their morning work as usual, but everything had felt off to Marlie, as if she were acting out a play for an audience she couldn't see. She'd been glad when they left the house to make a call that afternoon, hoping that a change of scenery would buoy her mood.

Instead, her sense of unease had only grown; the road was familiar, but every bend in it seemed to hold the possibility of some catastrophe. She hugged her mother's arm a bit closer and felt the deep sigh against her side before she heard her mother exhale it.

"Easy, Silas," Vivienne said, pulling on the reins.

The mule pulled up to a stop in front of Lavonia Burgess's small, neat house, one that made their simple shack look like so much plywood. Lavonia was a free Negro, like Marlie and her mother, but she made her living as a domestic, earning a better wage. She also didn't give away her services, like Vivienne always did.

"Should I let people suffer, if they have no money?"

It chafed Marlie that her mother was so kind to people who only visited when they needed her specific services, but Vivienne was right. Many of her customers were slaves visiting from nearby plantations to have their aches and pains tended to, and often their spirits, too; helping them was a small price to pay when you were already free.

"Cal stopped by my place earlier," Vivienne said as she walked into the front door and set her bag on the floor. "Boy said you was feeling your years today and needed my help. Is it your joints again?" The faint accent of the French she'd spoken on the island of her birth gave her words an enigmatic air, although she was mystery enough even when she was silent.

"Feeling my years? I bet you older than me, Miss Viv," Lavonia said with a cackle. The woman was aged, but not ancient. She was wrapped up in blankets, and a smile broke through the pained expression on her face. "I jus' don't got those witchy woman powers like you to keep me lookin' young and lovely. They say you two-facers don't age like reglar folk."

Vivienne simply smiled, the kind of smile that reminded Marlie of a cat stretching lazily in a bit of sunlight — just before it snatched your last bit of tripe and was out the door like a shot.

Lavonia cleared her throat. "It's not the rheumatics today. My stomach been botherin' me something awful." She paused. "I thought maybe it was something I ate, but it's mighty strange that ever since Jane Woods accused me of cozying up to her husband after Sunday worship, I been feeling sick as a dog."

"Mighty strange," Vivienne echoed. "Marlie, put on some water and make up a tisane for stomach troubles."

"She got the gift, too?" Lavonia looked over at Marlie and couldn't hide her slight shudder. "I shoulda figured with them eyes of hers."

Marlie grabbed the satchel and hurried to

10

the kitchen. The glass bottles of ingredients she pulled out reflected the sight she usually avoided: one normal brown eye, and one strange hazel green one that made people do the sign of the cross when she walked by them. Some people said it meant she could divine the future; after the dream she'd had, Marlie hoped they were wrong.

She set a pot of water to boiling, then pulled out a gnarled bit of pokeroot and whittled some pieces into the water. She uncorked another bottle and carefully poured out a dram of pine sap, and pinched up some Epsom salt from another. She stirred carefully, pretending to ignore the murmur of voices in the other room.

"You don't carry John the Conqueror?" Vivienne asked in a censuring tone.

"I'm a Christian woman," Lavonia said haughtily, then sighed. "I lost mine a few weeks back."

Marlie crept back into the room and searched for one of the dried roots in the satchel before her mother could ask. She handed the wrinkly oblong that was known to be a source of protection over to her mother and then sat behind her, already knowing what would be said.

"Sprinkle mustard seeds at your door every night. If the one who throwed at you come

here, don't let her inside. If you think she gonna try to hurt you again, toss salt after her every time she leaves her gate. After nine times, she'll leave you be because she'll be moving on to another town."

Marlie watched the way Lavonia's expression hardened as she listened and she knew what question was coming. "Can you —"

"I don't throw," Vivienne said, her voice low but firm. "I'll help protect you, break whatever roots she laid on you, but throwing ain't what I'm offering. Now take this and don't lose it this time."

Lavonia nodded, chastened, and as Vivienne dropped the root into the woman's palm, Marlie gasped. The world seemed to slow and blur, and then come back into clarity as reality overlaid a memory that she shouldn't have already had.

That happened in my dream.

It had. Every detail, down to the way the brown lines in Lavonia's palm crinkled as she closed her hand around the John the Conqueror. The unsettling caul of the dreamworld tightened over Marlie, sending her mind whirling. If that had been in her dream, and that part had come true, then . . .

"Take that tisane off the flame, *chérie,*" her mother said, turning to her. "We must

12

get home."

The ride back was silent, but not comfortable. There was a space between them on the bench now, as though Marlie's fears had taken a seat beside her. Marlie wished her mother would say something, anything.

"Yah, Silas," Vivienne murmured, leaning forward to shake the reins as she urged their mule onward. Darkness came swift on the mountain road, but Marlie could see that her mother's teeth were clenched tight when Vivienne leaned back and continued silently staring ahead of her.

"Maman, I —" The words died in her throat as they turned the bend in the road that led to the home she had always known.

The carriage parked in front was just as elegant as it had been in her dream, the horses just as large and muscled. In the dream, the cab had been empty, but had radiated a sensation of heartbreaking loss that had left her shattered and sobbing as she awoke. In real life, a driver jumped down and opened the door to the cab, and a young woman stepped out. A white young woman. Not many white folk came to Vivienne's house — they didn't understand her talent, and thought it dangerous. But this woman looked familiar even though she hadn't been in the dream.

Her black dress was clean and beautiful, simple, but obviously made of expensive fabric. It was probably soft against her skin, unlike the rough homespun Marlie was used to wearing. Her dark hair was pulled back into a sleek bun, held in place by shiny hairpins. Her lips were pressed together into a blanched line of determination, but her eyes showed her distress.

Marlie felt her world shift under her feet as the woman stepped down from the buggy. She threw an arm over Silas for support and stared, unable to look away from their visitor's eyes: two hazel green eyes that matched Marlie's single one. And the woman's ears stuck out too much, one higher than the other, a trait that had always embarrassed Marlie and that Vivienne said she'd inherited from her father. That was about the only thing Marlie knew about the man, but she had a feeling she was about to learn more.

"Been a long time, Sarah," Vivienne said. If she was surprised by their guest, she didn't show it. "I ain't seen you since you was a knock-kneed little girl."

Vivienne's expression softened, for just a moment, and Marlie imagined what her mother would have looked like when she was younger and even more beautiful. Marlie knew her mother had been a house slave. Had she cared for this woman as a child? Laughed and played with her, as she eventually had with Marlie?

Marlie hugged Silas tighter, feeling the calm, even thud of the beast's heart against her side. She was too scared to look at her mother. She already knew what was coming, could already feel the aching pull of her impending loss.

"Father is dead," the young woman said. Her lip trembled a bit. "Mother has gone to our holdings in Philadelphia, to live with her sister. I would have come sooner, but I discovered your letters only recently. And I agree with you. Marlie is a Lynch, and she should receive all the advantages that name can offer to . . . someone like her. You should have been offered more, too, after the — the misunderstanding between you and —" The woman struggled for words and her face reddened. "Father was wrong to send you away as he did."

"I got my freedom and hers. It's more than I would have had if I stayed." Vivienne's voice was sharp, and Sarah ducked her head as if she'd been chastised.

"Things are different at Lynchwood now," she said. "I'm seeing to it that the remainder of our slaves are given their freedom."

"And Stephen?" Vivienne asked.

"My brother is in Mississippi, with his wife," Sarah said. "I'm sure he'll agree with this decision, as he has with the other changes I've put in place. It doesn't matter what he thinks, in the end. I'll do right by her." She glanced at Marlie, and her expression softened. "I should have sent word ahead, but I just got the notion to come. I'm sorry."

"No need for sorries." Vivienne's hand was on Marlie's shoulder, suddenly, pulling her away from Silas and turning the girl to face her.

"Now, I know you're gonna be mad at me," she said. Marlie stared at the ground. She felt an anger so hot burning in her that she thought she might combust on the spot, taking her mother and Silas — everything she loved most — with her. But her mother's tears, rare as a unicorn's horn, doused those flames. The moon was rising, bright and full, and the tears shone silver in the moonlight as they tracked down her smooth, dark cheeks.

"Full moon means a parting of ways," Marlie said in a shaky voice when she finally met her mother's gaze. "I don't wanna go, Maman!" She threw her arms around Vivienne's slight figure and hugged her tight.

Vivienne hugged her back, and Marlie felt something close to weakness in a woman who'd only ever been strong. It frightened her. "I want you to have a better life than this: being the neighborhood root woman, only good for breaking a fix or getting rid of warts."

"Ain't nothing wrong with helping people," Marlie said stubbornly. "You always tell me that."

Her mother laughed low. *"C'est vrai.* But there are many ways to help people, and you're meant for something more. I know it. But that can't happen if you're stuck in the middle of nowhere, digging up roots. This is what's meant to be, *chérie."*

"Why can't you come with me?" she asked. "She'd let you, I bet. If you just asked."

"The people here need me, Marlie. And I can't go back to that place — it was no good for me. But it'll be different for you."

Marlie didn't know how long she held her mother. Didn't know how long she cried, or what she threw into her bag as she stumbled blindly around the house she'd spent all her life in.

"You're my family," Marlie said when she was finally able to speak. Her bags had been stowed and Sarah waited in the carriage.

"She is, too," Vivienne said. "And you're worth every bit as much as her and any of them Lynches. Never forget that."

"What if I poison her and come back?" Marlie asked darkly, desperation gripping her. She couldn't leave, just like that. It was all happening too quickly. "I can. I know things you didn't teach me."

Vivienne fixed her with a stare that made the hair on Marlie's arms stand up. "I raised you better than that. Now you can spend this last minute sulking and making threats you're too good to act on, or you can come here and hug your maman before she lets you go."

Marlie leapt into one more embrace, one that ended too quickly. Then she climbed into the carriage, smelling of dust and mule as she sat tongue-tied across from the woman who shared her eyes and her ears and her blood.

She clutched the John the Conqueror her mother had given her, hard, and wished for strength.

CHAPTER 1

Randolph County, North Carolina, April 1863
Somewhere outside of the prison walls, a
Kentucky Warbler chirruped, reminding
Ewan McCall of days spent searching for
flashes of brilliant yellow plumage in the
underbrush near his family's home. He
wasn't a man prone to nostalgia, but the
sound stirred something in him before it
was lost amidst the racket of hammer meeting metal and men shouting as they worked.

Ewan pulled his thin jacket, a poor barter
for a pair of shoes he'd purchased from a
guard, closer around him in the chill afternoon air. Some of the prisoners longed for
the warmth of late spring to arrive, but after
his bids at Libby, Castle Thunder, and Flor-
ence during the warmer months, Ewan
didn't count himself among them. Fleas and
other vermin reveled in the sun's warmth
like contented picnic goers; he didn't relish
the thought of what the prison would be

19

like when the first heat wave hit.

He didn't intend to be around to find out.

He rubbed his hands together and watched as prisoners laid pieces of curved metal over the creek that traversed the prison grounds; officers and infantrymen were lined up along the creek, some referring to the plans Ewan had sketched, others running back and forth carrying supplies. The project had given the men something to keep themselves occupied and, more importantly, it would benefit the prison population. The water source had served a number of uses for the thousand or so men in the camp, Union soldier and Rebel deserter alike, turning it into a source of disease. That would change now.

"Make sure the pieces are aligned correctly here," Ewan said, kneeling beside a sallow-skinned man who struggled with a wrench. "There should be an opening to allow for outflow when there's heavy rain."

The man nodded, clearly not as invested in the outcome as Ewan but, like most soldiers, willing to follow orders.

Warden Dilford walked up and stood beside them, gaze jumping anxiously between Ewan and the work being done. The man had come to Randolph around the same time as Ewan, and after four months of command still hadn't acclimated to his position of power. Given what most men did with power when they hadn't worked overmuch for it, Ewan was glad of that.

"So, because the prisoners will no longer be able to pollute the stream with their various, er, bodily functions, there will be fewer outbreaks of sickness and fewer deaths."

Dilford spoke slowly, making sure he understood Ewan's earlier explanation thoroughly, likely because he would soon be passing it off as his own idea. That was fine by Ewan. If Dilford claiming the idea meant it would be utilized at other prisons, all the better. Ewan had no need of glory; he was quite comfortable on the margins of life, observing. He also had other, more pressing reasons for avoiding attention.

"Yes, that's exactly it, Warden." Ewan stood, his gaze still fixed on the work, tracking the placement of rivets and nails. The small details were the only things one really had control over, though most men overlooked them in search of some grand purpose. Fools. Ewan knew that true power resided in life's minutiae, like exactly how far back a finger could bend before breaking or how much pain a man could take before he forgot about loving Jefferson Davis, the Confederacy, and even his own mother. But Ewan was in prison now, free from the kind of details that had become his field of study since the War Between the States had commenced.

A burst of noise erupted from a group of officers as they haggled over a small shovel with a soldier clad in a threadbare shirt. Ewan was surprised to see them clamoring for such base work. They lived in the nicer — relatively — clapboard accommodations instead of a patched-together tent like Ewan's, and generally avoided the lower ranking men. Ewan wasn't a lower ranking man, of course, but they wouldn't have known that. Ewan had gone to some pains to ensure that no one would.

Ewan noticed a fellow Union man from Ohio holding his hammer incorrectly as he battered at a nail, but ignored the itch to correct him. One need only worry about one's own faults, and Ewan had plenty to think on. The men at Randolph felt they didn't belong there, and with good reason, as they were generally imprisoned for the crime of fighting for the Union. That was one of the many differences between Ewan and his fellow inmates. He *did* belong there, and for the same reason.

When he'd enlisted, everyone had thought his reserved, peculiar nature meant he'd make a terrible soldier. They'd been correct. However, he'd quickly been given an assignment that made use of his attention to detail and his unbending sense of logic. Logic could be applied to all kinds of situations, and not all of them pleasant.

"You're a middling soldier, McCall, but it appears you can be of assistance to the Union in another way. . . ."

He scrubbed his fingers through the itchy auburn scruff that he still hadn't acclimated to. A daily shave had been sacrosanct before his capture, but the beard kept him warm in the Carolina winter — and unrecognizable to any Rebs he might have interrogated before his capture.

"The spigots along the sides will allow prisoners access to the water for drinking, washing, and cooking, but the metal laid over the creek will cut down on the detritus," Ewan explained to Dilford again, "as will the mesh over the opening of the pipe's entrance through the stockade. That will have to be cleaned, daily if possible."

"Detritus. Right. We can get the Negro workers to do that when they come clean the officers' quarters and the latrines," Dilford said.

"The slaves," Ewan corrected. "The term 'worker' implies that payment is provided to them for their services. It is not."

Ewan had learned to rein in the impulse for correction when in general company — his brother, Malcolm, and sister, Donella, had grown so tired of his pedantry over the years that they'd taken to throwing things whenever he went on a tear — but some things he didn't allow to pass without comment. If Ewan wanted to be more precise, he might call them illegally detained emancipated slaves, given Lincoln's recent proclamation, but 'slave' sufficed. If the Southerners couldn't bear to call their human chattel by the proper name for them, then why had they started this ungodly war?

"Warden, got some fresh meat coming!" a guard called out.

"The, um. They can ensure that's done," Dilford said, looking back over his shoulder to nod at the guard. "Thank you for your assistance."

He turned and walked off toward the watch house. Guards in gray uniforms strolled along the ramparts, their eyes trained on the dead line that surrounded the perimeter of the prison — so named because anyone who crossed it was a dead man. Ewan saw the next shift of guards approaching and noted, again, how the on-duty guards looked away from their posts for a minute or so as they chatted and traded friendly jibes with their replacements. Such details always had some kind of value, and Ewan was excellent at exploiting the finer points in life.

"We've been going back and forth about the location of this stolen artillery for an hour now. I see you're determined to be obstinate," Ewan said. *"In that case, maybe we should begin discussing anatomy."*

"Anatomy?" the Rebel soldier asked. "Sure, we can talk 'bout that, since I ain't got nothin' else to say to a yellow-bellied Yank."

"Very well." Ewan pulled out the long, thin strip of metal his commanding officer had provided him. "Let's start with the joints."

"Hey, Red, the library is here," his business associate Keeley said, sidling up with a grin and drawing Ewan's attention back to the present. The dark-haired Irishman knew that Ewan spent as much time as he could with his face between the pages of a book. He also knew that when the book cart came, so did more supplies for the little prison business that kept them both afloat in an environment that led men to desperation and despair if they weren't resourceful. Did Keeley suspect anything else?

Ewan fought the growing sense of urgency that pushed him to turn and search through the camp until he found the wagon of books — and the woman who pulled it. He spotted familiar faces among the Negroes who came every two weeks with an offer of succor for the prisoners from their employer — he didn't call them slaves because they were actually paid, or so he'd heard. The woman who dispatched her staff every other week, Sarah Lynch, pushed every boundary a person could in the Confederate South without waving the Stars and Stripes, but always stayed just shy of anything that could get her charged with treason. He'd seen her once, soon after his first arrival: small, straight-backed, and lying through her teeth as she convinced the warden that it was simple Christian charity that drove her actions.

Ewan valued honesty, but he wouldn't fault her for lies made in the service of the greater good. His brother, Malcolm, lied to preserve the Union, and Ewan had done much worse in the same service. Sarah Lynch's lies meant that the inmates at Randolph were able to live slightly better than most prisoners of war — and that information flowed in and out that otherwise wouldn't. It helped her cause that if the prisoners shared in the bounty of her farm's harvest, so did the soldiers guarding them.

The Rebel guards borrowed books from the same book cart, and the sick men of both sides asked for assistance from the woman he was currently seeking — not Sarah, but the woman whose gentle smile made Ewan question his principles each time she appeared within the confines of the stockade.

Something drew his gaze to the left, and there she was, kneeling next to a man laid out on the ground — one of the draft dodgers who had been hauled in by the Home Guard. The hunt for deserters had been in full swing since the winter, and their number at the prison camp grew every day. It was starting to seem to Ewan that the men in Randolph County who were against the Confederacy just might outnumber those who were *for* the blasted Rebels.

"This will get your fever down, John," she said, handing him a small bottle full of amber liquid, then digging into her apron pocket. "Take a sip when you wake up, at midday, and at night before you sleep. And chew one of these after you eat — do not swallow, you hear? That will help you keep your food down."

The sick prisoner took the handful of dark green leaves she pressed into his hand and nodded weakly.

Ewan's feet started to move toward her,

acting seemingly of their own accord.

"You know how my Hattie's doing? And the chil'ren?" John asked. "I don't think David can handle the sowing alone, and Penny kills every crop she touches. Nicknamed her Pestilence." He chuckled, then shifted uncomfortably. "Hattie was sick, last I saw her. I told her to stop bringing me food into the woods, that she'd catch her death or get caught by the militia, but she was too good to me."

"They're faring well," Marlie said. There was the slightest hitch in her voice before the word "well," as if she'd considered another less optimistic one. "The crops didn't take, but we've been making sure they've got food. Don't you worry about that."

John nodded and she gave him a pat on the shoulder, then stood and brushed the dust from her skirts. Her gray gown was well made but simple; it lacked the hoops and other gaudy accoutrements that would have distracted from her figure beneath it.

My kingdom for a crinoline, Ewan thought as he turned his eyes away from the clearly outlined curves that strained against the material as she bent to adjust her hem. He couldn't look away from her for long though; he'd counted to five once, and that

28

was the longest he'd lasted.

Her skin was a smooth light brown, throwing up undertones of yellow where the sun hit it. Her dark, curly hair was pulled back into a chignon, leaving her face, with its full mouth and pert nose, open for perusal. He'd noticed every detail of her face the first time he saw her, but it still took him aback with its loveliness every time. He'd once visited an exhibition of Greek art and seen a beautifully restored amphora. He'd been overwhelmed with the desire to hold it in his hands, an all-consuming urge that had nearly driven him to climb over the ropes separating the art from the public and seize it. The feeling that built in him when he saw Marlie was frighteningly similar.

She grabbed the handle of her cart and pulled, starting off in the opposite direction.

"Miss Marlie?" He felt a tickle of anxiety that she might leave before they had a chance to speak.

She looked over her shoulder at him and Ewan's heart leapt up into his throat. He knew it was anatomically impossible, but the strange shift in his chest and tightness in his trachea only happened when she appeared. He couldn't pretend it was simply the fact that she was a woman — other women had come and paraded along the ramparts, watching the imprisoned Union men like they were animals in a zoological exhibition, with little effect on him. Mastering his emotions had been the work of a lifetime, for both personal and practical reasons, and yet . . . there he stood, staring at Marlie like a raccoon caught in the grain silo.

Her mismatched eyes were still as shocking as the first time he'd seen her. It should have been an imperfection, one brown eye and one green, but instead it gave her an ethereal air.

Was that pleasure in her expression? It wasn't something he was used to seeing directed toward him, and his heart thudded a bit harder. If she knew him for what he truly was, those indentations around her mouth wouldn't have deepened as she smiled.

"Oh. Good morning, Socrates. I've been looking for you."

Ewan felt his cheeks flame at the nickname she'd given him after their first encounter: He'd requested Greek philosophy from her book cart, and when she handed him a book of mythology, he'd responded with a lengthy correction on the difference between the two. He hadn't meant to; something about her had jangled his nerves. The more attentively she'd listened as he droned on about the difference between Homer and Hermagoras, the more donnish he'd become. He'd finally cut himself off and proffered an apology, as he'd been instructed by his mother and brother, but she'd simply smiled indulgently and said, "Never apologize for sharing your knowledge," before moving on to the next man.

Ewan had wanted to kick himself. His older brother, Malcolm, had been gifted with the talent of making women swoon from a hundred paces, while Ewan could bore them to sleep within a hundred words. He thought flirting and seduction to be petty wastes of a man's wit, but for the first time he'd wished he knew what to say to make a woman — Marlie specifically — think him dashing instead of dreary. He chalked up the strange impulse to prison-induced boredom.

The next time she'd come, she'd handed him a book entitled *The Stoics of Ancient Greece.* There'd been comments penciled into the margins of the book, agreeing with or challenging certain points. It was in a copy of Plato's *Republic* that the first note directed to him had appeared on the flyleaf page. *"Dear Socrates, No one else in my*

31

acquaintance cares for my thoughts on a long dead Greek, so I shall share them with you. . . ."

She'd gone on to impugn everything he believed in, but that hadn't stopped him from carefully ripping the page out and rereading each looping word by the light of the fires that dotted the prison yard every night. He had several such pages, stuffed into his pocket. They passed a few moments discussing her thoughts each time she came, cordially, as if he didn't know the loop and slope of her words intimately.

"Hello," he said when he finally reached her. His voice sounded overly forceful even to his own ears, and he tried to inject a bit of diffidence into his tone. "I have another letter to send to my family, if that's all right. And I was wondering if you'd perhaps been able to procure the supplies I requested." He wondered more than that as he watched the corners of her lips turn up. The shape of her mouth, wide and lush, was perfection. Literally. He'd spent enough time reflecting on it to know it was symmetrical, harmonious, and well-proportioned: the Golden Mean in the flesh, and inspiration for thoughts that no man who was truly master of himself should be having.

She looked around, making sure no guards

were watching, and then handed him a small pouch, grabbing the letter at the same time and tucking it into her bag in a smooth, practiced motion. The bag landed in his palm with a metallic clink. "I have no idea what you need these for, but here they are. I have something else for you as well. I saw it and thought of you."

She thinks of me.

Marlie moved aside some books in her cart and pulled out a thin beige tome with black words pressed in block print on the front: *The Enchiridion.*

A peculiar feeling came over Ewan as he reached for the book. He distinctly remembered the first time he'd read it. It had been during one of the ever-increasing bad spells, with his father drunk and muttering darkly at his mother, who'd sat quietly doing the mending. Ewan had been frightened, as he often was when it came to his father, but his mother had focused on the intricate stitchwork that brought in money to the household, her expression unperturbed in the face of the unseemly abuse.

His brother, Malcolm, had watched the scene from the corner of his eye as he bounced Donella on his knee, but Ewan had cracked open his newest book, inhaling the musty scent of escape. The first words he read went through him like a bolt of lightning, illuminating a world that had been cloaked in darkness.

1. Some things are in our control and others are not.

Ewan had looked up at his mother and her steady hands and realized that the mending was in her control, while his father was not. He was still frustrated and still angry, but a new respect formed for his mother in that moment; what he had taken for a weakness, and tolerance of abysmal behavior, was actually a strength. Ewan read the short tome quickly, and then read it twice more before bed that night. The rules of *The Enchiridion* made more sense than "Turn the other cheek" or "Honor thy father." There was no need for forgiveness and false praise in this conception of life, only deciding what was essential and what was not.

His father was not essential. It was only a couple of years later that his father came to the same conclusion. If Ewan's quiet reprimands had helped his father to understand that fact, he did not regret it.

That *this* woman would give him *this* book — the book that had saved his life, if not his soul? Ewan wasn't superstitious, but even he could appreciate that this was a co-incidence of the highest magnitude. He could understand how a thing like this might make a simpler man believe it held some greater meaning, but he was not a simple man. The sensation of dizzy warmth he felt was simply gratitude, he was sure.

"This book means a great deal to me. Thank you." He ran his fingers over the textured cover, and when he looked up her gaze was following their path.

Her shoulders lifted and fell in a manner that indicated the gift was of no conse-quence, which was at odds with the warmth Ewan felt in his cheeks and neck and chest. She began moving away with her cart.

"Something told me you'd appreciate this sort of thing." There was a teasing tone to her voice that thrummed an ancient scar in him, the one that had sealed over the wound incised by the whispers of *"The boy is strange"* and the shouts of *"What kind of nonsense is he up to now?"*

"You didn't? Appreciate it?" He didn't know why the idea upset him — he was quite open to differences of opinion. *You cannot control the actions of others,* he reminded himself. But if she found this book, which was such an essential part of his being, ridiculous, then that meant . . .

She glanced at him, amusement dancing beneath those long, sooty lashes of hers. Little bolts of anxiety tightened at Ewan's neck at the thought that she might be amused by him.

"I enjoyed some parts more than others. I left my thoughts for you, in case you were interested in them."

"Always." *I look forward to your notes more than the books, and everyone knows how strongly I feel about books.* But he didn't tell her that. "Engaging the arguments of those who hold differing opinions is always a worthy use of one's time. It's how we strengthen our rhetorical skills and broaden our knowledge."

He sounded pretentious, ridiculous, but she smiled at him anyway and he had to fight back a groan at how sharply the slightest curve of her mouth cut into him.

"I'll have to disagree with that," she said. "Some arguments are not worth engaging. If you tried arguing for the validity of the Confederacy, this conversation would be over."

One of the things that drew Ewan to Marlie was that there was always a certain softness about her, but the look in her eye as she regarded him was serrated.

Ewan nodded his agreement.

"Quite right. There's discussion and there's tomfoolery." Even a confirmed pedant had some sense of decorum.

"Marlie!" a deep voice called out from a few feet away. "Time to go."

A black man, obviously older than Marlie but not old enough to be an uninterested father figure, stood watching them. He was standing beside one of the squabbling officers from earlier. The officer gave him a friendly clap on the arm and walked off.

Marlie's companion held a book in his hands that he quickly slipped into one of the large pockets of his wool coat. There was something in the movement that drew Ewan's attention — it was overly casual.

The man nodded toward Ewan; there was amusement in his gaze when their eyes met.

Get in line, son, his expression seemed to say.

Am I that obvious? Ewan's gaze flicked back to Marlie, not of his own accord, and he forced himself to meet the man's eye again.

The man shook his head and turned away.

Yes, I'm that obvious.

"Coming, Tobias!" Marlie gave Ewan a brief smile and then she was off, lugging her cart behind her. Ewan knew he should stop looking after her like a lost calf, so he turned to head back to his tent. He'd taken about four steps before he stopped and turned to the flyleaf.

Any man who believes he can control his emotions has already been bested by them, Socrates.

Turmoil across the yard caught his attention before he could process the words. Ewan slammed the book shut and shoved it into the waistline of his pants. The noise could be guards come to raid the tents and take whatever the Lynch woman had provided for the prisoners, as they were wont to do. It could have been one of the gangs preying on the weakest among them for the same reason. A man couldn't get too attached to his possessions in a prison, even a man who wielded some small amount of power, as Ewan did. You had to keep what was important to you close.

Across the yard, the throng of prisoners began to part and Ewan could see Warden Dilford hurrying alongside two men. One was slim and pointy all over, with squinty eyes and a long nose that reminded Ewan of a hungry dog glancing about in search of food. He was leading three or four men, all badly beaten, by a rope that bound each of them at the wrists with not enough space between them to walk without stumbling. Each time a man misstepped, the slim man gave the rope a vicious pull. Ewan winced. He knew how much damage coarse rope against skin could cause; he'd learned all about how fragile the human body was while carrying out his work.

"Got some more treasonous skulkers," the man said. "Worse than the Yanks, these skulkers."

"The word of my Lord is above the petty squabbles of man," one of the men responded. He was older, his skin leathery from a life working the fields. "You wish to force me to fight, but my only battle is righteous resistance to that which is unjust. Slavery and avarice are not just."

That drew murmurs of support from the crowd, likely from fellow War Quakers — those who followed the teachings of the Friends, but hadn't registered before the Conscription Act. All of the deserters fascinated Ewan, but these men the most. They chose not to fight out of a strong sense of morality, while Ewan had joined up for the same reason. Yet it was in committing the most immoral acts that he'd aided his country the most. He didn't regret being good at something so terrible — it had been made quite clear that he wasn't like other men, and this was just further proof of that — but he did wonder at the cost. If souls were real, his was irrevocably stained by what he had been assigned to do for the sake of the Union. Saying no had never occurred to him.

"Why should the poor yeomen fight for the rich slaver who can buy his way out of service while sacrificing those who have nothing to gain in this fight?" the man continued, encouraged by the crowd. "Twenty slaves is all that stands between a skulker and a righteous man in the eyes of Governor Vance!"

A larger figure lumbered up behind the man, sword drawn. He raised the weapon and brought it down, and for a moment Ewan thought he'd see a defenseless man hacked to death before his eyes. But instead the attacker leveled several blows with the flat of his sword, beating the older man like a beast of burden instead of hewing him like a fattened calf.

"That resistance will be whipped out of you once you reach the Camp of Instruction. We'll see what the good Lord says when you get to Raleigh," the man said, and then he looked up, bringing his face into full view for the first time.

Cahill.

Ewan's stomach constricted into a tight ball of disbelief, and a surge of anger and fear went straight to his head, leaving him with a raw, sick feeling, like a soldier dosed with too much morphine. Months and months had passed. Ewan had thought he'd come to terms with what happened in that Georgia farmhouse. The itch in his skull and the clench of his teeth told him otherwise. Cahill walked with a severe limp — Ewan knew precisely how the man had developed it — and his gaze swept over the prisoners like a wintry gale. When he got to Ewan, it lingered a moment, eyes narrowing.

He can't recognize you.

Ewan's instinct was to meet Cahill's gaze. No, that's not true — his instinct was to push through the crowd, grab the bastard's sword, and run him through with his own steel. But it was that exact instinct that had made Ewan question everything about himself. There was carrying out his duty to his nation, and there was what had happened during his interrogation of Cahill. There was the blinding rage at injustice that had left Ewan ashamed and Cahill with a brace beneath his trouser leg. There was the

41

knowledge that Cahill hadn't paid dearly enough.

Ewan scratched his beard and looked up at the darkening sky. The late afternoon sunlight wasn't enough to burn through the haze of awful memories Cahill had drawn up. Blood and laughter and brown bodies falling one after the other.

"Name's Cahill," Keeley whispered to Ewan as he sidled up beside him. Keeley was a man who drew information like other prisoners drew flies — it was why he and Ewan worked so well together. Casual conversation wasn't Ewan's forte. "He was the worst kind of overseer before the war. He's head of the Home Guard old Zebulon pulled together for sniffing out deserters, petitioned for the job. Vance has told him to do anything under the sun to drag skulkers out of hiding and into the service, and Cahill's more than happy to oblige. They say he'd do it even if Vance had turned him down, that's how much he hates skulkers."

Cahill was Sons of Confederacy, too, but Ewan didn't give Keeley that information. If he did, he'd have to explain why he knew about the hardcore Secesh group's existence and how he knew Cahill in particular was a member.

"I've heard some things, some nasty

things, Red. Holding men over campfires, toasting their bits like chestnuts. And sometimes they get ahold of a skulker's wife or kid . . ." Keeley spat, then wiped at his mouth with his sleeve. "Him being here can't mean nothing good."

"We're already in prison," Ewan said, clapping his friend on the back. "Things can't get much worse now, can they?"

Ewan didn't like lying, but sometimes you had to for the greater good.

CHAPTER 2

Marlie focused all her attention on the liquid working its way through the coiled glass tubes of the condenser in front of her, on the scent of perfumed steam pushing through plant matter and the drops that gathered at the tube's tip and dripped into the waiting bottle below.

She often wondered what her mother would say about her work space, which was both different from and similar to the one they'd shared in her childhood home. Leaves, roots, and bark of all types littered every surface, as they had in her previous life, but Marlie's walls were now covered with tacked-up schematics for new distillation processes. Small pots holding the many different medicinal plants she'd nurtured from clippings lined the windowsill and balanced on the edges of shelves stuffed with books on botanical medicine.

Marlie had once brought her *Illustrated*

American Botany with her for a visit and Vivienne had leafed through it disdainfully.

"You need a white man to teach you what you know in your bones?" she'd asked before tossing the book aside and returning to her work.

Marlie had tucked the book back into her bag and never mentioned it again, or any of the other books and what she'd learned from them. For Marlie, who had only ever traveled between her childhood home and Lynchwood, the books had been a doorway to the world. She knew of the latest advances from France, could test whether the specifications Helmhein of Germany suggested were worth recalibrating her production process for. She learned there were reasons certain plants elicited certain responses, reasons that could be quantitated and explained. Now when people looked at her strange eyes and called her a witch woman, she told them she was a scientist, something they found even more baffling.

Marlie got up and ducked through the door of the small room next to her work space to grab a few sprigs of dried rosemary for the decoction she was making. Baskets of the herbs and plants needed for her work covered the dark wood shelves and table-tops, and leaves crunched beneath her boots as she crossed the dusty wooden boards. Their comforting scents hung in the cool air that seeped in through the cracks in the window frame.

She moved between the drying room and her desk several times, her mind focused on the individual steps that would result in an effective tonic. Outside there was the noise of coaches making the weekly delivery from the Lynch farm, but it barely filtered up to her domain — work space, drying room, and bedchamber. The entire attic was hers. As a girl, she hadn't been sure whether it was because Sarah wanted to hide her from guests or an indulgence to make up for past wrongs, and it had felt lonesome. But she'd grown to appreciate having her own private space, and Sarah's love had made itself clear over time — her attention to Marlie's well-being was occasionally even cloying, which was one of the reasons why Marlie had never moved down to the rooms more fitting for a lady. The other reason was that Marlie wasn't quite sure she belonged there.

Sarah was her . . . friend. Benefactor. Partner in treason. *Sister* was what always came to mind first, but was never said. Sarah's father had been a slave master, though it was always explained that he'd only bought slaves to succeed in business with his Southern compatriots, as if that caveat absolved him. Marlie's mother had been one of the slaves he purchased. Everything else was conjecture, and after so many years, Marlie didn't know how to ask for more information.

You shouldn't have to ask.

She shoved the thought away, as she always did. She was lucky; most children like her ended up sold off or working their father's fields. Marlie had been granted a life of luxury. She was free. That should be enough.

Should.

She turned down the heat on the burner and then opened the copy of *Gulliver's Travels* Tobias had retrieved at the prison while she'd been talking with Ewan. The lending library had been a particular stroke of genius on her part. While the guards were bribed to allow Marlie, Tobias, and the other supposed slaves to carry out letters tucked away in the pages of their books, the real benefit was the pinprick messaging that allowed her to pass on information to the Loyal League, a group of Negroes and others dedicated to helping preserve the Union. She ran her fingertips over the page, retracing the messages she'd decoded earlier that day: EscAPe possible. wIll attEmpt aT Wan-

INg MoOn.

She put the book down and took a deep breath at what had been set into motion with a few pricks of a pin. Her acts of rebellion were small in the grand scheme of the war — other members of the Loyal League went undercover, put themselves in grave danger by fighting on the front lines of the war to reunify the nation. Sarah thought the little Marlie did to aid the resistance was already too much, but Marlie clung to each small victory as something her mother would have been proud of. She hadn't expected an escape to result from it, but she certainly wouldn't turn down a request for help. And though she wouldn't be participating directly in this escape, she knew Sarah wouldn't approve of her being even marginally involved.

So she simply wouldn't tell her.

She hadn't told Sarah many things, of late. She hadn't told her about the pinpricks or the new invisible ink she'd concocted to pass on what she learned to the Loyal League. She hadn't told her how much she spoke to the prisoners, either. She'd learned of troop movement in the Piedmont, and morale levels at Rebel camps — or the lack thereof. Each trip to the prison, Marlie gathered more intelligence, from her library

48

and from talking with the men as she treated their illnesses. And after each trip she realized how little she knew about the world outside of Lynchwood. A world she'd rarely been allowed to see because she was "safer at Lynchwood," according to her sister. Marlie had begun to understand that birds were kept in gilded cages because that was safer for them, too.

She'd met men from tiny towns as far North as Maine, from cities as large and bustling as New York. They had accents so different from the slow drawl she was familiar with, and spoke of places that she could never imagine visiting, even given the Lynch family wealth. And then there was Ewan. Another unexpected benefit that had arisen from her library, and one that had nothing to do with the resistance.

Marlie reached out and wiped a speck of dirt off a warm glass tube, and the thought of Ewan's finger sliding over the cover of the book she'd given him popped into her mind. There had been such reverence in that caress. If he treated his lovers with anywhere near the same tenderness . . .

She stood, rubbed her palms against her apron. There was nothing to be gained from thinking of such things, and so she searched for a better use of her time. She walked to the large rolltop desk on the other side of the narrow room. Sunlight poured in through the window, and when she grabbed up the stack of papers atop the desk, it was warmed through, hot in her hand like a living thing. Marlie stilled and closed her eyes, remembering for a moment the feel of her mother's palm against hers the last time she'd seen her. Vivienne had looked at Marlie as if searching for her reflection in a cloudy mirror, and then dropped her hand and turned away as if she hadn't found it.

"*Sometimes I wish I hadn't sent you there, you so much like them now. But that's the best protection you can have in this world,* chérie."

Marlie sifted through the pages that were smudged with dirt and sticky with pine sap. When she lifted them to her nose she could still catch a hint of the rosemary balm her mother had used to keep her hands soft. The packet had been delivered the year before, along with a trunk full of Vivienne's belongings and the shocking news of her mother's sudden passing. Vivienne had seemed immortal, and Marlie still hadn't reconciled herself to the truth, even after visiting her mother's grave. Sarah had seen to it that Vivienne had a beautiful tombstone, but the cold marble didn't ease the fact that her mother had died and Marlie hadn't known. Nothing had prepared her; she hadn't sensed a thing.

There'd been a time when Marlie had thought her dreams portentous, but she hadn't dreamt for years, and Vivienne's death hadn't changed that. She felt silly getting upset about what was simply another bit of superstition from her youth, but that didn't negate her sense of loss. She'd stopped dreaming, and that meant she would never see Vivienne again.

She sighed and leafed through the pages before her. Marlie had often wondered what her mother did in her spare time without a daughter there to fuss over, and she'd found out: Vivienne had told her story. The first pages were clearly older, meaning her mother had started putting her life to paper long ago. The memoir started in Guadeloupe, the island of Vivienne's birth, and Marlie supposed it ended in the home where she had grown up.

Everything Marlie had ever wanted to know about her reticent mother was inscribed on those pages, if she paid attention. Between the lines of a recipe for a salve for an aching back was the story of how Marlie's grandmother had pulled a muscle carrying a sick child on her back as she chopped sugarcane. The tisane to stop blinding headaches had been learned after Vivienne's sister had been struck in the head for talking back to the overseer.

All of the stories Marlie had been denied as a child had been delivered up to her, with one impediment: The text was in French.

"Ici mon passé écrit, pour toi, m'avenir qui vit," Vivienne had written boldly on the first page. *Here, my past written, for you, my future who lives.*

She'd once been able to understand most of what Vivienne said when she slipped into the lyrical language. It had been fascinating, like watching her mother turn into a different person before her eyes. Who was this woman who could make an *r* sound like a living thing taking flight, who could unleash a torrent of beautiful sounds that made even the most high-falooting Southerner sound positively provincial? But Marlie hadn't studied it in the ten years since she'd left home, and Vivienne had only spoken her somewhat clipped English in the times when she visited after. Marlie wondered if this weren't a final test from a mother who had always pushed her to learn more, faster. To be better than Vivienne had been allowed.

Marlie pulled out the French-English dictionary she'd ordered from Raleigh and began the slow, painful work of transcribing a language she was still learning. If preparing the tonics she sold to Weberly's Pharmacy couldn't keep her mind off Socrates, wrapping her mind around French grammar certainly would.

"Fait pression sur la feuille avant que l'ebullition." Marlie blinked at the words. She was only a fourth of the way through the pile, and some words were repeated enough that she knew what they meant. *Pression.* Pressure. To press. She thought of Socrates's fingers again and sighed, dropping her head into her hands.

She didn't know why she was drawn to him. In a camp full of men, all imprisoned for fighting the despised Confederacy, there were men more attractive than he. His hair was that shocking orange-red after all, his beard a darker shade that seemed out of place on his lean face. His nose was sharp, hacking its way forward between a heavy brow and clear blue eyes that were unsettling if they rested on you too long.

People often asked her if she had second sight because of her strange eyes, but Marlie thought it possible that Ewan could see clean through the mortal realm. There was an intensity to his gaze, as if he were examining every detail of the world around him to see how it fit in with his philosophy. She had the impression that most things did not. Perhaps that was why it made her skin warm and her heart beat faster when he approached cloaked in an air of uncertainty and blathered on about logic: It seemed that she had passed some kind of evaluation and had been found up to snuff.

A knock sounded at the door.

"Marlie? We've just had word from Diane Sims." Sarah's voice was high-pitched and excited, and that could mean only two things. Since Marlie hadn't witnessed the Union army sweeping in and reclaiming central North Carolina for Lincoln, she'd have to assume work was ahead. They'd have passengers soon.

"Come in," she called out. Before Sarah entered, Marlie quickly tucked the papers into a leather portfolio that lay on her desk.

Marlie pushed away the word *sister* and all it connoted and turned to Sarah as she entered the office, her nostrils flaring as the scent of the herbs hit her. She cupped a hand over her nose, as she always did.

Marlie reached behind her and pulled some of the books onto the portfolio, hiding it. As much as she loved Sarah, she didn't want to share this part of herself. The part that had been born on a plantation hacked into the jungle of a tiny island, dragged to America in shackles, and had still managed to create a source of happiness and fulfillment for itself through sheer ingenuity. Hiding yet another thing from Sarah chafed like an ill-fitting corset, but this was not for Sarah. Not yet, and perhaps not ever.

"What did Diane say? How many are coming?" Marlie asked. She took up a basket from a shelf and began gathering the supplies that were generally needed to tend to runaways. Before the war, when Marlie had first convinced Sarah that she should take her abolitionist tendencies one step further and allow Lynchwood to be a station on the Underground Railroad, the passengers had been slaves heading North toward freedom. The war had changed the demographics. More and more whites passed through, Union troops or Southerners who opposed the war, as many in the Piedmont region did. Marlie still considered Lynchwood a safe haven for Negroes fleeing enslavement, but she had learned that others coming through now might talk to her like she was the help and treat her work as what was due to them, as had happened with the last batch of Yankee soldiers who'd passed through.

Marlie focused on the fact that she was helping, and she didn't have to like a person to help them. But the contrast in the entitlement of the soldiers and the gratefulness of the escaped slaves was never lost on her. She learned something about the world outside of Lynchwood from that, too.

Whoever was coming, black, white, or native, would need the same care when they stumbled in, though: tonic of Sampson's root to clean the wounded feet of folks who'd traveled for miles barefoot or in rags that could barely be called shoes; red oak bark for blisters; sassafras for stomach upset; rhubarb for diarrhea; slippery elm for wounds or, for those who had found the trip extremely stressful, ulcers; chamomile for nerves.

"Three are coming, maybe four," Sarah said, ducking into the drying room and then reappearing with strips of linen that could be used for bandages. They'd formerly been the curtains in a guest room, but now served a more noble function. "Not sure who, but they're heading North like the others."

Marlie nodded as she continued gathering supplies. She didn't like talking much when there was tending work to be done. She needed everything inside of her to go quiet, to make space for the feeling that came when she had a patient in front of her who needed her help. Before, when she was young and foolish, she'd believed it was something outside of herself that told her whether to use sorghum or sassafras, rattlesnake root or Life Everlasting. But she knew better now: It was simply study and experience, not some otherworldly power. Sarah had tried to convince her that the feeling was the love of Christ, but Marlie doubted it was a blue-eyed man with long hair who worked through her.

You wouldn't mind having another blue-eyed man working through you. Heat charged through Marlie from her toes to the tips of her hair at the lewd thought. She wondered if there was a tisane to rid the mind of impure thoughts because she was sorely in need of it.

"Are you well?" Sarah walked over to her, concern in her eyes. She placed the back of her hand against Marlie's forehead. "Maybe you should take a dose of something. You're feverish."

The sound of horse hooves clapping against the path leading up to the house drove Marlie's stifled laughter away. They weren't expecting company, and refugees heading North certainly wouldn't draw attention to themselves with such a loud arrival. Sarah's eyes met hers, wide with fear, and she knew they shared the same thought.

The Home Guard.

Vance's militia was ruthlessly hunting deserters and anyone who helped them. Another war was playing out alongside that of North versus South, and in many ways it was more brutal. The once quiet countryside was soaked in blood, and the Union wasn't the cause of it — though anyone suspected of supporting them was at risk. Some of their most steadfast conductors, Friends and godless men alike, had been torn from their homes and families and imprisoned for their work on the Railroad and with deserters.

The hoofbeats drew nearer.

The Lynches had been suspected of Northern sympathies even before Sarah manumitted their slaves and began paying them a fair wage. And then there was Marlie, who was living, breathing proof that their ideas ran counter to that of the Confederacy. Her education and clothing and bearing were evidence enough. Had someone finally formally accused them?

Tobias pushed his way into the room then, rolling up his shirtsleeves. "I'll move the desk."

They'd already decided that Marlie's drying room, which was a valuable hiding space, should not be discovered. Marlie pulled the door closed and Tobias shoved the desk in front of it with two heaves. Once it was in place, it was as if the room didn't exist.

He turned to Sarah. "I'll answer the door, but you should be right behind me. I'm not trying to get snatched up by these sad excuses for soldiers." He was gone in a flash and Sarah tore out of the room after him.

Marlie put down the basket to follow and then paused to steel herself. She touched a hand to her chest out of habit, then remembered that she hadn't seen the John the Conqueror root she'd once worn for luck in years. When had she decided her mother's gift was no longer worth carrying?

"I'm so glad you've moved beyond those silly notions you had when you came here. You're a Lynch. You don't need hoodoo silliness to keep you safe."

Sarah had spoken similar words several times over the years, and Marlie? Marlie had laughed at the silliness as she clutched her science texts to her chest. But now, something awful tickled the back of her neck and made the fine curls there lift. The restless energy that had plagued her all evening coalesced into fear.

She moved to untie the tattered apron she wore over her dress, then stopped. Strange whites wouldn't tolerate a Negro woman sweeping down the stairs as if she were a member of the family, even if it was the truth. She tightened the knot on the apron strings, a reminder of how the world outside her home viewed her, as she walked slowly down the hallway. The telltale creak of the front door swinging open echoed in the foyer, and Marlie tensed, expecting to hear the clomp of boots and the sound of raised male voices. Instead Sarah gave a high, startled cry.

Marlie crept silently down the stairs, approaching the landing with a growing sense of dread. She couldn't shake the certainty that something terrible had arrived on their doorstep. She reached the bend in the stairs that was the last area from which she couldn't be seen and waited, trying to dispel the strange malaise that had enveloped her. Loss, was what it was — of what, she wasn't sure, but the feeling was familiar to her, and it wrapped around her throat tightly, like a threat.

"Oh thank heavens! I thought you'd leave us out there forever and I am plum exhausted." The loud, feminine voice that drifted up the landing was soaked in the accent of the Deep South, like sweet tea left in the sun too long. Marlie reluctantly turned the bend in the stairs and couldn't hide the sound of surprise that escaped her.

Stephen Lynch, prodigal older brother and master in name of the house they lived in, had returned home. He'd married a woman out of Mississippi for her family's money and discovered very quickly that they didn't suit at all. He generally spent all his time handling family business in Philadelphia, but had been stuck at their Southern estate when full-out war erupted.

He looked up at Marlie with baleful brown eyes, and then his gaze skittered away as it always did. Stephen worked to end slavery as well, in his own way, but always seemed discomfited by Marlie's presence. From what Sarah had told her, he had idolized their father; Marlie could understand why a living reminder of Mr. Lynch's perfidy would upset him, though it didn't make his rejection sting any less.

"Stephen has arrived, Marlie," Sarah said tightly as she looked back over her shoulder. "And Melody. General Grant has not given up his assault on Vicksburg, and their home was destroyed by cannon volley. We'll have the honor of hosting them until they can make further arrangements."

Marlie wondered if anyone besides her could feel the anxiety emanating from Sarah. She hoped Diane and the passengers would see the carriage and move on to the next station, but then she noticed Tobias go through the door and knew he would light the lamp that meant "no sanctuary." Her heart ached for whoever had thought they were reaching safe haven and would be turned away. Still, she feared more what would happen if they showed up and were seen by Stephen's wife, who didn't share his abolitionist sentiments.

"Further arrangements? These are the arrangements. I believe we'll stay right here until those yellow-bellied Yanks are sent to tarnation," Melody said. "I'm done with travel, and this house is much too large for one sad little spinster, now isn't it?"

Melody was nondescript: brown hair, brown eyes, and a figure that was neither plump nor slim. She looked up and Marlie smiled, only to be met with a grimace.

"Why is that nigger hanging about on the stairs?" The question came out so easily, trailed by an incredulous laugh. "Get down here and take these bags."

Marlie had been called that word before, but not often — folks knew her from her tonics at Weberly's and the free care she occasionally offered to the poorest residents in the surrounding counties. More importantly, she was a Lynch. People didn't have the nerve to call her such a slur, unless it was behind her back, and would most certainly never commit such a brazen act within the walls of Lynchwood. Not in the place that had been her sanctuary for almost half her life.

Her breath caught in her chest, stopped up there by the painful realization that, just like that, she was no longer welcome in her own home. The feeling of safety she'd felt for so long eroded beneath her feet as Melody looked up at her with contempt etched on her mundane features. Marlie stared back, her fingernails biting into the soft wood of the banister, not out of anger, but because she was holding on to her home for dear life.

"We don't use that word here, Melody," Sarah said. Her tone wasn't anxious anymore, it was calm and lower than a snake's belly, the voice she used when folks in the street slandered her Northern roots. "Not for Marlie, who is a member of the family, and not for any of the servants."

Melody giggled, but it tapered off when she realized Sarah hadn't been joking. "Silly girl, that's what they're called."

"Not in my house, they aren't," Sarah countered, and Marlie knew exactly what Sarah's face must have looked like: brows raised, cheeks starting to rouge.

"Darling sister, that sounds dangerously like Yankee rhetoric," Melody said, her head tilted to the side. "This is the South. The Emancipation Proclamation don't apply here, despite what Lincoln might have told you."

"I don't need a proclamation to tell me to treat other humans with respect," Sarah countered. "That's just the way things are done at Lynchwood."

Melody laughed, but there was no joy in it. "Whatever notions you might have, I'll remind you that this estate is actually in Stephen's name. As his wife, *I'm* mistress of the house now, and your thoughts on how things are done here are no longer necessary."

With that, Melody walked out of the foyer, her gaze taking in the room like a lioness surveying her new hunting grounds.

"I'm sorry," Stephen finally said. His voice was struck through with fatigue and he looked about as pitiful as a man could get, his suit wrinkled and his hat crushed in his fidgeting hands, but Marlie felt no sympathy for him. He'd just served as Trojan horse for an enemy who was now loose in their home, free to plunder and destroy. "I didn't know where else to go. Our home was no longer fit to live in, and she refused to try to make it to our holdings in the North."

"I'm just glad you're safe," Sarah said, hugging her brother. "It will be all right. Everything will be fine."

Marlie felt a sudden stab of pain in her finger and jerked her hold on the banister to see a splinter embedded in the pad of her finger. A feeling of surety settled on her as she watched a pearl of blood well up, one she hadn't felt so strongly since she'd left Vivienne. It pinned her to the ground as Sarah turned and smiled up at her reassuringly.

No. It won't be fine at all.

Marlie was struck by the fact that she'd never buried a gris-gris of safety at the gate in all her years at the Lynch home — first she had forgotten, then she had outgrown such ideas. But now evil had just waltzed into her home, and she hadn't made the most token attempt to prevent it. Vivienne would have been disappointed, indeed.

CHAPTER 3

"Now, Marlie, she might be kin to you, but I ain't a Lynch." Lace, the family chef, took one of the sharp wooden skewers on the counter and jabbed it through a piece of the seasoned meat in front of her. "I'm a free woman — I earned every cent used to pay for those free papers with my blood, sweat, and tears. I don't got to take any abuse from that woman."

Marlie's back stiffened as she rolled up another slice of veal for the dinner that night. She often helped in the kitchen when the arrival of guests meant she couldn't dine with Sarah, but she was always aware that her kitchen work was a choice, and not her job. Sarah discouraged it, and Lace occasionally wasn't in the mood to indulge her need for a diversion. That Marlie had been born free and was a member of the family and not the staff was something she could never forget, even when she had tried.

"I'm sorry, but I must say that this is one instance where being a Lynch isn't a privilege," Marlie said. "Melody hates me all the more for it."

Lace sucked her teeth and turned to stir the soup. "At least I just work here. I wouldn't tolerate a sour wench like that coming up in *my* house calling me whatever she thought fit. Ha!"

Lace shook her head as if conjuring a lethal fantasy; her thoughts likely didn't stray too far from the dark paths Marlie's imagination had taken to traveling of late.

Marlie took a deep breath. The two weeks since Melody's arrival had been awful. Marlie was intelligent, she was capable, and she'd thought herself above reproach. She'd experienced some of the injustices of racism, and read much about how they affected her race all across the country, whether they were free or enslaved, but in her small town she was so well known that few people were ever crude outright. Everyone used her decoctions and balms — her usefulness served as a shield to the everyday insults of racial hatred as much as her place in the Lynch household did. People tended to treat you better, to your face at least, when they needed something from you and couldn't compel you to work with a lash without consequence.

The shield of grace she'd built up over the years had shattered since Melody had taken it upon herself to reeducate Marlie in that regard; the instant Marlie ventured outside of her rooms, Melody would appear, berating the texture of her hair, the way her dresses hugged her curves "lasciviously," the color of her skin. She'd stopped calling her nigger after an argument with Stephen, one that had shocked Marlie because he'd actually stood fast against his wife, but she still referred to the rest of the staff that way.

And Stephen made Marlie almost as uncomfortable as his wife with the way he stayed ten paces from her but stared like she was a mythical creature stomping about the parlor. She didn't think he was being lewd — he was her brother, even if no one ever spoke of it — but he was still another landmine to avoid in what used to be safe ground.

Lace stopped stirring the soup and glanced at Marlie from the corner of her eye. "Back on the plantation where I grew up, there was ways to get rid of someone like that. You just went to the root woman, and she worked her tricks. Could get rid of anyone giving you a problem."

Marlie froze with a skewer halfway

through the roll of soft pink meat. Suddenly she was a child again, traveling with Vivienne. They'd gone to visit another conjure woman. Marlie had stood on tiptoe to peer through the window and saw a grown woman, face tear-stained and snotty like a child, holding an anxiously chirping bird in her hand. "This will get rid of his wife?" she'd asked, and then nodded and squeezed her hand into a fist. The chirping had stopped.

Marlie dropped the skewer, the feel of the meat suddenly disgusting. "You know that type of thing is just foolishness, meant to make people feel better but achieving nothing."

"Now that you got all them books, you too good for throwin' and all that, huh?" Lace asked. There was no venom in her voice, but the words stung all the same. Vivienne had never thrown hexes, but that was because she had *believed* in the power of such magic, not because she refuted it. Marlie felt a tightness at her throat, like the first time Vivienne had looked at her in utter disappointment.

Lace stared at Marlie, worrying her bottom lip with her teeth. "I remember when Sarah brought you home with her. That first day, I found you with a clump of clay from your mama's yard in your hand, trying to conjure a way back to her."

"It didn't work," Marlie said, surprised at how clearly she remembered the pain of that failed attempt. It was when she had truly understood that no matter how hard she believed in it, no matter her strange eyes and vivid dreams, she was powerless. The only power she had now came from the knowledge she had gained through her imported books on plants and herbs. "Besides, anyone who believes in that kind of thing knows that what you do to others comes back to you tenfold."

Lace grunted in assent, but grinned and looked away when Marlie took up a handful of salt, poured it into a cloth, and tucked it into the pocket of her apron. There was major throwing, and there was minor, and even if she didn't believe in it, it was better than doing nothing.

"Toss salt after her every time she passes through the gate. After nine times, she'll leave."

A little salt never hurt anyone.

"I have to go up to my rooms before dinner to fix up some general tonic," Marlie said. She also wanted to do a bit of translating of her mother's journal, one of the few things that made her happy since Melody's arrival. The total concentration required of the work would help calm her before the night's events.

The dinner Melody had planned for some Confederate big bug was sure to be a strain, even though Marlie wasn't invited. She was no stranger to being informed she couldn't attend dinner when certain guests came, but it galled more coming from Melody, in part because the stream of information Marlie had been passing on to the Loyal League had run dry. Being stuck in her rooms meant the only news she got was from Sarah, who spent her days accommodating Melody or comforting Stephen, and Tobias, who was sent to work at the farm more and more. She felt trapped; maybe she had always been trapped, but this was the first time she'd been aware of it, and it was a distinctly disagreeable feeling.

She moved quietly up the stairs toward the attic, but she wasn't the only one scuttling about. Melody was hunched before the door of Marlie's rooms, twisting a key in the lock. Every part of Marlie expected the door to swing open, and her mind preemptively recoiled at the violation happening before her.

Lynchwood had been her haven, but there

71

was one place in the world that was sacred to Marlie, and it wasn't the chapel. Her laboratory, her still room, her conjuring room — whatever one chose to call it — it was the only place where Marlie truly felt at peace. Where she could descend into the deep focus of grinding, separating, and mixing nature's bounty at the exact proportion to help save a life.

In the rage that consumed her as she watched Melody shake her head in annoyance and move to the next key on her key ring, Marlie remembered that she knew how to take a life, too.

Then the rage pulled back a bit as she imagined her mother's disappointment.

"Nous qui ont reçu cette cadeau dois choisir comment nous utilisons. Et comment elle nous utilise."

"We who've been given this gift must choose how we use it. And how it uses us."

She'd translated that passage the day after Melody arrived, serendipity she was sure. She couldn't harm this hateful woman, no matter how she was tempted, and she was feeling like Eve before the serpent at that very second.

"Is there something you need from my laboratory?" she asked sharply.

Melody jumped and the keys clattered to

the floor. She bent over gracefully, as if executing a curtsy, and retrieved them. "Oh, you people are always sneaking up on a body! I suppose that's why they call you spooks." She tittered behind her hand, but the gleam in her eye was hard.

Marlie gritted her teeth against the slur.

"I just wanted to see what you were up to in here," Melody said sweetly. "I've heard all kinds of talk about what your kind can get up to with those roots and herbs."

"I 'get up to' making medicine to heal people. If you need something of that sort, you can ask. Something for jaundice, perhaps?" She creased her brow in concern and studied Melody's face critically. There was a more pleasant way to warn the woman off, but she'd been pleasant in the face of despicable behavior since Melody's arrival and her reserve of pleasantries had just run out.

"I didn't know I had to ask to enter a room in *my* home," Melody said. She crossed her hands in front of her skirts, displaying the key ring and all that it symbolized.

"I guess I should expect you to burst into the water closet while I'm indisposed, too, then?" Marlie asked. She didn't know where the crude question came from, it was so unlike her, but Melody was like a poultice that drew Marlie's toxins to the surface.

Melody's lips pursed. "I told Stephen that no good would come of treating a darkie like she's one of us. At least the uppity ones downstairs still know their place. But you don't even serve a purpose in this household. You don't cook. You don't clean. Things would run just fine without you here." She let those words hang in the air as she stared at Marlie.

Fury sent heat rushing up Marlie's neck, made her fingers itch to reach out and slap the smile off Melody's face. Instead, she drew her back up straight and channeled Vivienne's inscrutable smile. "Oh, I have a purpose. Perhaps one day you'll come to understand it. Intimately."

She walked past Melody with her head high, close enough to brush against her in a manner just as symbolic as displaying a key ring. *I am here. I am a physical being and I will push back against any actions taken against me in* my *home.*

"You look like you need to prepare yourself before your guest arrives, so if you'll excuse me," Marlie said, knowing full well Melody was already decked out in her best for dinner. She pulled the key that dangled from the long chain around her neck and unlocked the door, slipping into the darkness and closing it before Melody could glimpse inside.

Later that evening, Marlie sat in a rickety chair next to the kitchen door with a pencil in one hand and a fried artichoke in the other. She took a delicate bite of the greasy deliciousness, then jotted into the back of the book beside her.

I've been mulling over what you said the last time we spoke, Socrates, about engaging with viewpoints different from ours. I must admit that I wish I could find whatever philosopher you learned that from and kick him in the shinbone. I could have asked you just who it was by now, but my trips out to the prison have been put on hold thanks to an unwanted guest in our home. It's a terrible thing, feeling like a stranger where you should feel most at peace. You know, I'd always imagined that were I placed in a situation that called for bravery, some inner strength would come to the fore, but all I've learned in the past weeks is that I am able to tolerate more than I am driven to change. Perhaps I'm becoming a philosopher, too.

Marlie paused, brushed aside a dollop of

oil that had dripped onto the page. Why was she sharing this with him? Usually she kept her letters restricted to thoughts on whatever book it was she was writing in; this was personal. She considered that maybe it was boredom, but the truth was that somewhere along the line she'd grown accustomed to her weekly conversations with Socrates, brief as they were. She'd grown used to sharing her thoughts freely with him; it only made sense that she'd continue to do so, even if he never received her correspondence.

The thought disquieted her. He was a friend, or the kind of man who could be, and it was hard to imagine a future in which she never saw that shock of red hair or received one of his too rare smiles.

Pearl, one of the serving staff, strode into the kitchen with a pained expression on her face.

"Any news?" Marlie asked. Pearl had agreed to be her eyes and ears during the dinner. Marlie wouldn't let Melody's presence stop her from relaying whatever intelligence she could to the Loyal League.

"Cahill chews with his mouth open and is over fond of his own voice, though he don't got nothing important to say. Melody, though. Melody!" Pearl shook her head.

"That wench almost knocked a plate out of my hand and then had the nerve to say I was clearing from the wrong side. The nerve! She wouldn't know French service if a frog kicked her in the eye."

"She delights in nothing more than trying to upset people," Marlie said. "You know you're excellent at your job."

"Thank you. She the devil's handmaid, I'm sure of it," Pearl said as she placed the skewers of veal olives warming on the stove carefully onto a serving platter. "Mr. Stephen look like he ain't slept a wink in ten years. Probably because she ridin' him all over the countryside every night."

Pearl finished the platter and began chopping parsley to place around the edges of the plate for decoration. Marlie hated the waste. That would go perfectly well in her Stomach Settling Solution.

"And you should hear what she out there saying! That anyone who's for the Union should be tarred and feathered, that she's heard there are Unionists in some of the most affluent households in Randolph — all the while smiling at Miss Sarah and asking her questions about what she's been doing to support the Cause! A viper in the nest never hissed so sweetly."

Marlie felt that horrible weight settle over

her again, the one that squeezed her with the certainty that something malevolent lay ahead.

"Ouch!" Pearl grabbed at her hand and pulled it in close against her. Marlie jumped up and saw the blood surging from a slash across three of Pearl's fingers.

"Oh dear. It's all right," she said, her voice soothing as she grabbed a cloth and reached for the hand. "Lace, can you bring me some of the Healing Tonic?" It was still strange to call it by the name she sold it under in the pharmacy instead of what she'd learned from her mother, but it was habit now. She stanched the bleeding and then applied the stinging solution before binding Pearl's fingers.

Hurried footsteps sounded in the hallway and then Sarah stumbled into the kitchen. Her expression was drawn. "*She* is in there raising hell about the wait. Is everything all right?"

Pearl tried to flex her bandaged hand and winced. "I'm sorry. I cut myself putting these greens on here."

"Oh, Pearl! Are you all right? Why does it seem like everything has fallen apart since she arrived?" Sarah thrived when she could put everything to order, but Melody's appearance had thrown everything upside down. "And she's out there taunting me, holding the fact that she can have Cahill haul me off to prison, or worse, over my head." Sarah placed a hand on her chest, which was rising and falling too quickly.

Marlie placed her hands on Sarah's shoulders and leaned forward until their foreheads were almost touching.

"She cannot prove anything," Marlie said in a low voice. "We've worked very hard to ensure that. Take a deep breath and head back out there. Think about all we've accomplished over the years. She's a temporary problem, and we'll eventually be free of her. I'll take over the serving while Pearl rests."

"Yes. Right as ever, Marlie." Sarah nodded, then let her forehead rest against Marlie's for a moment. "I'm so lucky to have you. I would have gone mad already if you weren't here."

A confusing mixture of emotions flowed through Marlie: happiness and gratitude, but also resentment that she was the one providing comfort. Sarah still had things that could keep her safe, even if Melody accused her outright: She was rich and white. That got a person far whether they were for the North or for the South.

Marlie had no such protection.

It grew clearer by the day that she was entirely dependent on someone who wasn't even completely free herself. The thought sobered her as Sarah pulled away, and she turned and approached the platter, trying to figure out the best way to carry the heavy thing.

Lace laughed. "Since when you know how to serve, Miss Marlie?"

"Would you prefer to do it?" Marlie snapped. "I'm sure Melody would love to compliment the chef again." Melody had sent back the duck soup from the first course, saying it was too salty.

Lace huffed and handed Marlie the platter. "Go on," she said. Her lips were pulled into a tight line.

"Sorry," Marlie said. Lace was even less protected than she, and didn't deserve Marlie's ire for a situation she had no control over, either.

Lace nodded in understanding, and then Marlie gripped the platter with two hands and started out of the kitchen. She marched down the hall, the warm porcelain in her hands feeling like a mortar that could go off at any moment.

From outside the door, she heard a rough male voice that wasn't familiar to her. "These cowardly Tory deserters, they're no

80

better than the Yanks. Worse in fact, because they're turning their backs on neighbors, friends, and country. They've grown bold and rebellious, pillaging those loyal to the Cause. I thought I'd be fighting boys in blue, but rooting out these skulkers is an even greater service, way I see it."

When Marlie walked into the dining room, she realized she had no idea what to do. The table was crowded with food, and there was no space for the increasingly heavy platter. Sarah had her back to Marlie. Stephen faced her though, and his tired gaze met hers for the briefest of seconds before he looked away. Marlie was tempted to walk over and dump the veal olives on his head, but then she saw him gingerly pushing one plate to the left, another to the right, until there was an empty space just large enough for her platter.

She didn't question his motives, just walked over and placed the heavy food down, then turned to leave.

"Ah! I see someone has learned their place," Melody drawled. "Refill my champagne, and Commander Cahill's." She turned back to her guest. "I tell you, darkies don't come more uppity than this one. That's what happens when you're lax with 'em. Back at my daddy's, it would be the lash for the way she walks about here."

Marlie kept her eyes down as she poured the bubbly alcohol. She waited for Sarah to point out that she wasn't a slave to be whipped, but that defense never came.

"There's a place for mongrels who get above themselves," Cahill said casually, as she filled his glass. "The women, especially. Fancy maids bring in quite a penny on the auction block, and soon learn their place in this world: on their backs."

Marlie jerked her gaze up at the brazen insult and came face-to-face with the man she'd seen at the prison last time she'd visited. He'd been pushing prisoners from the back of a horse-drawn wagon, kicking them down to the ground with their hands and legs tied so that there was no way for them to protect themselves as they hit the hard-packed earth.

He stared at her across the table, the coldness in his gaze worse than the hatred in Melody's. This man felt nothing at all; he regarded her as one does a fly while debating whether to swat it or shoo it out the window; he seemed the type to err on the side of swatting.

"I've seen those devil eyes before. Down at the prison with some other darkies giving out food and such." He put his glass down and turned to look at Melody. "You the one offering aid and comfort to those Yanks and deserters?"

Melody smiled brightly and pointed her skewer toward Sarah. "That occurred prior to my arrival. Regardless of what happened then, the Lynch household will never again offer succor to those who are enemies of the Confederacy. I'll see to that."

Marlie's stomach lurched like she was atop a horse that had just reared back to throw her. Her visits to the prison had been her sole source of freedom since the war had begun; it was the only time she'd traveled without Sarah, been able to make decisions without checking in with her ever-helpful sister. They hadn't exactly been pleasant, but they'd made her feel as if she was of use to her country. It was there that she had listened for information to relay to LaValle, and spoken to men who treated her as if what she did made a difference. It was there where her hope had been renewed, as she saw all the men willing to fight and die — or not fight and still die — in order to preserve the Union.

With one boastful sentence, Melody had snatched that away from her, too. The thought of no longer being able to help those who needed it took her breath away, and the realization that followed was just as painful: no more Socrates. No more conversations on philosophy. No more clear blue gaze and peculiar smile. He was the only person outside of Lynchwood she could call a friend. And she'd just lost him.

"Food from the farm is also distributed to the army hospitals and Confederate regiments," Stephen said quietly. His eyes were trained on his fork and knife as he cut his meat into ever smaller pieces. "Very little of it went to the prison."

"Very little?" Cahill's lip curled. "Should have been none. That prison is filled with Yanks, the enemy of this country, and skulkers — traitors to their own land, and their own kind. Scarcely a night goes by without deserters robbing or abusing some loyal citizen. And you see fit to coddle them once they're captured?"

"If you're speaking on abuses, you might bring up the fact that women and children are scared to leave their homes lest they encounter the Home Guard," Sarah said hotly, then caught herself. She was more composed when she spoke again. "I'm a Christian, sir. War doesn't change the fact that we're all God's children and that we must help our fellow man, especially the most misguided among them."

Cahill stared at her, and then let out a low, ugly laugh. "What Black Republican codswallop is that? The only God in these parts goes by Old Jeff, and anyone not for his dominion has chosen the side of the damned. You'd best remember that."

"Even Old Jeff cannot compel a man who does not want this war to take up arms," Sarah retorted. "If forcing a man to take your views on as his own were so simple, this rift between the North and the South would never have occurred."

Cahill smiled then, an ugly expression that held neither joy nor amusement. "Compel? I'm not here for any such task, Miss Lynch. I promised Governor Vance that I would smite all enemies to our glorious cause. If these men truly cannot be compelled, they will be exterminated."

He held Sarah's gaze until she shivered and looked away.

Melody took a sip of champagne, mirth in her eyes as she surveyed the table over its rim. "Well, what are you waiting for, darkie? Bring out the next entrée."

Marlie walked out of the room, numbness slowing her steps. Cahill's vile words were like a yoke thrown over her shoulders, and Melody's pleasure in them added to the weight. Sarah's silence was what nearly crushed her into the ground, though. She had defended the skulkers against Cahill's tirade, but had said not a word as he menaced her own flesh and blood.

In the kitchen, she picked up the book she'd been writing in and ripped out the page covered in her scrawling handwriting, balled it up, and tossed it into the flames.

"What was that?" Pearl asked.

Marlie watched as the paper burned down to ash.

"Nothing of import."

CHAPTER 4

. . . I did find many parts of the book to offer good advice, but all of this talk of logic makes me laugh. Is the desire to master one's emotions not at its root just another desire? Thus logic seems, to me, to just take those things which a man — or woman — might enjoy, and replace them with concepts that are invested with just as much emotion but simply more dreary. I'm not an ancient Mediterranean gallivanting about in a toga, but I believe I have the right of it. You can stay close to your ship, Socrates, as this Epictetus fellow endorses, but I imagine you can find other, more enjoyable, things to focus such discipline on if you strayed onto land every now and again.

Ewan hunkered in his tent and read the snippet of Marlie's last letter for what was, at a conservative estimate, the thousandth time in the month since she had left him *The Enchiridion.* Ewan had probably read the book itself as many times over the course of his childhood.

His original copy had been of a different binding, the wording slightly different, but the feeling it evoked remained the same. The original had been lost to him in one of his father's violent rages.

"How can this boy be of McCall stock," his father sneered, three days of nothing but whiskey and corn meal reeking from his mouth as he loomed over Ewan. *"I should have tossed him over the side when he did all that caterwauling on the boat, I should have. Always knew there was something wrong with him."*

"Ewan is a good boy," his mother said. *"Like his father is a good man when he has a mind to be."* Her voice was calm but firm, and Ewan felt that itch in his skull at the unfairness of it all, but knew he could not control the situation. Epictetus had given him permission to accept his father's rants and his mother's stoicism.

"Always defending him," his father said. *"Maybe he's a bastard, like little Donella. Maybe those English dogs weren't the first you opened your legs to, you —"*

"I wish I was!" Ewan was on his feet, tears

standing in his eyes not from fear but from anger. "I wish I was someone else's son. Donella is fortunate not to have your blood in her veins."

"Ewan." His mother's voice seemed far away, drowned out by the angry hammering of his pulse in his ears. Years of anger sharpened it to a sharp, precise spear of emotion that he aimed at his father.

"If you hate us all so much, why don't you just leave! We'd all be happier if you did."

The door creaked and he heard Malcolm's quiet footsteps — his brother hadn't had reason to learn stealth as Ewan had.

Ewan braced for a slap. His father had never hit him, but Ewan wanted him to. He was just a slip of a boy, but if his father hit him he would fight back. He would let loose all his fury and frustration. He wo—

His father snatched The Enchiridion from Ewan's hands and stormed over to the wood burning stove.

"Pa, don't," Malcolm pleaded from somewhere in Ewan's periphery.

"I'll be respected in my own home," his father said gravely. He threw the book into the oven and watched as it burned. Ewan watched too, hands clenched at his sides, fighting the desire to wail and kick and scream only for his mother's sake.

His father turned to him. His expression was sober, his mouth pulled into a frown. He laid the bottle of whiskey down and left the cabin.

Sometimes Ewan wondered at the cruelty he doled out during his interrogations and wondered if he weren't his father's son after all. He sighed and opened the book again.

Ewan had recalled *The Enchiridion*'s lessons often in the years after that, especially in times of fear and uncertainty, and they had always guided him well. Now Marlie had given it to him out of the blue. Marlie, who was his sole source of uncertainty in life. A prison could be escaped, a war won or lost, but the feelings she stirred in him defied such cut-and-dry categorization. They were not in his control.

He read her letter for the 1,001st time.

He couldn't even lie to himself as to the why of it — he wasn't searching for faulty argumentation in her words, although he was sure he could debate her definition of logic and her definition of desire.

Desire.

Her use of that word sent his brain veering sharply into the territory he'd become so adept at avoiding, and therein lay the problem. A life spent with his head buried between the pages of a book had fostered a formidable strength in Ewan's imagination, and when it came to Marlie, his mind was hell-bent on revealing just how easily it could take simple words and breathe them into life.

Before him stood Marlie in a toga, her smooth brown shoulders revealed by the draped white fabric. The curves of her calves as they emerged from beneath the pleated material as she took agonizingly slow steps toward him . . . perhaps she had just entered the chamber of a steaming private bath, one shared by just the two of them. Perspiration beaded on her skin, collecting in that sweet well just above her bowed lip and in the crevasse between her full breasts. He was already hard for her beneath the warm waters he was submerged in, and she stood before him, untied the belt of her toga, and let the fabric slide down over her curves. . . .

Ewan's cock throbbed painfully, and he folded the letter and slipped it back into his pocket with the others he'd removed from the books before passing them along. He'd thought destroying a book sacrilege until that first short note he'd received. Simple greed had driven him to carefully fold the page near the binding, first one way and then the other, before ripping it cleanly away. He should have known then he was in trouble.

A pulse of want rippled through him, like a disturbance at the surface of the water caused by powerful currents crashing beneath. His hand strayed down toward the tented groin of his pants. Self-gratification wasn't grouped with the many other things he denied himself, and yet . . .

He flopped back onto his hard bedroll and let his hand drop to his side. He wouldn't sully her by conscripting her into his fantasies, but his imagination was no friend to his resolve. When he had given himself release before, he'd thought of some generic woman, cobbled together superficial traits that had stirred attraction in him over the years. Blond hair, rosy skin, a seductive smile. But now the fantasy stranger who'd been his sexual muse for so long was unable to hold her shape. Her hair was now thick, curly, and dark, her skin the color of Carolina clay baked in the summer sun. And her eyes? One green, one brown, both looking up at him as that suddenly luscious mouth moved toward his cock.

Ewan took a deep breath and sat up, squeezing his eyes shut at the need that shot through him at the idea of sharing bodily pleasure with Marlie. And that was why he couldn't unbutton his trousers and have at it. With his previous erotic muse, he'd been in control of every aspect of his own desire. It had been safe. But when Marlie entered his fantasy world, everything spun out of his control, and all his composure was crushed beneath the weight of his want. Sexual pleasure was one thing. Wishing to lose himself in a woman and never come back up for air was another, even just in theory.

He needed to busy himself. That was the only way to keep his thoughts from straying to that which might be a danger to himself. It wasn't that he thought Marlie would hurt him, but allowing his want for her to proceed further most certainly could. She was too far from his ship, out along the rosy horizon of things that were not meant for men like him.

Whatever moral rules you have deliberately proposed to yourself, abide by them as they were laws, and as if you would be guilty of impiety by violating any of them.

That was toward the end of *The Enchiridion,* number fifty on the list, but Ewan thought it should have been at least in the top three. For breaking one's own rules was the greatest temptation a man could face, and that danger grew the more one knew of logic instead of lessening. If the leading minds of the Southern states could convince themselves this war was just, or it was a simple matter of autonomy, then a man could trick himself into going along with anything that suited his desires.

He reached beside the bed for the stack of small wooden rectangles he'd gathered from the woodpile, and the coil of metal wire. He grabbed the pouch of springs Marlie had given him, ignoring the throb in his chest when he touched the pouch that had been nestled in the pocket of her skirts . . . dammit. Maybe he'd stop obsessing if it hadn't been exactly twenty-seven days since he had seen her; he saved himself the dignity of recalling the hours. If the prison hadn't quickly lost the semblance of order that Dilford had managed and begun to descend into hell. If Cahill hadn't been the cause of it.

Cahill hadn't only come to Randolph to drop off the deserters he'd rounded up; he'd also been there to tell Dilford that the soldiers who'd been used as prison guards were being drafted into the Home Guard. The deserters were too numerous, and guerrilla warfare had erupted in the battle to bend them to the will of the Confederacy. Thus, the marginally competent guards had been replaced with men unfit for war — and even less fit to be prison guards.

In one fell swoop, all of the connections forged in Ewan's time at Randolph Prison had been lost. The new guards didn't understand the delicate balance of the prison economy. The import of food and greenbacks had gone dry because the first few Union men who'd tested the waters and tried to sell clothing or other goods to the guards had been beaten or worse for it.

They'd driven off the men who'd made a pretty penny setting up shop outside the prison gates, using guards as the middlemen for selling their wares. They'd chopped down the trees that attracted birds and other food sources beyond the meager offerings of the prison, which had reached sickening lows since the flow of food from Lynchwood had ceased. Rations had been cut and what they received was often rancid and wormy, as the guards skimmed the better-quality food for themselves and their families. Sadly, the worsening conditions ensured Ewan's newest venture would thrive.

He bent the wire strip efficiently, the task simple after several days of practice, and fitted each end into pre-gouged holes in the sides of the wood block. He screwed down the spring, building the tension on the little machine, and thought of Cahill. The man hadn't screamed all those months ago, tied down to a chair, the knee of his trousers soaked through with blood. Ewan had been sweaty, breathing heavily, and angry. Anger was nothing new to him — it was always there, really, just below the surface — and that was why his composure was so very important to him. Cahill had caused Ewan to lose that, and even though the Rebel was the one who now limped, he'd never broken. He'd been the victor in that makeshift inter-rogation room, and he'd known it.

An excellent reminder of what happens when you allow your emotions to get the best of you.

"Hey, Red, ya in there? There're some fel-lows interested in the product." Keeley stuck his fingers through the tent flap to an-nounce his presence.

Ewan double-checked that his Marlie-induced state had subsided, and then gath-ered the finished products. When he stuck his head outside the tent, he saw a group of pathetic-looking men huddled around it. Ewan tried not to feel pity for the men — pity served no purpose in this world. But then again, their well-being wasn't entirely outside of his control. The disturbance created by the new guards had initiated a chain reaction: Lack of trade meant a stagnation in the prison economy, one that matched the desperately deprived one that held the rest of the nation in its grip. Ewan couldn't do anything about the world beyond the stockade — not yet, at least — but reason dictated that his ingenuity be put to use for the greater good. He'd used the same thinking when gathering evidence from Northern traitors and captured Rebels. Moral laws, indeed.

Keeley, looking gaunter and grubbier than usual, pulled up a wooden crate and made a grand gesture toward it.

"Your audience awaits," he said, before grimacing through a cough and rubbing at his chest.

Ewan took to the box, imagining himself a great orator for just a moment. But instead of a crowd of Grecian intellectuals, he was met with the piteous sight of sunken cheeks and hollows under eyes. Clothes that hadn't been washed in weeks, and bodies that hadn't had access to clean water, made Ewan's eyes water. He didn't smell like roses himself — the guards rarely allowed the clearing of the grate that protected the water pipe, meaning now instead of detritus passing through, it was piling up, breeding the disease the grate had been intended to stop.

"Hello there, fine gentlemen of the Union forces," Ewan began. He paused, feeling suddenly aware that he was the center of attention. He worked past the discomfort, as he would if it were a physical pain.

"We ain't all Yanks," one man said irritably, and there were grumbles of approval from the crowd as it grew ever larger.

"Correct," Ewan said without taking offense. He corrected people as a matter of course; it was only right that he be open to receiving critique. "Hello there, fine gentlemen of the Union forces; deserters of the Confederate forces; Quakers and fallen Friends; Copperheads and Bushwhackers. Whatever offense you've committed against Jefferson, one thing is certain: If you're here, you're hungry. Food supplies have dwindled. Our new guards seem to enjoy using the five meters inside the dead line for target practice, so we can't grab birds like we used to. Desperate times call for desperate measures, and we passed desperate two trading posts behind."

"Get on with it!"

"Interrupting me is counterproductive to

my doing just that," Ewan said.

"Red," Keeley said, the nickname rolling off his tongue with a lilt of annoyance.

"Apologies. All right. We might be short on food here at Randolph, but if there's one thing we have plenty of, it's vermin." He pulled the project he'd been working on out of his pocket. "I have a solution to both of those problems."

"It's a rattrap!" someone called out. "Are you pulling our legs?"

Ewan held the trap up higher for everyone to see. "Yes. It is. No. I'm not." He looked around at the gaunt men. "We eat rabbit, we eat squirrel, we eat possum — why not rat? It's the only game willing to enter this reeking stockade."

There was an uproar but Ewan could sense when the men began to think realistically about their situations. "Believe me, I'd prefer roast chicken to roast vermin. But this is a matter of survival."

"And how much are you going to charge us for this survival?"

Ewan took a moment to survey the crowd. The interest that brightened the men's eyes made his stomach turn. This was what they had been reduced to: eager to scrabble over rat soup. He stepped forward and handed the trap to the man in front of him.

"Nothing."

"What do you mean?" the man asked suspiciously.

"I'm not charging anything. Whatever you all have right now you probably need it a sight more than I do. So, I will give the traps freely to several men, with one caveat — they must be used communally. No one person can own the trap or the rats it catches. They must be shared."

"And what if someone doesn't follow those rules?" another man asked.

Ewan simply stared at him. He didn't frown or smile or make any move of aggression. But he stared long after it had grown uncomfortable, until the man's lizard brain kicked in and realized that it was in a predator's sights. The man looked away.

Ewan turned to the crowd, and he let himself smile this time. "I assure you the greed won't be worth having that question answered." There were some grumbles, but no one challenged him. "Keeley, can you help me distribute these?"

"I can't believe you're giving our hard work away," he grumbled.

Ewan refrained from reminding Keeley that "our" was the incorrect pronoun, as Ewan had sourced the materials and constructed the traps himself.

"Good will is more valuable than greenbacks, these days," Ewan said in a low voice. His intent wasn't mercenary, but that didn't make the statement any less true.

"What's going on here? Prisoners aren't allowed to congregate!" There was a ripple in the crowd as a few of the new guards began to push their way toward Ewan. Ewan surreptitiously handed out the last of the traps to one of the prisoners as they dispersed.

"Nothing going on here," Ewan said, holding up his empty hands. One of the young soldiers ran up to him and grabbed him by the collar. Ewan, ever assessing, ran down the list of ways in which he could badly hurt the reckless fool — a quick turn to break his wrist, a chop to the throat to collapse his windpipe, a grab and reversal of that loosely held rifle. It would be so very easy to make the boy cry out in pain, but the easier something was to do, the more one should refrain from it.

"I never seen someone's arm bend like that without breaking, but you got that Reb to talk. You're a middling soldier, McCall, but it appears you can be of assistance to the Union in another way. . . ."

Doling out pain had come so easily to Ewan that the Army of the Potomac had

101

seen it as the only worthwhile thing about him.

He held his hands up at his sides.

The boy sneered, grabbed Ewan by his left arm, and pinned it behind his back. It was a clumsy maneuver, and Ewan helped the boy, tucking his arm back, pretending to grimace in pain. No need to embarrass him — a man with wounded pride was likely to act out unexpectedly. The boy angled Ewan toward the watch house, and then he wished he had struggled. There stood Cahill, staring at him with the same disinterested hatred that he'd last seen when the Union medics had carried the bleeding man out of the interrogation room.

Ewan's instinct was to stop struggling and meet that gaze, but he rejected that. "What're you holding me for?" he asked the young soldier, playing at shaking off the guard who held him. If he had actually intended to, the boy would be on his back. "Can't a man talk to his compatriots without being hogtied?"

The boy strengthened his hold and Ewan stopped thrashing.

"Cross," Cahill called out. "Come report what just happened with prisoner . . ."

"What is your name?" the guard said with a nudge.

"Homer," he said. "John Homer."

The guard called out the name more loudly, and from the corner of his eye he saw Cahill nod and go back into the watch house.

The guard released his arms. "You done caught the attention of the wrong man," he said with a coarse laugh as he pushed past Ewan.

Something ugly and violent rose in Ewan, the urge to run up on Cahill, to hurt him — again. It seemed Ewan hadn't exorcised himself of that particular demon, the one that was summoned by the sight of heartless men who had no qualms about destroying everything good in this country. Some in the Confederacy were motivated by their own twisted logic, but others, like Cahill, simply sought a venue to cause pain.

Perhaps you should sell mirrors instead of rattraps. Sometimes he hated his sensibility, wanted to rip it to shreds along with everything else, but that was why the same sensibility was so necessary. The uncomfortable itch that had tormented him since childhood stirred in his brain in a maddening whisper that presaged nothing good.

Ewan balled his fists at his sides and turned on his heel. He had no time for anger or what could come of it. It seemed his timetable had just been sped up: Cahill either already knew who Ewan was and that he was lying, or would figure it out eventually. He hurried across the yard, heedless of the cool spring rain that sent men scurrying for cover. The officers' quarters, where he should have been staying instead of in the tents with the enlisted men, loomed up before him. He'd avoided any mention of his actual standing and didn't intend to reveal himself, but he needed a quick change. If the guards were on the lookout for a bushy red beard later, and he knew there'd be a later, it would help to be clean-shaven. It wouldn't buy him much time, but every bit would help.

He walked in. "I need a shave," he said to the man who operated the rudimentary barber's chair in the corner of the room.

"This is for officers only, boy," the man said, a frown pulling at his jowly face.

"I know rank is quite important to a certain type of man," Ewan said. "But I'm going to have to be quite rude and inform you that I outrank you. So much so that I could make things very uncomfortable for you if necessary. All I'm looking for is a shave and I'll be on my way."

The man looked at him hard, and Ewan let everything inside of him go still, like he had when serving his country, by giving up his very humanity. Let this bastard deny him a shave —

Ewan closed his eyes against the buildup of anger and frustration. He thought of his mother's warm smile.

Breathe in. Breathe out. That's it, my boy.

He thought of Malcolm spinning a tale. Of Donella looking up at him with pride when he'd donned his Union blues. Of Marlie and her bright two-tone eyes.

He heard the sound of a chair being scraped back. "Have a seat."

Ewan sat, and the man began gathering his makeshift barber's tools.

"I'm guessing you don't feel inclined to tell me who you served under or what battles you been a part of," he said. Ewan had passed this man hundreds of times in the prison camp, but now the man narrowed his eyes as if really seeing him for the first time.

"No," Ewan said. "I'm not much for small talk."

The barber nodded, a grim smile on his face. "Your kind usually aren't, I suppose. I have to say I'm surprised to see you at this place if you're what I think you are."

"Small talk," Ewan said, and the barber began silently clipping.

Ewan thought about the man's insinuation as the dull scissors tugged at his beard. There was no good reason for him to still be at Randolph. He could have escaped if he wanted — he had before. But he'd been in various Confederate prisons for over a year now. He supposed it just went to show that he really wasn't cut out for war. That had to be it — there was no other reason for a man capable of escape to rest on his laurels while his country had need of him. None at all.

He closed his eyes against the sense memory of the shock that jolted his leg when he slammed his boot into Cahill's knee. He could still feel it, and the vicious pleasure he had gotten from it, if he thought about it too hard.

He focused on the room around him. A pile of muddy clothing was heaped in the corner. There was dirt caked deep under his barber's fingernails, despite the clean scrubbed skin of his hands. He heard the clomp of boots as a warm towel went over his beard; it didn't have the fresh barber scent he was used to, that was for certain, but he could bear it.

"We've done it," the officer who entered said jovially, performing a little jig, clapping the barber on the back. He recognized the man as the one who had been talking to Marlie's Tobias — as one of the officers who had quarreled over the shovel during the construction of the pipeline.

The barber gave the new arrival a quelling look and silently shooed him away, before adjusting the towel to block Ewan's view. Just before his sight was blocked Ewan took in the mud caked on the man's boots and pants, his hands dyed red with clay.

Ewan smiled beneath the towel. It was the little details that made all the difference.

CHAPTER 5

"What do you mean you can't go back to the tent? The temperature is dropping and it's gonna be colder than a witch's tit, spring be damned." Keeley handed Ewan his haversack, as he'd been asked, then shoved his hands into his pockets and shuddered.

"I'm afraid I can't hang about here any longer," Ewan said quietly from where he squatted beneath one of the lone remaining trees. Campfires opened up spots of light in an uneven pattern across the yard and he backed farther into the shadows as he checked the sack for the only item he'd really wanted: *The Enchiridion,* with Marlie's letters folded safely between its pages. Keeley had nothing else with him, which concerned Ewan. "I think some officers are going to scarper tonight, and I intend to join them. That's why I told you to bring your things, too."

"You make it sound as if leaving is a

simple task," Keeley said.

Ewan wouldn't call escaping simple, exactly, but it was certainly manageable. He simply hadn't tried too hard, for reasons he couldn't examine too closely. He was getting out and returning to his duty now, though. That was what mattered. Keeley would join him.

"What if these men are caught, and you're caught with them?" Keeley asked. He stopped, and his thin frame was wracked by an awful, phlegmy cough. "Besides, we have a pretty good thing going. We can ride out the war and —"

Ewan's firm shake of the head stopped the man's wishful thinking. "Whatever you're saying right now is motivated by fear, not logic. Be sensible, Keeley. You're sick and getting sicker."

"When the darkies come back, your freak-eyed lady can give me something to make everything right. They have to let them back in sometime, right?"

Ewan gritted his teeth against the way Keeley blithely dismissed the people he expected to provide his salvation, and against the thought that if Marlie did return, he wouldn't be there.

All for the best, his mind said, but his chest cramped in a way that belied that.

"Keeley, there's no guarantee of their return or that she'll be able to help you if they do," Ewan said, but he saw his answer in Keeley's dull eyes and closed-off expression. "Or of riding out the war here, for that matter."

"Well, there's no guarantees out there, either," Keeley said, shoving his hands deeper into his pockets. He shrugged. Twisted his lips.

Ewan sighed. His mind was spinning counterarguments, but common sense was no match against stubbornness and Keeley was as stubborn as they come. "You can have my tent and bedroll. Dig into the ground at the head of the bedroll and you'll find a metal tin with some greenbacks to use if these guards ever come to understand that their purpose here isn't to kill us."

Ewan didn't have much hope in that coming to pass, but he'd taken out what he thought he'd need for safe passage and could only hope that Keeley would be able to make use of the rest of it.

Keeley nodded, then reluctantly stuck out his hand, which Ewan grasped firmly.

I wish he would . . . I wish . . .

He stopped. He'd learned long ago that wishes were about as useful as a holey fishing net. Wishes hadn't kept his mother and siblings safe from his father. Ewan's logic had done that. And though he should have regretted how things had turned out back then, the day his father had taken his rifle, walked out into the woods, and never come back had been one of relief for him.

"Be safe, Red."

Ewan nodded but didn't offer the same platitude. He knew Keeley was already searching for the next man who could be useful to him instead of thinking of how he could be useful to himself. Ewan didn't judge him for his weakness — not much at least.

Keeley stumbled off, and Ewan felt a pang of guilt as the man stopped and looked helplessly about him, then continued on until he melted into one of the clusters of prisoners. Ewan pulled his gaze away; he had to keep track of those who held the key to his success, not those who wouldn't even believe in the possibility of their own.

The barber and the other officer sat around a nearby fire, close to the darkness that rimmed the yard. Two other officers sat with them. He could hear their crude jokes, and then the songs they sang, but as it grew closer to time for everyone to retire — and for the nightly shift exchange for the prison guards — he noticed first one face disappear from around the firelight, and then another.

Ewan crept in the shadows between fires, keeping his steps silent. For a moment, he was a child again, creeping past his father as the man stared bitterly into the distance. Those years of living like a skittish cat had trained him well — no one paid heed as he passed the various groups of prisoners. Men talked and bluffed and gambled as they did every night at Randolph. Guards lazed about, as drowsy and ready for sleep as those they kept watch over.

Ewan walked on, toward an area that made the best sense for digging an escape tunnel. It was one he'd scouted out himself, although digging out had been one of several plans he'd come up with. Each plan had its dangers, but digging had also required a group of conspirators and he hadn't trusted anyone besides Keeley.

Trust?

Ewan's trust only extended so far. Keeley knew nothing about him. If they were ever to meet again, the only thing the man who had been his closest friend in the prison would be able to recall was his name, maybe, and his restless energy. No one really knew Ewan, and that was for the better.

As he approached the looming wall of the

stockade at the farthest point of the camp, he caught sight of shadows moving within shadows. It wasn't a trick of the eye — it was the possibility of freedom.

The men had dug at the point farthest from the watch house. When the guard's shift change occurred, they had their backs to this point for the longest period of time, and it took the longest for their replacements to arrive.

Well done, officers.

"And to think, I was worried about losing nearly a stone," one man whispered. "But if it helps me shimmy through that tunnel, it'd be worth it. Come on, men. Abe's waiting on us."

Ewan crouched in the darkness, close enough to make out the men's figures as the first man crawled down into the hole and began making his way through. A joke broke the silence between them every now and then, but not the tension. Forcing oneself into the earth driven only by the hope of emerging on the other side was a mad type of bravery, even for a man well-acquainted with the threat of death.

"Okay, who's in next? Down you go, Hendricks."

Ewan glanced about in the darkness, checking to see that none of the new shift guards had arrived early or none of the old shift guards had turned back. He was hoping the following men would move at a quicker clip, or he'd be in trouble. That was when he heard it.

There was a quick, sharp groan from the direction of the escaping prisoners. Not one made by men, but by wood. He heard something snap loudly — rope? — and then a more prolonged groan.

"Shit, it's coming down," someone shouted, fear overriding the imperative for quiet. Ewan couldn't see it, not in this darkness, but he could hear the steady groan and the popping of twisted fibers and came to the only logical conclusion: A section of the stockade was falling. It appeared that although the men had had the sense to pick the perfect place to escape, they had chosen to dig near a point of support in the hastily erected wooden fence.

"Jesus. Run!"

There was an ungodly moan and then an impact that echoed through the camp loudly enough to wake the dead. Dirt and debris carried by the fence's impact with the ground prickled against Ewan's face.

The attempt was over, it seemed . . . or was it? The officers had scattered as soon as the fence began to fall, but now a section lay on the ground, leaving a wide-open path. A cool breeze pushed its way through the opening, cutting through the stench of the camp and funneling the scent of pine to Ewan.

He didn't think. One moment he was crouching, the next he was sprinting forward, hopping onto the remains of the section of fence and running along it toward freedom. His execrable excuse for shoes tapped loudly against the wood with each long stride, and the logs rolled this way and that as he ran, forcing him to readjust his balance with every step. Behind him he heard a commotion. A gunshot rang out and he wasn't sure if it was aimed at him or some other unlucky prisoner.

Think only of the next step. And then the next.

He hopped down onto solid earth, and relief shuddered up his leg at the contact. The ground was no different from what he'd just been crouching on, and he was still deep in Confederate territory, but he felt the fury of Athena springing from Zeus's forehead surge through him as he leapt into freedom. He made no clarion call to the sky, however; he was no god or goddess, just a mortal who would now have to cower and crawl his way toward Union-held territory.

"Mmmmph!" He almost bypassed the muffled cry, but then he saw the vein of caved-in ground, and the pale hand sticking up in the moonlight. For a moment he thought to keep running; it was logical after all. Instead, he stopped and quickly began scooping up fistfuls of the soft dirt until a face was slowly revealed. His barber.

"Thank you," the man said. His breathing was labored, his eyes wide as he strained against the heavy dirt. He was wiggling his way up through the soil, slowly, and Ewan tried pulling at his hand to speed things, but to no avail. Another shot, closer this time. More shouts, and the baying of a hound.

"Go," the officer said. "Go quickly! Toward the river!"

"Good luck," Ewan said. He didn't think of what would happen to the officer when he was found. He hoped that by some turn of chance, he'd find his way out, too. But he followed the man's command, running heedlessly because caution was a luxury he no longer had.

The dog howled again, and was joined by another.

Breathe in. Breathe out.

He repeated the phrase in his mind as he

had been taught when he was a child, giving himself a single task to focus on.

Breathe in —

Ewan ran into something solid and thick at chest level, the hard *thwack* of it knocking him down onto his ass. A tree branch? No, it was an obstruction made of flesh; solid as oak, but all too human. He looked up and was able to make out a dark figure in the pittance of moonlight that shone down.

"Where are the others?" The whisper was harsh, hurried.

A bit of relief loosened the muscles in his back, which had been tensed and ready to spring upon the man. It seemed the appendage belonged to an ally and not a foe.

"Captured," he replied, easing his way back. Just because he was an ally of the officers didn't mean he'd be one to Ewan. "They brought down the stockade with their tunneling."

There was a heavy sigh, followed by shouts from the direction of the prison.

"Let's move. Now." A hand reached down and interlocked with Ewan's, the strong grip levering him up. Ewan made out the man's shape turning in the darkness. After that his focus was fully on the man's back, struggling to keep up, to move silently, to not fall and be left behind as they dashed through the dark woods. They crashed through trees, splashed through shallows in the river to evade the scent-seeking dogs. After what seemed like ages, Ewan realized he could no longer hear any sign of pursuit. He wasn't sure if that was because they were no longer being chased or if the beat of his heart and the wheeze of his breath blocked out all other sound.

Ewan ran without heed of his surroundings, his sense trained on keeping up with his ally in the darkness. He regretted his tunnel vision when his foot came down into a hole and he fell forward, painfully wrenching his ankle.

He didn't cry out as pain blasted through his ankle. "I've injured my ankle," he said calmly, even as he struggled to his feet.

"Can you walk?" came the terse response.

Ewan tentatively tried to rest his weight on his injured ankle and bit back a low grunt as a million hooks of pain pulled in different directions as he applied pressure.

"I can manage." He took a step toward the man's voice and his ankle gave out from under him. He collapsed again, catching himself on his hands this time. "You can leave me. You've helped enough. Thank you."

Ewan felt nothing at the thought of being left. It was often the most sensible solution to a problem, though rarely used because human decency and logic sometimes sat on opposite sides of the fence.

"I won't," the man bit out. "Besides, if you get picked up by a patrol, you could lead back to us, and I can't take any chances."

"I wouldn't talk," Ewan said. He wasn't lying.

"So you say." The man sighed. "I knew something like this would happen. All right, come on then."

He knelt and pulled Ewan's arm over his shoulders, sliding an arm around his torso to support his weight. They made their way slowly, Ewan trying his best not to be a burden. They soon arrived at the perimeter of a property. There they came upon a shack — Ewan could make out the silhouette of a large house in the distance — and the man used a key on the padlock that held it closed.

"In here for now," he said brusquely, but his touch was gentle and slow with his own fatigue as he helped Ewan inside.

"Thank you," Ewan managed. The words seemed inadequate, but the man gave his shoulder a pat and then moved back into the night, closing and locking the door behind him.

Ewan sat slumped against the wall of the shack, imagining what else filled the dark space. Gardening implements? Food? Weapons?

The bodies of men too poleaxed to verify who was aiding them and why?

He lay with the dull sensations that throbbed through him, accepting the burst of red behind his eyes when he shifted his leg too quickly and jarred his ankle. He breathed through the pain. The stitch in his side and the dryness of his lips, his battered feet encased in shoes that had lost their soles miles before they reached wherever he'd found himself. All of those painful things were simply reminders that he was alive, ones that he dearly needed from time to time.

Ewan started up into a sitting position at the scratch of a key searching for the lock, although he hadn't heard any footsteps. Had he fallen asleep? Likely.

The door opened and two figures stepped in, closing it behind them. A match was struck and held to the wick of a candle. The brightness dazzled him at first, and then he was sure he must be dreaming, because there was Marlie's face illuminated in the circle of soft light. Her hair was braided into a crown on her head, like the laurel of antiquity, and her shoulders were bare save for a fold of white material.

Had his fantasy come to life?

Then the light flickered as she made some adjustment. She pulled her robe closed, a dark, heavy wool that covered her to the neck.

She stepped closer, and then those eyes that haunted his fantasies went wide. "Socrates?"

"I've been called such before," he said, his pain well and truly forgotten. Ewan realized that his mouth had curved up into a smile, rather inappropriate given his current situation. He frowned, hoping to balance it out into some semblance of seriousness. "I also go by Ewan McCall."

The man who had guided him stepped into the light and Ewan recognized the same wry expression he'd seen a month or so ago. *Get in line, son.*

"And you're Tobias," Ewan said. "Thank you for your help."

Tobias seemed a bit taken aback that Ewan knew his name, and he heaved a sigh when he turned to Marlie.

"You've injured your ankle, I hear," she said in that lovely cadence that he heard every time he read her letters to himself.

"He wouldn't be here otherwise," Tobias said. "I told you —"

"Well, he's here now, so let's see what we can do." She knelt before him and lifted his leg up so that the heel of his foot rested between her thighs, and Ewan let out a strangled sound that she mistook for pain.

"I'm sorry." Her hands went to the hem of his too-short pants, raising them a bit to get a better view of his ankle, and her brows drew together at what she saw. Ewan's gaze was so fixated on her face that he didn't notice what her hands were doing until pain radiated through his ankle. He didn't allow himself to cry out.

"Can you move your foot this way and that?" she asked.

"Yes," he said.

She stared at him. "So do it."

Ewan let out a pained laugh at his attempt. "Perhaps my injury is graver than I imagined."

"Perhaps." She began pulling off his shoe, gently, and Ewan found himself caught in a strange matrix of arousal and pain — and embarrassment. She was fresh and smelled of flowers, and he needed a scouring to be anywhere near clean. Still, she didn't wrinkle her nose as she settled the heel of his bare foot back between her thighs, squeezing to hold it in place as she examined it. Ewan was acutely aware that she wore nothing but a shift beneath her robe.

"Looks like a sprain. A bad one. I don't think you'll get far if you try to go anywhere for the next few days."

"Sarah is going to have my hide for this," Tobias muttered, pacing behind Marlie.

"She said no *new* operations," Marlie said. "This was already in place. Besides, if you hadn't gone, what would have become of him?"

"Him? What about the others? I went for a group of men, not one."

"Even one man is worth saving," she said, a serious tone to her voice that Ewan had never heard before.

Tobias finally stopped pacing, his sigh indicating his acquiescence.

"He can rest out here for a spell, I suppose," he said, peering over Marlie's shoulder as she worked. "Melody's been sticking that pointy little nose of hers everywhere in the house, but here is safe enough."

"Hm. I'm not sure I agree." Marlie's voice was softer now, distracted, as she opened a bottle and soaked a strip of cloth with its contents. A strong herbal scent filled the air — Ewan picked up notes of sage and peppermint — and then she began wrapping the cool, damp cloth around his injury. "This shed is away from the house, that's true, but he might be discovered at any time."

Ewan watched the scene before him play out with detached curiosity. He combed through every bit of gossip he'd heard about Sarah Lynch: freed her slaves, paid her black staff, probable Unionist, gave freely to those imprisoned by the Confederates. At the prison he had assumed that Marlie and Tobias were at the same level, but there was something about the dynamic between them. He was deferential, as if he worked for Marlie. Which meant . . .

"Are you a Lynch?" Ewan asked, only realizing how tactless it was when both sets of eyes narrowed in his direction.

"The Lynches have the distinction of holding me in their ranks," she said without looking up at him. He assumed the jolt his ankle received as she worked was a co-incidence. Tobias rolled his eyes and resumed the conversation Ewan had interrupted.

"Melody never came out here before," he said. "You think she'd be caught dead doing anything close to work?"

Marlie's lips pursed. "She hasn't come

here *yet,* Tobias. But she could, and she likely will eventually to see what else she can try to claim as her own. Or if she keeps hinting to her Home Guard friends, Lynchwood might be searched. There's only one place she has no access to, that would be overlooked in a search, and we both know it."

"No," Tobias said, drawing himself up tall. "It's too dangerous. We need to go get Sarah."

One corner of Marlie's mouth turned up, as if the idea of danger was exciting, and Ewan felt the pull of her despite his throbbing muscles. "You knew it was dangerous when I asked you to do this, and yet you went out into the night to help those men. If I ask you to put yourself at risk, I must also be willing to do my part. I will handle Sarah." She finished wrapping Ewan's ankle and sighed. "Besides, one malnourished Yank won't change our odds too much, given everything else."

They looked at Ewan at the same time again, Tobias annoyed, Marlie unreadable.

"Do you know how to be quiet, Socrates?" she asked.

He nearly laughed, thinking of all those nights curled in a corner with a book in front of him; he'd peek over the top after slowly turning each page to make sure the quiet *swish* hadn't caught his father's attention.

"I'm well practiced in the art of silence, Miss Marlie."

Finally, she smiled at him, and it was like the cool breeze that had induced him to run toward freedom back at the camp. Something danced through him, and he tore his gaze from her face. No feeling should have been dancing, prancing, or otherwise happily making itself known at the sight of her. Fantasizing about Marlie had been one thing, but this was reality, and in reality he was a man who was neither worthy of her nor available for attachment.

He forced himself to his feet, taking the pain and focusing on it instead of Marlie's beauty.

"Come with me," she said.

CHAPTER 6

Marlie had been attempting to decode the letter she'd received from a Mr. LaValle, one of the higher-ups in the Loyal League, for nearly twenty minutes. She'd dipped her finger in a dish of milk, spread it over the surface of the paper, and calmly waited for the scrawling black text to appear once the SS fluid was activated. She'd glanced between the words and her Polybius square, drawing out their hidden meaning. But she hadn't been able to move beyond the second sentence on account of the distraction caused by the escaped prisoner she'd impulsively decided to harbor in her home. Ewan was separated by the wood backing of her desk and the wall it was pushed up against — and he'd been silent the entire day — but she could *feel* him.

Her nerves were frayed, her mouth was dry, and her hands shook every time she picked up a pencil, and not just because the

127

man she'd spent an unseemly amount of time thinking about had been secreted into her private quarters. When she sent Tobias to complete the mission they'd undertaken on their last visit to the prison, she'd thought he'd be leading the group of men away from the prison, not bringing home an injured man in need of aid. Perhaps Sarah had been correct; Marlie was not prepared for this. She'd downplayed the danger when talking with Tobias, but now that she was sitting in the quiet of her rooms, ears straining for any sign of movement from Ewan, she realized just how foolish it had been to propose this. It was reckless, dangerous, and improper — and Marlie fairly hummed with excitement in spite of those things. Or because of them.

She turned her attention back to the page, willing herself to focus despite the fraught situation she was in. After a few moments of decoding, she finally had a complete message.

I thank you for your continued information about Cahill and his Home Guard. Reports confirm that resistance to the Secessionists is strong in your area, and shows no sign of slackening. A Dr. Johnson has reached out to Union Forces about the

Heroes of America, whom you mentioned in your previous correspondence. It appears that what we thought were welcome pockets of local resistance are transforming into a coordinated anti-Reb front. I understand why Governor Vance is so eager to crush these groups and present a united Confederate front — Europe is watching, after all. But so are we. You are the only one of our people who's had contact with the group; if ever the opportunity arises to build a stronger link with the Heroes, you have our full support.

Marlie put the letter down, her already overtaxed mind struggling to reconcile what she'd just read with reality. Her involvement with the League had occurred by happenstance, a natural acquaintance born of whispers here and there from conductors and escaping slaves. Helping the officers escape had fallen to Tobias, and had been independent of her interactions with the Loyal League. This was the first time anything had been asked of her beyond basic information, and Marlie wondered if La-Valle would laugh if he knew whom he was asking. Marlie Lynch, who had spent more time with plants than people and never left her home without an escort. Who, these days, was hardly brave enough to leave her rooms.

Marlie Lynch, who has a Union man hidden in her home. She allowed herself to feel a bit proud of that bit of daring, to feel as brave as the detectives she'd read of. However, she was no detective, and the dispatch reinforced something that had been nagging at her all day: The danger of the Home Guard was clear and immediate. The area was crawling with them as they tried to flush out the skulkers; the other Railroad conductors had even temporarily ceased their work because of the danger. Thus, in addition to a woman who would turn them over to the authorities at the drop of a hat under her roof, Marlie also had irrefutable proof of the Lynches' Unionist leanings and no idea what to do with him once he recovered beyond leaving him to his luck.

And Sarah . . . Marlie still hadn't told her. That morning, Melody had forced Sarah to go a-calling with her, visiting the neighbors Sarah hadn't spoken to in years — the dyed-in-the-wool slave masters who wouldn't acknowledge Sarah in the street and published thinly veiled threats against her in the local paper.

What she'd thought to be one secret to protect Sarah from worry had grown into out-and-out deception. She didn't think Sarah would force Ewan to leave, but part of her was worried about how she would react. Sarah always wanted Marlie to err on the side of caution, to not do too much too fast. She'd been stunned by Marlie's volunteering to go to the prison herself. She knew nothing of the agreement between Tobias and the officers to lead them from the prison. And she'd certainly never had an inkling of the fact that Marlie had been talking with the men enough to grow fond of one of them.

Marlie tried to imagine what she would do in Sarah's position, if she were told that a strange man whose presence put them all at risk was holed up in the attic, but each time she could only think, *Well, it's Socrates.* That was an explanation that wouldn't pass muster.

How could she explain the interactions she'd had with him? The letters she'd written when she'd thought that the walls of the prison and society would stand strong between them? How could she explain that the last time she'd seen him at Randolph, he'd looked at her as if he knew her, and it'd made her feel as if maybe she wanted him to? His blue eyes were pure ice, but when they'd rested on her she'd felt their heat. It'd been like the realization she had the first time she'd traveled into the winter cold without gloves: Ice could burn.

And his safety now rested on Sarah's reaction to Marlie's omission of facts. Her fears put into stark relief the nature of the relationship between them; Sarah could say "no" and Ewan would have to leave, despite what Marlie wanted or believed was right.

There was a sliding sound beneath her skirts and Marlie jumped, nearly toppling back in her chair. She righted herself, then peered under her chair and saw a slip of paper on the floor.

Miss Marlie,

I thank you once again for your kindness. I have a question that is most unbecoming, but the result of not asking even more so: Is there some manner in which I might make use of the necessary?

Your most humble and
obedient servant,
Socrates

Marlie stood and looked about: In the mad rush to secrete him into the house, she hadn't left him a chamber pot, and she knew why. She'd meant to bring him one after fetching remnants of the previous night's dinner for him, but when she'd walked into the room with his plate he'd been stripped to the waist, balancing on one leg as he washed off the grime of the prison camp. He'd been a reeking mess when he entered — she'd never seen him within a stone's throw of clean — but there he'd been, beardless and shirtless, the ropy muscles of his arms and chest illuminated by candlelight.

Marlie had placed the plate down on a bundle of rosemary and left him to the rest of his ablutions without another thought of his other bodily needs. She'd been too distracted by her own.

She moved to search about for a pot and then realized that his request was likely urgent if he'd been moved to write that note. Could he wait while she searched closets and cabinets? The house was silent as she considered her options; everyone was out, and if anyone returned suddenly, they couldn't gain entry to her rooms.

She hesitated; this was courting trouble. However, Marlie and trouble were already on a first-name basis, it seemed.

She quietly pulled the desk away from the wall, not too far since Ewan was all lean muscle, as she'd seen for herself. She slid her hand over the wall until she felt the ridge where the door had been cut into the wall, and then she pushed. It swung inward, and his face appeared in the opening, the slightest frown pulling at his lips.

"I'm sorry to be more of a bother than I already am, but . . ." His whisper trailed off.

She shook her head to show he was no bother to her, and then motioned for him to squeeze out of the opening. She had looked down at him as he crouched in the doorway, but now he was standing at his full height and she had to look up into those eyes that always made her feel as if he were peering right into her.

Her face warmed.

"There's a privy in my bedchamber," she whispered. "There's a plumbing system, so . . ." Finishing that sentence would rend the already frayed propriety of their situation, so she turned and began walking to her room. He was a smart man; he could figure out the mechanics of a rooftop water receptacle and gravity.

There was no noise behind her, but when she looked back he was tight on her heels, and she startled. He'd said he was quiet, and apparently it hadn't just been an appeasement.

How can a big man like him move so silently, even while injured?

"Is the painkiller I gave you working?" she asked quietly. "I have laudanum, though I've been saving it for dire circumstances."

"I've seen too many men fall into laudanum's embrace to ask for it," he said, his voice low but clear. "And I assume that you have given me the treatment you think best, which is fine with me."

Marlie didn't know if all those words meant he wasn't in pain; he'd talked cheerfully with an ankle so swollen and ugly he should have been in tears.

She stopped at the door of her chamber and pointed out the privy, then returned to her workspace.

She stood beside her desk, fiddling with the decoding square.

He is just another passenger on his way to freedom.

He was at her mercy, and even the thought of anything further was inappropriate. More importantly, she reminded herself of the obvious: He was white. She'd been immersed in white society for the past ten years, had white blood in her veins, but she was a Negro woman in a country that was fighting a war to keep people like her enslaved. It didn't matter that Socrates was

135

for the Union. She wasn't a fan of his devotion to logic, but it didn't require much to see that her fascination was an unwise one.

"They take what they want because nothing is denied to them, Marlie. But taking is different from loving. Problem is, it feels a lot like loving 'til you find out otherwise."

Her mother's words surged up from the recesses of her mind. What had they been discussing — perhaps the white boy at the general store who always paid her too much attention when they went into town? She didn't remember, but at the time she'd thought her mother overly careful; now she understood she'd been giving her a warning.

" 'O, mickle is the powerful grace that lies, in herbs, plants, stones, and their true qualities.' "

The low voice startled her, and she turned to find Ewan looking over her equipment with those keen eyes of his. He seemed to be entranced by the vapor gathering in the coils and the low hiss of steam releasing as the medicine distilled. Ewan looked over her distillation system how most men looked at a shapely ankle. Maybe that was what drew her to him; that he was a curious man in a world full of incurious ones.

He reached out a hand to touch, and then

seemed to think better of it, as if sensing that she wouldn't like that. He was correct. She'd worked hard to assemble and calibrate her apparatus, and he could keep his hands to himself — even if they were very nice hands.

"The Apothecary put us all in a bad light with that irresponsible plan of his. I would have told Juliet to go home and perhaps drink some calming tea," she said, moving to stand beside him. She should have ushered him back into the drying room. She didn't. "I admit I'm surprised that someone so committed to the Stoics would be a fan of Shakespeare."

Something resembling a smile, but not quite, pushed up at the corners of his mouth.

"I was a child with a limited library who spent all my time reading and rereading what was available," he said, then gingerly lowered himself to a kneeling position to look up at the still from below. "My father was rather fond of the tragedies."

The words were delivered without inflection, but there was something in his grip on the edge of the table that belied his measured delivery.

"You didn't find it romantic, then? Star-crossed lovers and such?" she asked.

She felt foolish as soon as the words were out of her mouth, could taste the residue of an implication she hadn't intended. She squeezed her eyes shut and when she opened them he sat with his head tilted, as if actually giving the question thought.

"I'm not very well-versed in the topic, but I'd have to argue against two dead adolescents being romantic," he said. "I did find many of the passages to be quite moving, though, before the poison and suicide and such. 'Did my heart love till now?' "

The question hung in the air between them, resonating between the motes of dust caught in the late afternoon sun that streamed through the window. He looked up at her, his eyes wide and searching, and for a moment Marlie could scarcely breathe. There was warmth in the depths of those eyes, she could see now. Warmth in the flush that spread over his broad cheekbones.

He turned back to the still, all of his focus on the apparatus before him. "Your alembic is quite . . . smooth. And sturdy."

Marlie cleared her throat and focused on the still, too. She hadn't wanted him to read anything into her words, and she wouldn't search for any meaning in his. She'd rather discuss science than sonnets anyway; there was less room for misinterpretation there.

"I'm not surprised you found the most ancient piece of equipment here," she replied, brushing a finger over the blown-glass ball. A candle below it heated the liquid inside, pushing the vapor down a long glass tube that ended in a small opening, where it dripped into a waiting vial. "It serves its purpose, but great advances have been made since the days of your Greek alchemists." Her hand drifted over to the more modern metal still, glistening bronze with multiple condensers projecting from its sides like unwieldy appendages.

"An acolyte of modern science, I see. So you don't believe in the balance of the humors?" he asked, one auburn eyebrow raised. "I'd say the country is suffering from an excess of phlegm right now. Maybe you could whip something up to take care of that?"

He grinned at her then, and Marlie felt a sharp pinch in her chest at the beauty in the creases around his mouth and the crinkles at the corners of his eyes.

"I'll set to it immediately," she said, fixing her gaze on the still, which was a more proper resting place than the face of a man she was giving shelter to. She moved one bottle from below the dripping end of the coiled tube, replacing it with another without wasting a drop in a practiced move. "Lynch's Mint Tisane will break that right up."

He was quiet for a moment and when she glanced at him again, he was watching her hands.

"I didn't realize you did this all on your own. All of the salves and tonics you brought to Randolph —" he said, and then nodded to himself once as if it met his approval. Marlie didn't know why that one nod made all the hours of work seem more worthwhile.

"You seemed to keep quite busy there," she teased. "I'm sure you would have had your own distillery in the works, eventually. McCall's Moonshine."

"I don't drink," he said, and she noticed the tightness in his body again, one that was instinctual, how a child shies away from a hot stove after having been burned once. He caught himself, and turned to her with some approximation of a pleasant expression. "How did you come to this line of work?"

It pleased her that he called it work. Most people treated it as a hobby despite her hours of reading, study, and testing new formulas.

"Plants and their healing properties have been a part of my life for as long as I can remember. Some of the first memories I have are of going out and collecting leaves and roots and making them into things that helped people. It was when I moved here, with my . . . with the Lynches, that I began to study more modern techniques of distillation and processing." She pulled a battered and dog-eared book down from the bookshelf and handed it to him. "This was gifted to me soon after I arrived. I was having a hard time acclimating and Sarah thought it might distract me. She was right."

She could see the curiosity on his face as he took the tome on medical botany from her and began flipping through its pages. "You didn't always live here?"

A diplomatic question.

"No," she said. "I came here when I was thirteen. Before that I lived with my mother, in the east of the state. She wanted me to have more opportunity than she'd been given, and when the opportunity arose she sent me here."

"Are you still close with her?" he asked. He flipped a page and his eyes scanned back and forth slowly as he read. He dropped a fingertip to the page, just beneath something she'd written in the margin. She hoped it wasn't from that brief, embarrassing period when she'd been smitten with Tobias and taken to scrawling his name surrounded by hearts in all her books.

"I was. I visited with her a couple of times a year, but she's passed on now." She waited for the awkward expression of sympathy, the withdrawal, the polite way of saying "let's not linger on such unpleasantness." Even Sarah, who'd lost her own mother a year before Vivienne, didn't indulge Marlie. It simply wasn't done. She'd read Ewan's Stoics, and knew what they'd say about the grief that was lodged like a splinter between her shoulder blades.

He looked up from the book, and she knew it had to be a draft from the faulty window jamb, but his gaze felt like a caress. "That must have been quite upsetting for you, to lose her by degrees."

It was a tactless observation, and not exactly sympathetic, but Marlie still swallowed against a sudden roughness in her throat, as if a handful of bristly bark had cropped up there. No one had ever understood that — that she hadn't lost her mother once, but every time she'd gone to her mother's with a trunk full of fancy dresses and heavy books, and then left Vivienne behind for Lynchwood. Each time she'd gone home, the distance between her and Vivienne had been more apparent, even if their love had remained the same.

"She never got to see all of this," Marlie said, gesturing toward the still and the books. "She refused to come here. Understandably so. And when I offered to buy her things to make her life easier, she said the old ways had worked just fine for our ancestors, and they'd work for her. I wish I had been able to share what I've learned with her."

Marlie experienced the sudden sensation of nudity that came with unexpectedly revealing one's feelings to a stranger and crossed her arms over her chest. She didn't know why she was telling him these things, just as she didn't know why she'd picked up the pencil and written to him that first time. It was as if some unknown force squeezed at her until she gave up a private part of herself to him.

The sounds of hooves clapping in the drive drew both of their eyes to the window, though she was the only one who moved toward it. He stepped farther into the shadows of the room.

Marlie watched as Stephen's carriage and horses rolled up to the house, and she felt the familiar sense of dread that enveloped her every time Melody was near. She moved back to the side of the desk. "You should go back inside now."

Despite having work to do, despite the danger, she wished he could stay a little longer.

Utterly ridiculous.

"Yes. Right. Thank you, again." He snapped the book shut and brushed past her to slide behind the desk. She pushed the desk back against the wall firmly once he was through, as if she could seal the feelings Ewan stirred up in the drying room with him. She leaned her head against the top of the desk and exhaled shakily.

Ancestors, help me.

She drew a deep breath and then sat down, only to jump again when a knock sounded at the door. She imagined she would be jumping at every sound until Ewan was on his way. She tucked the letter on her desk into a botany book and pulled a pile of blackberry bark over the decoder.

"Yes?"

"It's Sarah." The response was terse — Marlie knew that tone. Sarah was furious. Had Tobias told her?

Marlie opened the door and Sarah stormed in. She pulled off her gloves in a fit of pique and then threw them down on the ground and kicked at one of them.

"The nerve," she spat, glaring at Marlie.

"As if this isn't my home and my life being turned upside down for the sake of some godforsaken man!"

Marlie's lungs contracted and her skin went cold. She'd known Sarah would be angry, but not this angry. Sarah was her closest friend, which superseded the tangled web of family secrets between them, and Marlie hated when she was upset, especially if she was the cause of it.

"I'm sorry," she said. She reached a hand out and Sarah grabbed it, held it fast, but gently. Marlie didn't understand the disconnect between word and deed.

"No, I'm the one who's sorry, Marl," Sarah said. She squeezed her eyes shut in a face that was flushed pink from anger. "While visiting those horrid people today, we heard that there had been another skirmish between the Heroes of America and Vance's militia. Some of the resisters' wives were captured and are being imprisoned as incentive for them to come forward and join the army. In retribution, Cahill's lodgings were burned down in the early hours of the morning."

Marlie's skin pricked as the feeling came back into it. Sarah wasn't angry with her. She didn't know about Ewan at all. That still left Marlie with the job of telling her, but she would attend to that soon enough.

She took a deep breath.

"Was he hurt?" Marlie asked. "I'd hate to waste the burn salve on such a repulsive man, but if you need my help —"

"Marlie, she's awful." It was then that Marlie realized Sarah's hands were shaking. "Don't you see? As soon as Melody heard, she rushed us over to the garrison where Cahill had gone and invited him here. Into our home."

Marlie dropped her hand and stepped back, the room spinning around her. Hosting Ewan was dangerous enough, even without Melody's noxious presence, but Cahill was the accelerant that could send her life up in flames. Beyond that, the man had flatly stated he considered her good for nothing more than being a white man's plaything. How could she be expected to live with him?

"No. Surely Stephen won't allow this."

Marlie struggled against the panic that was building like steam in a glass coil. Ewan's presence. Her Loyal League ties. Her safety and that of everyone at Lynchwood. They were already in danger, but Cahill's arrival would multiply that a thousandfold.

"Stephen lets Melody do as she pleases,"

Sarah said in a shaking voice. "She said it's our duty to provide assistance to such an upright Southern man, and that not offering would convince people of my Unionism. He'll get here later tonight and we're to treat him as an honored guest." She swiped angrily at her eyes. "I thought having that adder here was a violation, but this?"

Marlie's mouth worked, but no words came out. She had to tell Sarah about Ewan, but the shock of the situation was too much.

"Well," Marlie finally managed. "This is inopportune."

Sarah gave a harsh laugh. "Perhaps there's one way in which this isn't so bad. It will certainly throw suspicion off of us once people learn that he's lodging with us."

Marlie startled, tried to hold herself steady against the dizzying realization that hit her. *Surely no one will suspect Ewan's presence with Cahill here, because only a fool would attempt such a thing.*

"Sarah, you must know —"

"Sarah! Where are you, sister dear?" Melody's voice echoed up the stairwell and into the room. She had steered clear since Marlie had implied that some ill might befall her if she entered. "Lace is being stubborn, but I know we must have finer linens for Captain Cahill's bed."

"We'll just have to be careful, is all," Sarah whispered, giving Marlie a fortifying hug. "No more passengers, no more Unionist work, until we figure this out. We'll get through this."

Marlie nodded numbly, and then slumped into her high-backed wooden chair as the door shut. Her head swam like she'd imbibed a dose of laudanum. If she didn't know better she might think some higher power was punishing her for her deception. She pulled open the drawers on her desk and began rifling through the sundry items that had collected there over the years. When her fingers grazed the square of soft red flannel, she tugged it free and stared at it.

She hadn't made a gris-gris since she was a girl — when she first arrived she'd tried to lay a trick that would allow her to return home. Nothing had come to pass, though — and Marlie had eventually educated herself enough to move past such ideas. But in her moment of overwhelming panic, this was the first remedy that had come to mind.

She took up a slip of paper and wrote *"Free me from Melody's presence"* on it, then rolled it up tight and laid it in the middle of the cloth. She dropped in a sliver of Life Everlasting, and a few dried leaves of sage; a three-element gris-gris. She tied it up into a little pouch and splashed a bit of the alcohol she used in her distillations onto the fabric and watched as it absorbed. She closed her eyes and envisioned her mother and that curious smile of hers, and prayed that the charm would work.

Chapter 7

Socrates,

I noticed when I gave you your meal that you'd cleaned and tidied all of the clippings and roots in the drying room, and even created labels for them. I must remind you that you're supposed to be staying off of your ankle, but I give you my thanks, as Sarah is always chiding me about the mess. Were you fibbing when you said you didn't know much about botany?

— M

Dear Marlie,

No need to thank me. I have a restless mind, and whatever activity I can find to distract it is a blessing not a bother.

My ankle is much improved thanks to your skillful care.

My botanic knowledge mostly lies in which plants to avoid (poison ivy) and

which berries not to ingest (learned through harsh experience). The *Illustrated American Botany,* and your drawings in the margins, helped with much of the categorization. You've a deft hand.
Your Obedient Servant,
Socrates E.M.

P.S. I've noticed you spend much of your time in your workspace. I hope you do not remain about for my sake. I don't want to impose on you any further than I already have.

S.E.M.,
If you flatter my drawings I can only assume you are in need of Lynch's Clear Vision tonic, and shall get it to you posthaste.

I linger in my rooms because leaving them has become a gauntlet I'd rather not face. As your Epictetus would say, the world beyond my rooms is not in my control. Melody has begun receiving callers, and she can't have someone who looks like me but wears fine clothes and doesn't do the serving walking about. There is also the problem of Cahill, the Captain of the Home Guard, who has settled in to his comfort and delights in disturbing mine. I try to remain optimistic that my increased time up here will result in great advances in my work.

Since we've touched on the topic of imprisonment, how did you end up at Randolph?

Y.O.S.,
M

Dear M,

I'm sorry to hear about your current circumstances and must admit that the news of Cahill living under your roof is distressing. The man is dangerous, and I hope you are rid of him shortly.

I have quite the knack for getting captured and have been imprisoned at no fewer than three Confederate facilities during my two years of enlistment. Randolph was by far the most amenable, for reasons of location and access to literature. The first time I was captured was while heading home on furlough to meet my brother Malcolm's bride. The prisoner exchanges were still occurring then and I was deemed valuable enough to be traded to my freedom, though not for some months. The second, after a fort I was stationed at was taken by Rebel forces. This last time, I was captured while making my escape from the second prison. I would view it all as unlucky if I didn't find the war deeply unpleasant and entirely ridiculous.

Your Obedient Servant,
Socrates E.M.

S.E.M.,

What do you find ridiculous about the war? Is it not noble to want to keep our country united? Or to fight for the freedom of an enslaved people?

Y.O.S.,
M

Dear Marlie,

I believe the war to be ridiculous because I believe this nation to be ridiculous. The very basis of our nation, the Declaration of Independence, states that it is self-evident that all men are created equal. And yet every aspect of our law and political climate have stated otherwise by creating a hierarchy between white, colored, and native, rich and poor. Thus, this nation was inherently divided, from its very conception. To pretend otherwise is illogical. To add to this foolishness, the Southern legislatures secede on the basis that their rights have been infringed upon, when the only right being disputed is whether to hold other men in bondage for something as inconsequential as the color of their skin. Thus, I argue that our nation is ridiculous, and has always been so.

Don't take this to mean that the war isn't worth fighting. It is an honorable fight against the most despicable facets of human nature. I can expound upon this subject for much longer, but I trust you understand me.

Your Obedient Servant,
Socrates E.M.

P.S. How is it that a woman of your standing was allowed to enter the prison? I am forever grateful for this, but also even more perplexed now that I understand your familial situation.

Dear S,

If you understand my familial situation, do tell. I'll be honest when I say it leaves me quite perplexed.

You have siblings, correct? Well, I suppose I have two, but it has gone unspoken. Sarah brought me here and called me family, and that is what I've remained. I have never been called "my dear sister" or even "my maddening sister." Funny how such a small thing as being given a proper title can seem large when given enough time to reflect on it. I would say it's silly, but it would also be silly to sell a tonic without a label and assume everyone knew what malady it healed.

While there may be ambiguity about my standing in this family, there is none where the world at large is concerned: People who do not know me assume I have neither family nor "a situation," and barely afford me the title of woman. For further discussion, please reference your letter about the inherent ridiculousness of this nation.

Yours,
M.

Marlie,

I know man is perhaps the most ignorant creature in all of creation, so I will not comment on how violently I disagree with any assessment of you that doesn't hold you in the highest esteem.

I have a dear older brother and a maddening younger sister, and, while never explicitly discussed, I assume that to them I am the confounding middle brother. I also have a sister-in-law now, but my tour of Confederate prisons has prevented me from making her acquaintance as yet.

Yours,
E.M.

P.S. If I might bother you once more for the necessary, I'd be obliged.

Ewan was anxious as the door pushed open, and not just because he'd drunk too much from the canteen Marlie had provided him with and his need was truly pressing. He'd spent many nights at Randolph Prison fighting fantasies of Marlie, trying his best not to dishonor her. He'd fended off thoughts of the curve of her breast, and how her shoulder would feel cupped in his palm as he pulled her toward him. But his physical desire for her had been the least dangerous thing, it seemed.

Reading the notes scrawled in her botany books — equations and comparisons with other texts, her own thoughts on how something could be improved — showed him she was a rigorous thinker just as much as their exchanges did. Hearing the toneless hum that was usually followed by the tinkling of glass bottles and tubes made him ache to see what her face looked like as she concentrated on her work. Glancing at the base of the door to his refuge a thousand times a day after noticing that first slip of paper peeping through, in search of the next note . . . that was a sensation Ewan had never experienced. Agitation was no stranger to him, but the feeling that consumed him in those spaces — sometimes hours, sometimes minutes — when he awaited her response seemed some kind of retribution for the pain he'd caused others. That Marlie was smart enough to know better than to create evidence of his stay but continued to slip scraps of paper into the room anyway made it all the worse.

He should have been focused on getting to Tennessee, back to the work his superiors had insisted he was made for. Instead he was passing notes and mooning over Marlie like a teenaged fool. He'd read all the old newspapers piled in a corner: Union morale was low, and victories were few and far between. What information had gone undiscovered while Ewan had puttered about in prison? He couldn't think on it. He found he also couldn't think on what he'd be returning to once his ankle healed and he made his way back North. Perhaps that's why thoughts of Marlie had become such a fixation.

He climbed through the door carefully, favoring his good ankle, and squeezed past the desk and there she was. It was only when he realized that she wore her night-gown and a wrapper that he wondered at the time. Time of night was all he allowed himself to think of, not how seeing her in such a state was a new stroke of intimacy between them.

"I'm sorry to disturb you again," he said. He tried to think of what his brother, Malcolm, would say; something witty and dashing and perhaps slightly provocative. "I've got a rather small bladder, it seems."

She looked at him with raised brows and he understood immediately that Malcolm would not have said such a thing. Speaking with Marlie was comfortable in a way he hadn't experienced with anyone else before, but that didn't mean he could do it without making a hash of it.

"It's no bother," she said, gracing him with a polite smile. "I was working on something. I haven't slept well these last three nights, and having a bit of company wouldn't hurt." She tucked some papers into a leather portfolio and placed them into a drawer. Her hair was down, curls brushed out into a thick, downy blanket that floated past her shoulders.

"I'm sure my presence plays some part in your lack of sleep," he said. Now that he looked at her, he could see that darkness shadowed the delicate skin beneath her eyes. His thumb pressed into his pants, a much rougher caress than the one he imagined sweeping over her face.

She led him to the WC, stopping in the doorway to her bedchamber. "Between Melody and Captain Cahill, and a war raging in the surrounding woods, I have quite enough to keep me up nights. A Union soldier in the drying room is an interesting diversion at this point, which tells you all you need to know about the goings-on outside these rooms."

Ewan kept his facial expression blank, composed, at the sound of Cahill's name, despite the flare of anger, and the familiar wash of shame when he remembered the feel of the man's body caving beneath his blows.

Although Ewan loved the Greeks, he had never been a fan of their Fates, and it seemed they held him in the same esteem. For Cahill to show up first at the prison, and now at the place that had provided him sanctuary, seemed like something out of the old tales, with grim adversaries who could not evade a final reckoning with their nemesis. Ewan reminded himself that although Cahill embodied the toxic hatred that now stained the nation, smiting him would do nothing to help mend the country. It didn't stop him from wanting to do it all the same.

Marlie turned back to her work, and Ewan made quick use of the WC. He had rigged a way out of the room on his second night there: a pallet with wheels that he could slide under the desk and push it away. He was proud of the work; Marlie would appreciate such a device. He absently wondered if telling her that would lessen her stress or increase it. It would create less work for her, not having to monitor his needs, but it might disturb her to know he could enter her room at any time — not that he would abuse her trust in him. Ewan fastened his trousers and decided to keep quiet unless she asked specifically.

He tried to keep his focus blinkered as he passed through her room on his way back to her work space, but he was overly observant by nature, and he couldn't help but notice all the small, intimate details that marked the room as specifically Marlie's. Her toiletries lay scattered over a dressing table, bottles of perfumes and jars of oils. The dress she had worn that day was folded over the back of a chair, as if she had been too tired to hang it. A white apron with streaks of green where she'd rubbed her fingers against it had slid to the floor. A sachet of dried rose petals rested on her pillow, and a silver-backed hairbrush lay in the middle of the bed.

He thought about her hair, how soft and inviting it looked, and imagined how it would feel to gather it into his hands. His fingers curled against his palms as he limped back into her work space. She stood at the window, peering out as she finished plaiting her hair into a single braid. Ewan smelled flowers as he stepped closer to her, and realized the enticing scent of wisteria was from the oil she used to smooth her hair down.

"There are militiamen about," she said, nodding her chin toward the window. "Cahill's Home Guard. I feel silly and ungrateful — I've lived a life of luxury compared to so many, no matter their race — but each day I feel as if I lose another part of my home, and I resent that. I just have to remind myself that no matter how dire the reports in the papers, the North will prevail and all will be well."

The certainty in her voice pricked at Ewan. How could she say such a thing with surety? She could lose more than her home with Cahill about, and luck could not ensure her safety.

You could, he thought. His hands curled into fists as a sense memory of the same fists pummeling Cahill until his knuckles were raw and he couldn't tell if the blood was Cahill's or his own; a macabre blood brothers' oath.

Ewan could take it no longer.

"Please be careful of Cahill, Marlie," he said, trying to keep his voice calm. The beginnings of a headache gathered between his eyes. "Fortune is no shield against men of his ilk."

Men such as me.

"I admit that I find his behavior troublesome, but he wouldn't harm me in my own home," she said. "I'm a Lynch."

Her voice wavered — she was less certain in the Lynch name than in Lincoln's, it seemed. It was the only thing standing between her and Cahill, so Ewan had to hope it would be enough. He remembered the expression on Cahill's face as he'd sat tied to a chair. He hadn't said a word as Ewan had punched and pricked and poked, his calculated efforts fraying as Cahill remained silent.

"*You murdered those men in cold blood, without their weapons, without respect,*" Ewan bit out, holding his anger at bay. "*I will know who gave you the information about the Negro battalion, and I will know what else they've told you.*"

"*What men?*" Cahill asked. The question was casual, despite the sweat streaking down his abraded face.

"*The detachment of Negro —*"

Cahill's loud, sharp laughter shocked Ewan into silence. The man had been emotionless throughout the interrogation, but now he shook with laughter. Tears welled in his eyes, though they were still emotionless.

"*I didn't kill any men, son,*" Cahill said. "*I killed a bunch of animals playacting as soldiers that needed to be put down. It had to be done to preserve the purity of this country. Of the American people.*"

"*What's pure about men who can't survive without leeching off of the work of others?*" Ewan asked.

Cahill stared at him, no longer laughing. "*I'm fighting for the future of this country, and so are others like me. If a darkie ain't a slave, then there ain't no place for him here. I did my duty, and that you don't realize that is why the South will never subjugate itself to the yellow-bellied Northmen."*

It wasn't his words that broke Ewan's composure; it was his conviction. It was the way he smiled, as if pleased with himself. It was that Ewan knew no amount of logic would change a mind corrupted with ideals of racial superiority. Cahill embodied everything wrong with their country.

Ewan lunged for him.

Ewan wiped at the sweat the memory had pushed out on his brow. "I hate that he's here in your home. I hate that war puts you in the path of men such as him. I hate that we live in a world where this illogical war is even being fought."

Ewan had never said the words aloud.

Marlie moved away from the window, turning toward him with questions in her gaze. Ewan braced for whatever she would ask of him.

"Why did you join the army? You seem to detest everything about it, and . . . it's hard for me to imagine you on the battlefield with a gun instead of a book."

Ewan grimaced. In his hands, a book could be much more painful than a gun. He'd once ripped out a rich, heavy page of a book, folded it to a sharp point, and pushed it into the bed of a Reb's fingernails until he had revealed the location of float-

164

ing bombs strategically placed to disrupt the naval blockade. And he had slept soundly afterward.

He wouldn't tell her that though.

"I don't subscribe to zealotry based on accident of birth, but the South is wrong and the North is right, generally speaking. A man owes his country service in times of need, and when Lincoln called for volunteers I answered." He paused, trying to convey how a path that might help the tumult in his mind had opened before him. "And I thought that the army could provide me with the kind of discipline I needed. I imagined that it would be orderly — I like order, you see."

She likely wouldn't understand if he told her how badly he'd wanted to believe that the drills and routine of army life would be what he needed to quell the tumultuous thoughts that sometimes rose to the surface of his mind unbidden. Thoughts that could turn to angry action if given no vent.

"You speak as if you were a wild child who needed to be brought to hand, Socrates."

He remembered those times when his breathing exercises weren't enough to stop from lashing out, the disappointment on his mother's face and resentment on his father's. "Some considered me as such," he said.

"Am I to gather that the discipline offered was not what you imagined?" she asked. The hint of a smile tugged at her mouth; it was the slightest movement, one that telegraphed understanding, empathy, and Ewan felt it as if her lips had grazed him. He generally looked at a person's mouth when they spoke — he'd been told his gaze was too intense often enough — and never had one been as compelling as Marlie's. Heat coursed up the back of his neck from that simple millimeter of movement, and he regretted his lack of proper dress. His collar was limp and did nothing to hide his high color.

He cleared his throat.

"I enjoyed certain aspects — the physicality, the training, learning tactics and maneuvers. But I thought it would make me a better man, and there I was mistaken. War makes no man better, and most assuredly not me." He thought of what he'd learned as a counterintelligence interrogator — how to make another man bend to your wishes in the quickest manner possible. As in every other part of life, there was generally one technique that produced the fastest results: pain.

That was the life that awaited him once his ankle healed and he made his way to Tennessee. When Ewan had first been imprisoned at Libby, he'd subscribed to the widely held belief that the discord would be settled quickly. It hadn't been hope, but common sense. Fighting to maintain a practice that required the subjugation of one's fellow man while crying freedom was preposterous. Could a great country really be laid low by such unsophisticated ideas? Ewan had thought that reason would soon prevail, but bloodshed and enmity — and certainty that each battle would be the decisive one — had stretched out day after day. The end of the war had turned into a moving oasis, ever on the horizon and always just out of reach. A crushing victory was needed for the Union to end things, and men like Ewan helped provide tacticians with information that could bring about such a victory. So he'd spend the foreseeable future hurting others and being told to be proud that he could stomach it.

"Ewan?"

He looked at her, unsure what was in his eyes, but Marlie's lips parted.

"I'm sorry. For whatever you've gone through." She took a step toward him, and then her hand was resting on his shirtsleeve.

The feeling that grabbed him fast at her touch was something to marvel at. He imagined that was what peace felt like: a woman like Marlie touching your arm and looking up at you, her eyes full of understanding.

But Marlie understood nothing of him. If she did, she'd neither touch him nor shelter him. She wouldn't offer him her pity when he had reserved none for others in carrying out his duties. Ewan did not regret his work, but he couldn't expect anyone else to accept it.

"Such is life," he said. He stepped away toward the entry to his refuge, but the sensation of her touch lingered even then. "All this killing to prove which men can own which other men and in what capacity. If anything I've done has helped bring us closer to ending the institution of slavery, then it was worth it."

He had to believe this was true.

"So, you believe the South is wrong on a moral level."

"On every level," he clarified. "Morality being one of the higher tiers."

"I've wondered . . ." She took a deep breath. "I've wondered how you can idolize antiquity, and fight against slavery? Greece was a slave society, was it not?"

Her gaze met his now and Ewan felt pinned by it. This was a moment when reading others' emotions was not an asset, because he could see the disappointment in the tightness of her mouth. That was a look he was well acquainted with.

"Yes," he said. "But slavery wasn't race-based there, you see."

"But they still owned other humans?"

"That was one fault of their society, yes," he said, crossing his arms over his chest. "One I do not endorse. 'It is the mark of an educated mind to be able to entertain a certain thought without accepting it.' "

"All right," was all she replied.

A flash of irritation at her tepid response set things off kilter in his world; was she judging him, as others had? Then he thought about the books Marlie had brought for him, the great philosophers he revered so much. She had read the books, too, had seen the blithe talk of slaves. She was free, but her people as a whole were not. How had those passages read to her? What must she think of him? He'd met enough Copperheads in the prison, and flat-out racists in the ranks of the Union army, to know that wanting to maintain the Union and wanting to end slavery were not mutually exclusive.

"I suppose I always just . . . looked past it." He unfolded his arms. "I've had the privilege to pick and choose what spoke to me from those passages. To me, it is history. I was mistaken about that, though. It is not history when we fight this war. It's just . . . I very much needed something to believe in. The Bible made me feel like a sinner, but *The Enchiridion* made me feel like someone, though separated by time and country and mother tongue, had understood me."

The words surprised Ewan; he'd never had to justify himself. His behavior had always been accepted as strange, but no one had ever cared why he read and thought as he did. When people had asked before, it hadn't really been a question, more a statement of how bizarre they found his interests.

Marlie looked at him and slowly nodded. "I suppose people find what they need where they can. I certainly feel the same way about my *Illustrated American Botany*. And not everything in the pages of the Bible is kind and just, either. Thank you for explaining."

He felt peculiar, knowing he had brushed aside an element as large as slavery. It was logical: The society was long dead, living on in the words of its philosophers. But he knew American slavery to be a horrible stain upon the world. Would it be brushed away so cavalierly when people read of America in some distant future? Would it be a footnote, an aside? That thought troubled Ewan.

Something occurred to him then. "One constant throughout history is this: Every society built on slavery has fallen. I suppose that should give us hope that the Union will prevail."

"I've never believed otherwise," Marlie said. Her voice was guileless, her eyes wide and hopeful.

He looked at her a long moment and wondered if she would feel the same if she'd been in the trenches with soldiers pissing their pants, men who barely knew how to use a gun or follow a direct command. Then he remembered how each time she walked into the prison, her smile had been a beacon amidst the misery. Yes, she would feel the same, for Marlie possessed an ineffable quality that shone through even in dire situations. Ewan wondered what it felt like to give oneself over to hope, logic be damned.

Her gaze dropped to the ground and he understood he should stop staring at her and return to his hiding space. He slipped into the darkness and pushed the door closed, leaving his hand pressed against it until he felt the decisive bump of her desk meeting the wall.

CHAPTER 8

Everything in the receiving parlor was as it had always been — it was one of the few rooms that Melody had not left her imprint on by rearranging it to be more to her taste. Marlie found that although the glossy piano and the suite of dainty rosewood furniture had not changed, except for a bit of fraying on the raspberry silk upholstery, the room felt different. The gilt pier mirror across the room reflected her sitting serenely on the chaise lounge, book in hand, but the tension that filled the room had no reflection, surrounding her like a malevolent being.

Perhaps it was the sound of the Home Guard milling about outside the window, the raised voices of the men going through their afternoon drills piercing through any illusion that their home was still theirs. It was strange that sharing her small space with Ewan gave her a sense of freedom, while sharing the whole of Lynchwood with the militia made her feel caged in.

A tingle of panic swept down her back at the thought of Ewan, as if Melody might overhear her most private contemplations and soil those, too.

"How was your visit to the Sloanes' plantation?" Marlie inquired, taking a sip of the nerve-soothing tea she had brewed. She savored notes of blackberry, chamomile, and beneath it all, valerian root, one of the more dangerous plants in her arsenal. She tried to repress the ugly thought that followed — how easy it would be for her to get rid of Melody, who sat across the room playing euchre at the card table with Sarah.

She'd been unable to stop thinking of things like that since she'd made her gris-gris. Lessons from her past, learned or warned against at her mother's hip, had begun coming back to her, as if tying off the little red sachet had unlocked something that Marlie had hidden away beneath the science. She'd felt a sense of control that had nothing to do with the Lynches' money or name in undertaking that small act. More importantly, she'd felt hope. The night she'd made the gris-gris she'd startled awake, not from a dream but from what might have been the start of one. She'd smelled rosemary in her room though she hadn't used it for days.

Maman.

It had likely been her imagination, but sometimes imagination was the most effective tool a woman could wield.

Stephen sat in a chair in the corner of the room, out of sight of his wife but able to listen in on the conversation. He didn't do much talking; he was reading a newspaper, glancing up at Marlie every few moments. She had already offered him two benign smiles, and now she pretended that she couldn't feel it when he looked over at her.

"It was quite pleasant," Sarah said. "They had very strong coffee, which must have cost them a fortune. They mentioned that several of their slaves had run off to the contraband camps, which was quite a nuisance to them."

Sarah took a sip of her tea, and Marlie knew it was to hide her smile.

"They received a letter from their son that presented in rousing detail how his regiment repelled Grant and the Yanks from taking Vicksburg," Melody added. "Grant and Sherman have been trying to scratch their way in like possums ready to spawn, but our brave boys won't let them gain entry."

"Perhaps they'll give up entirely and you

and Stephen can return home soon," Sarah said cheerily as she picked up the cards to shuffle them.

"Oh, I don't think that will happen," Melody said. "We've received a letter saying our home is being used as a center of defense, damaged though it was, providing shelter for several officers and their men while they strategize. Even if I wanted to go back, we couldn't impose on men undertaking such an important task. We'll be at Lynchwood for a while yet, right, Stephen?"

He puffed on his pipe. "Perhaps. We could always find a way to get to Mother in Philadelphia —"

"Enough, Stephen!" Melody's voice burst forth with passion, a sudden change from the mask of sweet refinement she had been wearing. "I've told you that I refuse to indulge this silly plan, and I will not discuss it any further! There are no amusements for me in Philadelphia, and I refuse to be surrounded by cowardly, darkie-loving Yankees."

"I understand, darling, but if you gave it some thought —"

Melody shot a dark look across the room. "It's bad enough that you haven't the fortitude to fight, or the wiles to support the South in some other way. This talk of heading North only further disgraces you, which I must say I didn't think was possible."

The tension in the room was suffocating, and the sound of heavy, dragging footsteps on the carpet that lined the hallway sent a spike of agitation through Marlie. She wished she were back upstairs, that she had never ventured down to begin with. Then she glanced at Sarah, saw how her face had gone pallid. She caught her gaze and smiled, lifted the teacup to her lips, silently encouraging Sarah to drink, too. She didn't regret being there for Sarah, though her reserve faltered when Cahill walked into the room.

He removed his hat and bowed toward Melody and Sarah, gave the pretense of an acknowledgment to Stephen, and then walked over and sat decisively in front of Marlie. He did not acknowledge her cordially, but glared at her. She didn't know why he acknowledged her at all, if her presence bothered him so, but he sought her out at every opportunity.

"I hadn't seen you about, Fancy. I thought perhaps they'd come to their senses and sent you out to the fields, where you belong," he said. His voice was calm and low, but his expression frightened her. He had the look of a man who would enjoy nothing so much as to crush her beneath his heel, like an insect. A keen affront at such a look from such a man rose up in Marlie, pushing out a tart response.

"I could say the same for you. Alas, it appears we are both to be disappointed," she said, then sipped her tea, trying to look unaffected despite the way her stomach twisted and plunged.

You are not brave enough to issue such challenges, some desperate segment of her consciousness reminded her. Perhaps it was right. She should be quiet and unassuming, given the secret she held two flights of stairs away, but apparently her rebellious side had begun to bloom, like a nightshade that unfurls when shrouded in darkness.

"I've spent much time in the fields, actually," he said, leaning forward a bit and regarding her with that cold gaze. "I was an overseer for a plantation in Charlotte. Spent my days keeping lazy darkies like you in line. You may think yourself high and mighty in this parlor, but you wouldn't have lasted five minutes under me."

Marlie's body went taut with anger at the derision, and implication, in his tone. His gaze wandered over her body then back to her face, and though it was still cold, there was a new threat there, a gloating reminder that men like him could do anything to women like her and this society would laugh and clap him on the back.

"*The man is dangerous,*" Ewan had written, and Ewan was not the type who was prone to exaggeration.

Her bravado faltered, and she blinked back tears.

Maman, why did you leave me to these people?

Marlie was Daniel in the lion's den, but she was by no means sure that she'd make her way out. And the lions at least had a reason to eat Daniel; it was their nature. Melody and Cahill regarded Marlie with a hatred and disgust that chilled her to the bone, just because she was a Negro. Was that simply their nature, too? Cruel subjugation of their fellow man?

"Commander Cahill," Stephen called out. His voice was overly loud, and when Marlie glanced at him, his color was high. Still, his words were civil when he had the man's attention. "What is the latest news? Have you had much luck routing out the deserters?"

Marlie put down her teacup and clasped her shaking hands together. She had never heard Stephen speak of the war so directly, and she had to wonder if he wasn't purposely drawing Cahill's attention away from her. A tiny ember of gratitude warmed her; she'd often wished that he would be less remiss in his brotherly duties. If he had chosen now to finally act on them, she could not help but feel some gratitude, tempered by the fact that his wife was the one who had created this situation.

She was also grateful that she might learn something to report to LaValle, which she'd been unable to do.

Cahill rose and walked toward Stephen, stopping to look down at him. "They grow bolder every day. Just this morning we got word from a metalsmith that a group had held him hostage these last two days, tying him up while they used his tools to repair their weaponry. He said there were whites mixed with darkies and savages; they count in their ranks those from the most deplorable sectors of society."

He looked over at Marlie. She sipped her tea.

"I heard that they've had some recent successes," Sarah said, turning over a card daintily. "They've elected leaders, begun holding drills, and despite the lawlessness of some, are shaping themselves into a formidable militia."

Stephen ran a hand over his whiskers. "I must admit, they're rather more organized

180

than I had assumed from previous reports."

"Well, reports are all you would know of, as you lift nary a finger to help the Cause in this war," Cahill snapped. "All men are welcome to join the Home Guard, but you have not. Why is that?"

"Sir," Sarah said, smacking a card down on the table. "If you consider feeding and housing you and your men as lifting nary a finger, you are welcome to take your leave."

"Now, now, Sarah," Melody chided. Just three words, but they may as well have been a backhand across her husband's face. Stephen looked down at his hands.

Cahill looked at Sarah a long while, then stood, straightening his uniform, before limping back toward the door. "I've got men to lead," was all he offered in response. "Governor Vance has said that these Lincoln-loving Tories must be routed out and destroyed posthaste, and I'm not a man who shirks his duty."

A chill crept over Marlie's skin. Even bloodier times lay ahead for the region, and Cahill seemed happy to do his part in the carnage that would ensue.

"Oh, do wait a moment, Commander, there are some things I must discuss with you." Melody pushed up out of her chair and sped across the room in a rustle of hoops and swinging skirts. She took Cahill's arm as they left the room, sparing not even a glance at Stephen.

"Not all men gain their power by crushing those less fortunate than them," Stephen said, finding his voice too late. "The people in this region resist the Confederacy because they own no slaves or they detest the institution. Killing the poorest of your people to bring them to heel shows how inadequate a government this is."

"Quite," Sarah said. "And that the strength of the men laying out has increased with the formation of the Home Guard, not diminished, gives me hope that this war will end in the manner we have been hoping for."

She looked about, as if Melody were hiding around the corner waiting to pounce on any pro-Northern sentiment.

"Yes, this war is changing many ideas of who is capable of fighting, and how. I've read about the colored regiments fighting for the Union now," Stephen said, speaking directly to Marlie for the first time in recent memory. "The papers here revile them, but by all other accounts they have acquitted themselves honorably."

Marlie didn't know how to respond. Was this some attempt at kinship? As if she should be happy that her people were now seen as worthy enough to be cannon fodder, after everything else they'd been through? She felt thoroughly annoyed by something she'd never considered: Why should Negroes have to fight at all? She thought of the parts of her mother's memoir she had translated, the tales of men and women working themselves into an early grave or being beaten if they resisted. Whites had created this problem, why shouldn't they resolve it themselves?

That wasn't realistic, unfortunately, but it didn't change the fury the realization brought to the fore. She looked from Sarah to Stephen; they would not understand such a sentiment if she were to express it. She was gripped by a sudden, aching loneliness, the surety that neither Sarah nor Stephen had any idea who she was at all.

"It must take a great strength of will to go directly from toiling in the fields to taking up arms against one's oppressors," she said diplomatically.

"And luckily you shall never experience either of those hardships," Sarah said. "You are quite well taken care of here, aren't you?"

Marlie stiffened. She didn't consider herself taken care of — she worked, earned

183

her living, but that's exactly what she was. Exactly why she had never felt freer than when venturing out to the prison and helping those men of her own volition.

But with the Lynch money paving your way.

"I believe I will retire to my rooms," Marlie said.

"You are always in your rooms now," Sarah said. "I know things are difficult for you with Melody and Cahill, but they are difficult for me, too. Can you not tolerate a bit more for my sake?"

Marlie felt an inarticulate anger rise in her, and the first words on her tongue were neither kind nor true, so she took a moment before opening her mouth. "Sarah, I am sure things are difficult for you, but have you not heard the way Cahill speaks to me and the things he insinuates?"

How could Sarah not see? She was protected by her rank in society and the color of her skin, and Marlie had no such protection. Marlie felt the spinning disorientation of vertigo even though she was sitting. She found fault in everything now, it seemed — she'd always wanted to change the world, but never had she realized how maddening so many aspects of it were. For a moment she doubted her sanity, that everything the person she loved the most said chafed at her.

"I understand, but I just miss how things were before," Sarah sighed, and Marlie's anger diminished, replaced by affection for Sarah and sadness that it was strained. The work of treason had united them, and now that their joint operations were stalled, Marlie felt as if an ever-widening gulf was opening between her and Sarah, one she desperately wanted to ford.

"I do, too," she said. "But war brings change, and none of us shall pass through these trying times unscathed."

Sarah bustled over and sat beside her, taking up her hand. Her expression was serious. "Cahill hasn't taken any liberties with your person, has he?"

"No," Marlie said, shuddering at the thought. "He seems to take pleasure in inspiring fear in me, and I hate giving him the satisfaction. But I *am* afraid."

Sarah placed an arm around her shoulder. "Forgive my thoughtless request, Marlie. You're right. Perhaps it would be best if you remained out of sight until things have quieted down."

"No, it would be best if he were kicked out of our home," Marlie said, that headstrong voice rising up in her again. She

185

glanced at Stephen, who quickly looked away. "Since no one is willing to do that, yes, perhaps it's better that I remain in my rooms."

She patted Sarah's hands, then left the parlor, stopping by the kitchen to prepare a basket of food before walking up the stairs to her room. She was both furious and elated. She had been encouraged to make herself a prisoner in her own home for the sake of Melody and Cahill, but then again, she had just been given leave to spend her time as she wished instead of skulking around the parlor, flinching every time Cahill turned his gaze on her. As she entered her room and locked the door behind her she felt the weight of the outside world fall away from her shoulders. She knew that her situation with Ewan was far from normal — and most definitively temporary — but the freedom found in the moments spent talking and sharing with him had become important to her. Perhaps too important.

She tied on her apron and began gathering the ingredients to test out a new deworming tonic that she hoped could be of use. Then she glanced over at the desk and sighed. She didn't investigate what the sensation in her chest might be, but she followed its impetus, walking over and pulling the desk back. The door opened and there was Ewan's face, all sharp angles and freckle-sprayed.

"Here are some biscuits with lard," she said. "And I can put some tea on the burner if you'd like." She nodded her head in the direction of her work station.

"Tea would be excellent, if you're having some, as well," he said. "Thank you."

She put the kettle on.

He sat with his legs stretched out on the floor before the door, chewing his biscuit with great concentration. "These are wonderful," he said. "Reminds me of my mother's."

Marlie knelt down and prodded at his ankle, then sighed deeply. "Have you ever felt . . . as if the earth had shifted and you ended up on one side and your family on the other?"

He simply looked at her, the moment stretching out long enough that Marlie could regret asking.

"I'm sorry, that is none of my business. Your ankle seems to be healing well."

She pushed herself to her feet, the loneliness she had felt in the parlor making its presence known once more.

"I gather you don't mean physically," he said.

She shook her head.

"I believe that I was born on the other side of a gulf such as the one you speak of," he said quietly. "I have always been the odd boy, the strange young man. I asked too many questions, or turned the conversation to things that pleased me and bored everyone else. Easily frustrated and eternally restless. I'm sure you've noticed these traits." He paused then and looked up at her, and Marlie saw the slightest hint of vulnerability, as if he expected her to tease him or say something cutting. She remained silent, and he continued. "When I got upset as a boy I would have terrible tantrums that humiliated and frightened my parents. I made the voyage from Scotland to the States even more traumatizing, I've been told. And once my father lost control of his drinking . . . yes, I understand such a feeling."

Marlie felt a bit of the tightness that had gripped her since the tension-filled expedition to the parlor loosen a bit. "How did you manage?"

"Well, I realized I could not close such a gulf — that was not in my control. But I could learn what pleased my family and what didn't, and what pleased me about pleasing them. Even though the gulf still exists, there are bridges, and those allow me to get along with my family and vice versa."

Marlie nodded appreciatively. "I will give thought to what bridges I may be able to build. I'm not used to feeling this way about Sarah."

"She is your sister, no?"

She felt that exasperation rise in her again, and the word came out forcefully, as if meeting a challenge. "Yes."

"Well, if you've survived this long without ever wanting to secede from her then you're doing better than the nation as a whole."

Marlie allowed herself a bit of laughter and was rewarded with a startled smile from Ewan. "Thank you, Socrates. This has given me some comfort after a trying day."

"Anything I can do to put you at ease, I will do gladly." The words were not spoken suggestively, but were so earnestly delivered that they left Marlie flustered and warm. It didn't help that her imagination took the word *ease* and spun off with wild abandon imagining all the things it might mean.

"Good night," she said, pushing the desk forward.

"Good night," he replied, closing the door. When the desk was flush against the wall, she remained leaning on it, trying to discern why everything in her was straining toward the man on the other side.

Simple infatuation, and nothing more. It will pass.

Marlie had to believe this was true. She knew better than to think anything else could occur.

CHAPTER 9

Ewan gripped the rough wooden beam that
bisected the attic space and pulled the
weight of his body up, going slow enough
that he could feel the burn in each muscle
of his arms and abdomen. He reached the
summit of the motion, exhaled, and lowered
himself back to the ground. Then he did it
again.

He tried to pull himself up again and his
arms refused to follow through on the command. Since coming to Marlie's home, he'd
doubled and sometimes trebled the length
of his exercise routine — modified to avoid
jostling his ankle — not because he was vain
but because it was the only outlet for the
frenetic thoughts that ricocheted about in
his mind. The letters passed back and forth
between him and Marlie, slid beneath the
door of the room that both protected and
imprisoned him, were his lifeline to the
world, and to Marlie. With each letter, she

grew in his estimation, and the distance between wanting and having grew ever further, too.

Each time she asked him a question about what he'd done during the war, or what post he was returning to, was a reminder of why he needed to pull any unrequited feelings he had for Marlie out by the root. He didn't regret what he had done for his country, but the fighting he did was different from shooting across a battlefield or wrestling in a trench. One could be morally right and yet still irrevocably stained, but he wouldn't sully Marlie with the truth of himself.

"I count him braver who overcomes his desires than him who conquers his enemies, for the hardest victory is over self."

Aristotle's words were generally a bit too optimistic for Ewan's taste, but the man had the right of it sometimes. Ewan was feeling very brave of late.

He'd already separated and organized all the dried plants that had been hanging in the room, again, using a different organization system. He'd asked Marlie what work needed to be done, and had set to labeling bottles and mixing to her measurements. After that had been completed, he'd gone through the books. Reading usually calmed him, drawing all his attention from reality and into the text, but being trapped in a room just out of reach of the person he most wanted and the person he most hated was bringing to the surface feelings that made concentration a hard thing.

The bothersome itch that seemed to emanate from deep within his skull had come back, driving him to distraction. He hated the feeling that had plagued him as a child; even in the prison camp he'd been able to work and barter and fix things to keep his mind clear. He hadn't felt all turned around in such a way since before his father died. No — that wasn't true. There had been one time since then.

Cahill.

The day he had first encountered Cahill was supposed to be calm; Ewan had been returning from another mission. The town was supposed to be free of Rebels, having been captured by the Union. The farmhouse was supposed to be safe — occupied by Negro men drilling for the day when Lincoln said they could fight in Union blues, officially. The sound of gunshots and panic had greeted Ewan and his fellow soldiers; a cowardly ambush.

There was a knock at the door in the wall, almost too quiet to be discerned, but pulling Ewan's mind away from that horrific day all the same. He ran a hand over his sweaty face, unlatched the door, and pulled it open. It was only when he saw those dark, delicate brows raise toward the ceiling that he realized he wasn't wearing a damned shirt.

"Pardon," he said, turning to grab the shirt he'd tossed aside. He winced as he pulled his arms through the sleeves. "I may have overtaxed myself," he said as he began buttoning.

When he turned, Marlie was still standing in the same position. Her brows were back at the proper longitude, but her lips were slightly parted and she stared at him as if he'd been wearing nothing but his boots. He heard a tinkling noise and realized it was the tray she held in her hand — the glass was brushing against a bowl of something delicious, on account of how her hands trembled.

He'd frightened her. Part of him wanted to soothe her, but it was better for her to be frightened. It showed she was as smart as he knew her to be.

"I — I brought your dinner," she said. "Everyone else has gone to a town hall meeting, so if you'd like to come eat in my rooms, you can."

"Are you sure?" he asked.

"No one can get in," she said. "And we'll hear them arrive."

He looked into those strange eyes of hers, wondering why she'd ask him to dine despite the risk. They spoke through their notes during the day, and his nightly trips to the necessary had become nightly conversations. But his meals during the day were usually taken in the drying room.

As he looked at her, one corner of her mouth tipped up into an awkward grin and her shoulders hunched, only by a millimeter, but such things caught Ewan's attention.

She's lonely.

There was the strangest searing twist in his chest at that realization. Although solitude was his preferred state, he didn't mind being around other people. He was adaptable, and even the crowded confines of prison camp had been bearable. Anything was bearable, when it came down to it — that was his personal philosophy. But there was a difference between bearable and tolerable, and knowing that Marlie had been lonely while he was just a few feet away was intolerable.

"Sure, if it's not too bothersome," he said. "Having a different set of walls to stare at wouldn't hurt."

"Your ankle is nearly healed, so we can start figuring out how to get you up North," she said. "I'm sorry that you've traded one prison for another."

Being cooped up so close to her was surely some form of torture, but not in the manner she imagined. "Marlie, you do yourself a disservice with that comparison."

She smiled, just a twitch of upturned lips, but Ewan soaked it in as if she'd caressed him. Maybe he had some of the McCall charm in him after all. He stepped out into the room, and she stepped back, placed his tray on her desk, and then turned to her work.

"I ate downstairs in the kitchen with Lace and Tobias," she said. "They insisted I take advantage of Melody being gone since I've been passing most of my time up here. Tobias also wanted to interrogate me about whether anything improper was going on between us."

Ewan paused, thinking perhaps he'd misheard since she said it so calmly. Had she really just spoken those words so plainly? Perhaps she wouldn't have if she'd known how much time he spent trying not to think about exactly what Tobias was asking about.

"What did you tell him?" He moved the chair to the side of the desk so he could watch her as she worked.

She poured a premeasured cup of distilled water into the bottle, then corked it and placed it onto the shelf of an instrument he hadn't seen her use before. When she'd filled the small shelf, she used a strap to secure the bottles, then wound a key. The shelf slowly lifted and lowered on one end and then repeated the motion, slowly mixing the contents of the bottles. Ewan was almost distracted from the conversation by the ingenuity of the device. Almost.

"I told him we were living in sin in several ways, but that given our circumstances we didn't have much choice," she said.

Ewan tried very hard not to focus on the ways they *weren't* living in sin. *Taking the Lord's name in vain, perhaps. We haven't done that.*

She glanced at him. "He wasn't pleased that I sassed him, but I told him that you were an honorable man who wouldn't take advantage of the situation."

Ewan remembered the looks Tobias had given him. "Is he courting you?"

Marlie laughed quietly. "Tobias has never seen me as more than a sister, which would make his courting me quite uncomfortable. As would his marriage to Lace."

Feelings of possession were infantile and

not the sort of behavior Ewan indulged in, but if he *were* that kind of man, he would have been powerfully pleased by the fact that Marlie wasn't attached to Tobias.

"What about you?" Marlie asked. She kept working, but Ewan noticed that her efficient movements slowed. She picked up the wrong bottle, then knocked a bowl of dried leaves askew.

"Well, I believe Lace would take exception to Tobias courting me, as well," Ewan said, and was rewarded with Marlie's delicate laughter as she collected the leaves that had been tossed onto her worktable.

"You know what I mean," she said. "You've mentioned your parents, a brother and a sister, but no sweetheart or wife."

Ewan didn't quite understand. "Because no such person exists."

Or has ever existed. And that's how I like it, he reminded himself.

"Truly? From what I'd read in the papers, it seemed every soldier had a lady pining away for him at home." She glanced at him, then back at her work. "Seems a bit hard to believe you're not one of them."

Ewan wasn't sure, but she might have been complimenting him.

"I never found a woman I'd ask to wait for me," he replied. No one had exactly petitioned for the role, either, after receiving a lecture or three.

She smiled full-out now. "Ah. I can only imagine the high standards you would have for a sweetheart."

Why did she find this amusing?

"Let me guess," she continued. "She'd have to have memorized *The Enchiridion,* be able to speak several languages, and shoot a Rebel from fifty paces —"

"If you think that's the case, perhaps I've misrepresented myself," Ewan said quietly, though warning signs were going off in his head. "I have exactly one."

She tilted her head. "And what's that?"

"Cognitive superiority." He didn't allow himself to expound on ways in which a woman might demonstrate such a thing; for example, teaching herself medical botany, designing her own still and constantly improving upon said design, and engaging in spirited philosophical debate. She needn't know that.

Marlie let out a quiet laugh. "Actually, that fits you perfectly," she said. There was no derision in her laughter or tone, nor was there any inkling that she was aware how perfectly it fit her, too.

"What are you making?" he asked before taking a bite of chicken, helpfully changing the subject. People not perceiving the obvious were a terrible bother to him, and he couldn't risk pointing out this particular oversight on her part.

"There's a fever going around in the children in nearby towns." She didn't take her eyes from the line of glass bottles she was filling. "I think they're weak from hunger — so many of the farms have gone to seed because the husbands are either hiding in the woods to escape Cahill or off at war, by force or by choice. Conditions are perfect for a terrible sickness to set in, as if we haven't had enough loss. Tobias will be carrying these out to families tomorrow."

At Cahill's name, Ewan couldn't help but grip his wooden spoon more tightly.

"How has it been, with Cahill?" he asked. He hadn't revealed his connection to the man. How could he explain that to Marlie? The last bit of his ego couldn't have her thinking he was a monster. Not thinking — knowing.

Her shoulders rose on a sigh, and her posture was stiffer when they fell again. "It's going as well as one could imagine. Melody treats him like a king while constantly berating her own husband for not joining the Confederate forces himself. She abuses poor Sarah every chance she gets, and hints at her Unionist leanings. It's a miracle Cahill hasn't questioned her, or worse." Marlie paused in her work. "They say he does terrible things. Captures the wives and children of men who don't report to muster and —"

She stopped and looked back at him.

Ewan swallowed the chunk of potato down a throat that had suddenly gone dry. He knew very well what Cahill did to get what he wanted. He'd allowed himself to be dragged down to the same base levels. He wasn't proud, but the only regret he felt was that he had let Cahill live. If Ewan hadn't, Marlie would have never encountered the man.

"I've borne witness to the type of terrible things you mention," he said carefully. He considered telling her that he had witnessed such things because he had carried them out.

"Oh, how dreadful. I'm sorry." Her expression was one of such tender concern for him that any idea of confessing was tossed aside. Telling her would only cause her to fear for her safety, and that wasn't in question.

Not from you. But Cahill . . .

"A great many shocking things are carried out in the name of North or South. Sometimes, they're necessary. I've had to inure myself to that truth."

"Such cruelty doesn't disturb you?" she asked. Her gaze roamed his face, likely searching for some indication that she had misunderstood him.

"Wanton cruelty disturbs me. Cahill acts not out of necessity, but because he enjoys hurting others. There is no logic behind his actions, simply a sadistic pleasure in the pain of others."

Marlie's eyes were wide, the muscles of her face tense. "Yes. You said he was dangerous, and I'm afraid you weren't mistaken."

Ewan had to take a deep, slow breath, as he had every time his mind traveled to the ugly possibilities Cahill's presence had opened up. Marlie had the Lynch name, and her family, to protect her. He'd told himself that over and over again, but he couldn't stop himself from asking. "I hope I'm not overstepping, but has he exercised such behavior toward you?"

Her lips pressed together. She shook her head, clutched the bottle in her hand a bit too tightly.

"Marlie." If she had been hurt and hadn't told him . . . His scalp began to prickle.

"He's been . . . less than agreeable. That's all." She paused, considering her words.

"It's nothing I should say in polite company."

"You just saw me without a stitch on above the waist. As you made clear to Tobias, we're past polite," Ewan pressed. Marlie turned back to her work.

"He said that the best place for a woman like me was working as a fancy maid." Her voice was low and full of shame, as if *she* were somehow at fault for such distasteful behavior. "He's taken to calling me 'Fancy' now, when he sees me around the house. And the way he looks at me . . . you'll understand that I do not want to encounter him alone. That is why —"

Ewan dropped the utensil and it was only when he felt the twinge in his ankle that he realized he'd jumped to his feet as well. He lowered himself back into his seat when he saw the flash of concern in her eyes, but he didn't pick up the spoon. He was worried he might snap it.

"Breathe in. Breathe out, Ewan." His mother's brogue drifted up into his mind.

He'd been sure that he had better control over himself — he'd worked so hard for every bit of that control — but the thought of Cahill degrading Marlie was too much to take, especially knowing what he knew of the man. But Marlie knew nothing, of either

203

Ewan or Cahill, and he didn't want to frighten her any further than he had.

Assuage her.

"I'll kill him if he tries to hurt you," he said. His words were calm, but her eyes opened even wider, and Ewan understood too late that death threats weren't quite the way to make a woman feel safer with you. He was already imagining her telling him to leave, that she shouldn't be cooped up in a house with two men she feared.

"You say that as if you mean it, and you know exactly how you'd do it." She held his gaze.

"I'm sorry." He looked down at his hands. He wouldn't descend into Lady Macbeth's madness, but his hands were stained with the blood of Rebels and traitors to the Federal cause. Some said that made him a hero, but Ewan simply felt empty.

"Did you?" she asked. "Mean it, that is?"

He couldn't bring himself to meet her gaze, and the awful feeling was starting deep in his skull again.

"I don't want you to be afraid, particularly because you and I are in much closer quarters than you and he." Ewan forced himself to pick up his spoon from the ground, to hold it normally. "I wouldn't hurt you, Marlie. *Ever.* But him? Yes, I mean it."

Better for her to know what kind of man she was dealing with. He owed her that, at least.

He felt something light on his shoulder and almost shrugged it away until he realized it was her hand. It was warm through the rough fabric of his shirt, and when he looked up at her she wasn't frightened. Her dual-toned eyes were glossy, but she regarded him as she always had.

"Let's hope it doesn't come to that. Do you want to help me clean the still when you're done eating? I could use the help."

Ewan had been struggling against rage and anger but he was abruptly inundated with a dizzying combination of warmth and gratitude. She was giving him something to do with his hands, a distraction he desperately needed.

Like running them up over the curve of her hip, pressing your fingers into the softness there . . .

Ewan blocked those thoughts away. He recalled a line of Epictetus. *"Destroy desire completely in the present. If you desire that which is not in your power, you will be wretched."* He already felt like a mangy wretch, plagued by impure thoughts that alternated between violence and passion. He'd not entertain such thoughts in Marlie's presence.

He should have gone back into the drying room, but he nodded instead.

"I would like that." He ate the last bites of his food, not because he was hungry, but because she had given it to him, and then moved to stand beside her as she began dismantling the still. He watched her carefully, helped her lay the pieces down, and tried to remember how to put them back in the right order. She spoke as she took it apart, her low voice calming him as she explained the pieces and what they did. He already knew for the most part — he'd already begun thinking of ways to improve the device after reading her books and hand-drawn schematics in the flyleaves. But as he listened to her talk, he realized she was already aware of every improvement he would have suggested and had come up with alternatives that he would never have been able to synthesize.

"It's a pleasure to watch you work," he observed as she refit the final tube back into the body of the still. He had nothing to do with it, but he glowed with a sense of pride at her knowledge and ability. "You're so very . . . competent."

Ewan blushed as he said the word, for truly he could think of nothing he held in higher esteem. He felt as if he'd just admitted everything, but she simply glanced at him with a grin.

"This is my life's work, so I'd hope so," she said. "I've spent more hours working in this room than I can count."

"Didn't your studies take up your time?" he asked.

She shook her head. "I had a tutor for a bit. I couldn't continue my education otherwise; there was no school for free Negroes nearby, and I was too Negro for the others despite the family name. I don't quite fit in anywhere but these three rooms. I don't mind, though, so no need for the pitying look."

Ewan didn't think he was capable of pitying looks, but perhaps he had been mistaken.

"How did you make friends?" he asked, then wished he hadn't. It was the way her smile faltered before she caught herself, like a bird with a hobbled wing trying to take flight.

"I have Sarah and Tobias and Lace and Pearl," she said simply. "I have everything I need here at Lynchwood."

Ewan had seen the way she moved

through the prison camp, smiling at surly men, offering aid to everyone without judging whether they deserved her kindness, or even appreciated it. Her smile had made even the worst men among them respond in kind. He wondered now how many people besides the prisoners had ever been lucky enough to see it.

"I've never been terribly good at making friends," Ewan commiserated.

"You had that Irish fellow chasing after you like a puppy at the prison, and I saw men stop and talk to you all the time." She paused. "Not that I was paying much attention."

A little bud of warmth opened in Ewan's chest, and he tried to crush it. She was friendless and that was the only thing she saw in him — a friend.

"I suppose," was all he said in response. He didn't like to think of what had become of Keeley. "Why do you have a Polybius square?"

There was generally only one use for such a thing — decrypting private messages. Marlie had just said she didn't have friends outside Lynchwood, yet the square sat at her desk beside correspondence. Ewan couldn't imagine what use she would have for it though; Marlie was too open, too naive, to be engaging in espionage. Then again, she was brazenly sheltering him in an occupied home. Ewan considered that perhaps it was he who was the naive one.

She glanced at the corner of the decoding ring sticking out from under a pile of papers. "Oh, is that what this is? I found it in the pages of a used book. Are you in the habit of examining a woman's personal belongings so closely?" Her words landed lightly, cushioned by her teasing smile. Ewan might have believed her if she hadn't tried to distract him by pointing out his tactlessness — it was unnatural for her, even if she was correct.

He bowed his head, deciding not to press her. She owed him no explanation and demanding one would be bizarre, no matter how his curiosity was piqued. "I apologize. I have a hard time not noticing things, but that doesn't excuse my rudeness. I saw it sticking out from under that account of a slave revolt."

"You mean this?" She picked up the stack of papers, her gaze jumping back and forth between it and Ewan. "You speak French?"

Ewan shook his head. "I can't speak it, really. I can read it, though. And Latin. One of my teachers gave me a set of books he no longer needed, and I found the exercises to be quite soothing."

She was staring at him now — not really at him. Through him. She handed him the top page and then took up a pen and a fresh piece of paper. "What does that say?" she asked.

Ewan should have felt put on the spot, but this was an interaction he wouldn't have to worry about. This was something in his control.

" 'The master beat another man that day,' " he began. His cadence was slow as he eased back into language. He'd translated a few intercepted correspondences in the last year, but they had been completely different from the vivid personal tale he was reading. " 'They wanted us to be afraid. We were not. When that is everyday life, fear becomes useless. All they beat into us is hope, because hope is our only chance for survival.' "

He looked up to see Marlie bent over her desk, dipping and writing, dipping and writing, her hand moving furiously but the expression on her face torn between happiness and something like wonder.

"Should I continue?"

"Please."

They worked like that for the next two hours, stopping only when the sound of a carriage pulling up alerted them that the house would soon be occupied by the enemy once again. She rubbed her ink-stained hands against her apron. "Time for you to go back inside."

Ewan reluctantly followed her. He was a refugee, not a guest, and he had been lucky to get out of that space for as long as he had. He still wished they'd had more time. It seemed he always wanted more when it came to Marlie.

"If you want to give me those papers, I can translate the rest," he offered after he'd slipped back into the secret room. "A paltry repayment of your kindness. And I wouldn't mind a task to keep me occupied."

It was more than that. A light, unfamiliar sensation suffused his veins. His French had been one of the many courses of study he'd been told would serve no purpose, and now it had one — and no one was hurt in the deployment of it. Being able to read the text clearly pleased Marlie. He wanted to please her.

"No." Her voice was harsh, but then she said more gently, "Perhaps you can help me again tomorrow. But I prefer to keep my mother's papers with me. They're all I have left of her."

Something throbbed in his chest at the

211

fact that those were her mother's words, and she'd shared them with him. The door started to close, but then the thin line of light widened again.

"Ewan?"

"Yes, Marlie?"

"Thank you."

Then there was only the soft scrape of the desk and darkness. Ewan didn't want to conjecture why her thanks filled him up like an amphora. He was wretched enough as it was.

CHAPTER 10

It was so strange to me. Back home, I could go for days without seeing a white face. There were so many of us slaves, and although the laws that held us in bondage were strictly and harshly observed, we lived our own lives amidst the terror. I learned that life was different for the American slaves. They were watched always, by master or overseer. Some were even made to sleep on the floor of the master's room, not given the opportunity to even dream freely. Even their magic, their healing, had become a shadow of what I had learned on the island. And now I was one of them. Why had fate chosen this path for me?

Marlie placed the quill down and looked at Ewan. Three days had passed since he'd begun helping her with the translation work; Marlie spent even more time in her quarters than ever. Her world had for so long been no larger than Randolph County, and even the trips into town to shop and bring her wares to the pharmacy, and the occasional visits to the small farms to minister aid, had been few and far between. Sarah had always thought it safer for Marlie to stay at Lynchwood.

When the Fugitive Slave laws had been enacted, making free Negroes even less safe in their daily lives, those trips every couple of months had ended. She'd spent mornings in the nearby woods collecting roots and plants, but with bands of soldiers and impressment gangs wandering about, even that had become too risky. Her world had been scaled back to the house; the trips to Randolph had only been approved because Marlie had forced Sarah to see their utility to the Cause. Her utility. The arrival of Melody and Cahill had taken away that last freedom, and more; her days and nights were now spent in the three rooms that comprised her quarters.

She should have been more disturbed by that, but there was Ewan. His presence softened the blow of her undeserved punishment, quite a bit more than it should have. He was actually interested in her work, and helped her without complaint. She could talk to him about the different species of sassafras, and the difference in extract of bark and root and leaf. She could talk and talk, more than she ever had it seemed, and when she was done, he wanted to know more.

She had learned much from him, as well, about philosophy and politics, and anything except the War Between the States — that had fallen into the category of things they didn't discuss after those first few days. Because discussing the war meant discussing the cause of it, and even if they were both on the same side, that didn't mean there wasn't still a hierarchy between them that was enforced with brutality in every corner of the land.

"I must go show my face or Sarah will come around looking for me to make sure nothing is amiss," she said with a pang. Marlie felt no small amount of guilt that she hadn't told her about Ewan's presence, but Sarah was so very put upon every time they spoke that Marlie couldn't bring herself to give her more reason to worry. And perhaps, just perhaps, there was a part of Marlie that enjoyed having one thing in her life that Sarah had not sanctioned or provided for her.

There was also the fact that every moment

Marlie spent with Ewan, she was also spending with her mother. He'd become Vivienne's mouthpiece, speaking her words into being. She'd thought it would be a simple exchange of words, but she quickly realized how wrong she was. Translation was an act that revealed as much about the person doing it as the text. The way his expression grew tense with anger as he parsed certain lines, or solemn with respect. The way he smiled when he came across a particularly sharp observation. How the passages sparked memories in Marlie, and her resulting stories had the reciprocal response in him. He learned about her childhood in a small shack in the piney woods. She knew all about his mother, older brother, and younger sister. Little was ever said about his father, but that empty space in his stories spoke volumes, and she was sure the spaces in her stories did, too.

Their translation felt like a greater intimacy than if he had pressed his mouth to hers, though she couldn't help but wonder what that would feel like, too.

She tried very hard to remember that she was doing him a favor in harboring him, and he was simply returning it, but Ewan was giving Marlie her own history, and the line between appreciation and something stronger grew slimmer with each translated phrase. It wasn't just Vivienne's words that drew her to him, but his intelligence, and his own words, which, although sometimes too blunt, always resonated with her. Talking to him was easy. Too easy.

Because you're living in a fantasy world.

Marlie couldn't deny that they were living apart from reality. In the shared space of her rooms, they laughed. They spoke of family and favorite books and the best kind of pie. They debated scientific theories, and Greek, and Latin. They didn't speak of war and the possibility that the Union would be forever rent asunder. They didn't speak of the way people would look at them, a Negro woman and a white man laughing intimately, if they were on the street instead of in her rooms. They brushed hands and knees and shoulders — accidentally, of course. The room was small after all, and translating quietly required their sitting close and speaking in whispers. . . .

Ewan put down his pages, the expression on his face like a man waking from a dream. "Oh. Right. Of course you have other things to attend to."

Marlie reminded herself that this was a fantasy world for him, too. All too soon, he'd be off on the dangerous journey toward

Tennessee and, if he made it back to his regiment, facing possible death at the hands of Rebel forces. The reality of war intruded into their private space, and she pushed away the thought of harm befalling him.

"I have quite the same feeling I had as a boy, when my mother would make me put my book down and come eat supper," Ewan said. "It was like leaving a beloved friend behind."

They'd been translating Vivienne's recollections of her arrival in the US — how she'd been sold off after the rebellion, thrown onto a ship bound for the edge of the earth for all she knew. She'd arrived at Briarwood, the Lynches' farm estate, and was acclimating to life as an enslaved person in a new and strange land. The passages were fascinating, as her mother struggled to reconcile her gift and beliefs with her life on the plantation.

"I'm loathe to leave her words behind, too. I wish she had told me these things when we were together," Marlie admitted. When she looked at Ewan, he was scrubbing a hand over his eyes. They'd been working for hours — neither had been sleeping well, and they'd begun to work in the middle of the night, coincidentally while no one was up and around to disturb them.

"My father shared too many of his memories with us, especially after getting his hands on hard drink," Ewan said. "A parent eager to share isn't as marvelous as you might imagine."

Marlie studied him, the way the fine auburn hairs of his stubble shifted from the frown on his face as he looked into the distance. Then his gaze jerked toward her abruptly, focusing on her much more intently than could ever be considered appropriate.

"Careful of Cahill," he said. "The news reports you've brought me all say that the Home Guard has been having a string of successes against the draft dodgers, that they're preparing for a large-scale maneuver against them. Nothing makes a man more dangerous than a bit of success."

His fingertips brushed lightly over the back of her hand, sending a thrill through her, but he hesitated, then pulled his hand away.

"I can finish translating this section, if that pleases you," he said, and oh, Marlie did not need to hear that last phrase from him. He smiled, a full smile that set her heart beating apace again. "I admit, I want to know what happens."

"No, Mr. Socrates. If I must live with the

suspense, so shall you." She stacked the papers neatly — one part the original and one part the translation — and tucked them into her drawer.

"I'll take this instead," he said, reaching past her to grab a book from the shelf. His face came perilously close to hers as he leaned forward, so close that if she moved forward just a bit . . .

His gaze went from the book to her face, down to her mouth, and did not move. This close, Marlie could see the first spots of pink on his cheeks and how quickly they spread, accenting his sharp cheekbones. He'd stopped breathing — she'd feel it against her lips if he was. His head moved forward the slightest bit, then he stood abruptly.

Had she imagined what had just passed? Her racing heart testified that something had almost happened, but she couldn't bring herself to think on the missed possibility.

"I've had enough reading for the day, actually," he said, his voice suddenly terse. "I quite enjoy the translating, but all the talk of spirits and gods was tiring."

The warmth Marlie had been feeling after their near collision iced over like a lake in deepest winter.

"Pardon?"

"It's quite difficult to understand how a woman as obviously intelligent as your mother could believe in such things."

Marlie was on her feet now, too. "What gives you the right to speak of my mother and her beliefs that way? What gives you the right to judge her? Or anyone?"

Ewan's brows drew together. "Be logical, Marlie. If there was any truth to these hexes and hoodoo, why wouldn't every slave master in the States have been struck down?"

"If there was any sense to the logic of the dead white men you and many of those slave masters so revere, why would there be cause to strike them down? And yet you do not dismiss their work as nonsense."

Ewan scrutinized her expression, his face impassive. Marlie did not want to know what her face looked like because she felt as if she could throttle him for so deceiving her.

"You've said yourself that you know now that science, not spiritualism, is the right of things," he said. "Why are you upset if you don't believe in it, either?"

Marlie stared at him, shocked at the tears welling up in her eyes and hating the fact that she had no answer for him. She didn't believe in those things, did she? If so, why

221

did Ewan's words make her want to rage? Sharing her mother's writing with him had been a joy for her — had he been judging her mother the entire time?

"If the work is tiresome, your assistance is no longer necessary," she said, tucking the papers into the portfolio and placing them under a pile of notes.

Ewan's mouth opened and closed, like a catfish caught out when the creek runs dry. "I meant no offense —"

"And you managed to offend despite that. I must go, Ewan. Now."

He moved back behind the desk. When she heard the latch of the small door, she slid the desk back and leaned her head against it, in the thrall of a strange sorrow. Part of her hoped that when she returned Ewan would have vanished, so she wouldn't have to face him again. How could she? His words felt like a betrayal of some unspoken pact between them. She'd thought he understood her — or perhaps what she couldn't face was that he understood all too well what she had become.

She left her rooms, taking a deep breath as she locked the door behind her, then crept quietly down the stairs. She had once moved about the house confidently, but now she tiptoed like a thief. She wore only simple dresses that required no crinoline so that her skirts made the barest rustle when she walked. She had gone through a period after her arrival at Lynchwood when she'd purposefully stepped on the left side of the third stair from the bottom, its groan announcing her like a butler, but these days she carefully avoided anything that would bring her attention.

She'd almost made it to the kitchen when a hand touched her shoulder. Her heart pounded as she whirled about, but it was only Tobias, a concerned look on his face. "Marlie, you told me you was gonna tell Miss Sarah. About that thing. You haven't. What you think she gon' do if she find out I've been hiding information from her? I ain't her blood like you."

Marlie's anger at Ewan slipped away, replaced by chagrin.

"I'm sorry," she said. "It was selfish in the extreme of me. I thought I was preventing her more worry, but I've only pushed it onto you."

"You know I can't stay mad at you, Marl, but this is getting out of hand." He sighed and shifted uncomfortably. "And Lace and me are wondering what all you're getting up to with that man that you never leave you rooms now."

223

"Tobias! Absolutely nothing!" Her voice was high and heat rushed to her cheeks. It wasn't a lie. "Making the tonics that bring greenbacks to the house and keep us in health."

Tobias held up his hands. "Okay. *Okay.* Ain't no business of mine. But I know you don't have much experience, and a man is a man — men like to sniff after women, and you all so close up there, he might just catch your scent, if you see what I mean." He sighed. "I just want you to be careful, girl."

"Believe me, I am. But if sniffing is the problem, I'm safer in my quarters than with Cahill and his men down here." She tried to keep the indignation out of her voice, and the shame. Another part of the fantasy world in her rooms was pretending no one knew what she was about — that no one conjectured. And that's all it was, thank heavens, conjecture. Tobias didn't know that Ewan came out of the drying room and spent hours upon hours with Marlie. That they talked about everything under the sun except those things that could hurt them. At the very worst, he might think they'd engaged in something carnal. That would have been the least of Marlie's problems. She knew all about a man's body, even if just from a strictly scientific standpoint.

That she was growing more interested in Ewan's heart and mind was the issue.

There was a familiar quick-paced slap of slippers on the floorboards and then Sarah appeared, smiling with relief. The smile twisted the dagger of guilt into Marlie a bit more. How could she hide anything from Sarah?

She hasn't ever even acknowledged you as her sister, or your place in this family. Why is she entitled to know anything?

The angry thought shot to the surface of her thoughts just as Sarah engulfed her in a hug. Where had that come from? Surely Marlie wasn't angry about something as silly as a label, after all Sarah had done for her.

"I'm so sorry you're forced to skulk about in the attic like Mrs. Rochester," Sarah said, and then released her. Marlie felt like she'd played a round of her childhood game: closing her eyes and spinning until her head felt scrambled and like it just might float off her shoulders. Maybe it was all the time spent in Vivienne's world, with Ewan, but things between her and Sarah suddenly seemed even more misaligned.

"I'm fine," Marlie assured her. "I get to hide away while all of you are forced to be pleasant and accommodating to those you disdain. That has to be much harder."

"Anything for the Union," Sarah said in a low voice before taking a fortifying breath. "This morning I reminded Cahill that while he is welcome here, his militia is not. They've been availing themselves of our hospitality and food for days, while Melody smiles and encourages them. Men have started to sleep in the parlor and last night they were bivouacking in the yard. The azaleas are ruined, and worse than that —"

She threw up her hands in frustration and Marlie knew what she meant. They could undertake no operations while the enemy lounged casually in the garden and made himself at home. Except that, unbeknownst to Sarah, they already were. Marlie's stomach tumbled thinking about a house crawling with Rebs with a Union man hidden away in her rooms. What was she to do?

Tobias cleared his throat, then cleared it a bit louder, his gaze boring into Marlie.

"Are you well?" Sarah asked. Her brows raised in concern. "Who knows what sickness these men are bringing with them? Another reason they need to find another base of operations."

"I'm fine," he said. "Just been feeling out of sorts for a little while now." Another meaningful look at Marlie.

Marlie felt slightly ill herself, but it was pure nerves. "Sarah, there is something I've been meaning to mention —"

The pounding of hooves and sudden racket of men's celebratory shouts outside drew their attention.

"Oh no." Sarah lifted her skirts and jogged into the parlor, toward the window looking onto the front of the house. What she saw made her raise a hand to her mouth in distress.

For an instant, Marlie thought to turn tail and run back up to her rooms, and the impulse frightened her. She was no detective, but she'd been doing Railroad work for years, had set up her own business in a white town, had walked into a prison teeming with men. Why should she run from Cahill? Still, she thought of their previous encounters, and the frown that marred Ewan's face every time he spoke of the man.

There was the noise and commotion of men dismounting, and another kind of ugly sound.

A heavy thud, and then a shout. "Get up! You mangy skulker." The sound of a fist connecting with something solid, and a muffled cry of pain.

Marlie joined Sarah at the window. A slender man with a cruel face was standing

227

over a bound boy writhing in the middle of the lawn where, until recently, Sarah and Marlie had occasionally had picnics. The boy was a horrid puce color, and Marlie rushed out the door, leaving her logic behind her.

"He's suffocating!" she said as she rushed past the cruel-faced man and went to her knees. She pulled away the dirty strip of fabric that bound his mouth and turned him to his side as he retched. Only a lifetime of experience with the scent of bile and sickness kept her from doing the same.

"David?" John and Hattie's son, one of the many children she had tended to over the years, coughed weakly and retched again.

There was a sudden, sharp pain in her side and Marlie was sprawled behind the boy, clutching at herself as if that could stop the pain radiating from her rib cage. Cahill stood above her, his face impassive, as if the mud from his boot weren't caking the side of her dress. "Roberts, I told you that these curs were to receive no aid."

"This darkie came out of nowhere, sir," Roberts said. His hand went to rest on the pistol holstered at his side and Marlie's breath stopped in her chest for a moment. Her mind went clean as a steamed vial, un-

228

able to focus on more than the pain in her side and the gun that could be drawn at any second.

"Release my boy, now!"

The cry came from the far side of the lawn, near the entrance. Three women stood there, faces grim. Their dresses were the plain homespun of the local farmers' wives, cheap and ragged from overwear. One woman stood near the front, older and obviously less afraid than the other two, and Marlie recognized her stern expression. Hattie. Her daughter Penny cowered behind her, with a woman Marlie didn't recognize.

"Ma!" David's cry was pitiful, and though the woman's hard expression didn't change, she held her eyes shut for a moment. When they fluttered open again, her gaze was fixed on Cahill.

"You Rebs are already starving us to death, then robbing us o' the little we have," Hattie said. "You took my husband and now you wanna take my boy? No. Release him this instant."

Her voice, the anger and the fear and the resentment bound up in it, echoed back from the trees.

"Presumptuous trash," Cahill said. "This is no boy. He lost that designation when I caught him bringing supplies to those malingerers in the forest. If he's man enough to aid the draft dodgers, then he's subject to the laws of the Confederacy. He is going to serve his nation, as we all must serve during these times. You're lucky I didn't shoot him on sight."

Hattie didn't cower at Cahill's words.

"We just poor farmers. Ain't got no slaves and don't believe in no slaves. Why should my boy fight so rich men can keep on living off the work of others? Gimme my boy, or you'll regret it. Your luck gonna run out eventually; the Heroes will see to that."

She lifted her hand and pointed a finger at Cahill, and Marlie understood that a different type of conjuring was going on, even if Hattie didn't: the power of a mother's love throwin' against the man who would take her boy away. That was a powerful thing, but not so powerful as it should have been.

Cahill grimaced. "I see where he learned his disobedience to the laws of the land. You're one of these pathetic women, bringing food and vittles to deserters who cower in the forests like vermin, and you think I should fear you?" he asked.

Hattie didn't answer.

"Aiding those who would subvert the Confederacy is punishable by imprisonment or death. Roberts, give me your gun." He held his hand out, his eye still on the women.

Roberts started. "Sir? For a woman?"

"If she holds truck with criminals, she's subject to the same law as them. Your pistol. Now." His fingers moved in a beckoning motion.

The two younger women scrambled back into the forest, tugging at Hattie's arms, but she shoved them off and stood fast.

Marlie looked up. Cahill was squinting to take aim. David thrashed as he fought against his bonds, trying to get to his feet. The militiamen looked on, unsettled but unwilling to question their commander.

So much of the claptrap of the Confederacy was about how their women needed to be protected, but Cahill intended to kill this one. Marlie realized that, just as she didn't fit Cahill's conception of a woman, neither did an impoverished farm wife in a raggedy dress.

There was silence, except for the cock of the gun and a single syllable, tinged with a hint of French and soaked in Carolina Southern that resonated in her head. *Move.*

Marlie darted up toward Cahill's arm, her own arms stretched upward, just as his finger pressed into the trigger. There was a loud report that echoed across the lawn and into the trees, sending the birds flying, and then she was knocked away hard and thrown to the ground again. As she landed, she could see the back of Hattie's skirt as she took flight into the trees.

Marlie's ears rang, and she couldn't hear the birds that she saw flying overhead. She felt strange as she watched the birds winging away, like she was seeing a memory playing back against the slate gray sky. Then Sarah was by her side, running her hands over Marlie's arms, her sides.

"Marlie! Has he hurt you?"

Marlie was not unhurt, but she hadn't been shot. "I am fine," she said.

"Come now. Come." She pulled Marlie up to her feet, pulled her through the militiamen and into the house, glancing back over her shoulder every few steps. It was only when they reached the house that Marlie looked back, too.

Cahill was still looking into the trees after his escaped quarry, but he had no reason to track Marlie's movements: He knew exactly where to find her.

CHAPTER 11

Ewan was shaking. He was shaking and didn't know what to do with the rage that made him want to lunge and kick and lash out.

"Breathe in," his mother had told him when he was small and that feeling came over him, her lilt soothing. "And then breathe out. Then do that again. It's the only way we get through life, my boy."

His mother knew better than most how to move past the terrible things life could subject a person to. The only time he'd ever seen her break was when she'd discovered his father dead by his own hand, when he'd finally grown ashamed enough to put an end to the wretched abuse he'd laid down on his wife and family for years. That had been Ewan's only regret — that after that last argument with his father, when the man had grabbed his gun and stalked into the woods, Ewan hadn't found him first. He'd been glad that his father was gone from their lives and hadn't understood why his mother mourned him.

"It's been weeks. Why is she still so sad?" Ewan asked as he and Malcolm watched their mother stare blankly into the fireplace.

"Love," Malcolm said. His expression was pinched and serious, as if their father were still there. "Nothing good can come of it. Remember that."

It was their father who had first inspired Ewan's impulse to lash out and cause pain, as well as the desire to control such base emotions lest he emulate the man he hated. But when he'd seen Cahill attack Marlie, all the years of training, all the methods for funneling the ugly bursts of energy — they all fell to the wayside. He'd wanted to hurt Cahill, again. Worse than he had before. And when he saw Marlie stand up unharmed, he wanted to pull her back up into her rooms and hide her away from the world with him.

Why hadn't she listened when he'd warned her to avoid the man? Instead she'd run right at him.

Ewan pressed his fingers into his scalp, as if that could relieve the frustrating itch that began in his skull and grew each time he thought about what he'd seen.

When the shot had gone off and she'd been thrown to the ground . . . at the angle from which he'd viewed the scene, Ewan had been unable to piece together what had happened. For a brief, terrifying instant, he'd been certain Marlie was dead. Certain that he'd let Cahill kill her.

Even the memory of the despair that had near caved in his chest left him reeling in a way none of his wartime experiences had. In the wake of their near kiss, he'd said the first thing that had come to mind that would put space between them, and had hurt her deeply. When he'd seen Marlie lunge for the gun and heard its report, he'd been sure that she was gone and that he would never get to make amends. And she still hadn't returned.

Remember the nature of anything which pleases the soul or is loved. If it is an earthen vessel you love, remember that, for when it breaks you will not be disturbed.

He'd told himself Marlie was just a woman, like many women, as *The Enchiridion* counseled. If she were broken, he would not be disturbed. Whether she lived or died was beyond his control.

He'd told himself that as he exited the drying room. He'd told himself that as he'd opened the leather and translated pages of

235

Vivienne's memoir. He'd written out passages with shaking fingers and a mind too distracted to take in their import, just so her mother's words would be waiting for her when she came back.

He'd told himself he would not be disturbed if she didn't come back. It was beyond his control.

She had to come back.

What if she's injured? What if he's hurting her? Ewan knew what Cahill was capable of: anything. The image of him interrogating Marlie came to Ewan riding on a wave of nausea. He would go to her. He had to. But then logic, damned logic, kicked in. *If you go running into the house searching for her, you put her at even greater risk.*

The risk to himself was immaterial. But he refused to be the one who'd sealed Marlie's fate because his nerves wouldn't let him be. During his first battle, the soldier beside him in the trench dug into red clay had been jumpy beyond measure. As the drumming of the Confederate battalion they were to face drew nearer, Ewan had watched in dismay as the man had jumped up out of the trench and charged, too anxious to wait for the order to do so. The battle had gone pell-mell after that. It might have anyway, but Ewan would never know, nor would the men killed by the gunfire the soldier had attracted.

He would wait. She was just a woman. He would w—

The sound of the key in the lock startled him up off his seat and toward the drying room door.

Breathe in. Breathe out.

He heard steps, and after several of them he recognized they were hers. He knew the sound of her footsteps like the melody in his favorite song; recognizable in any variation. The heavy drag of these ones revealed her fatigue.

He sat on the bundle of fabric that made for a bed — it wasn't soft or comfortable, but it was still precious in those dire times, when every scrap was put to some use. That wasn't lost on him.

He heard the scrape of the desk only by straining — she'd grown adept at moving it quietly in his days there.

He felt her before he saw her, moving toward him in the darkness like a specter. Then she drew nearer, and he could make out her faint silhouette in the moonlight seeping through the curtain. She settled next to him on the pile of fabric, more substantial than shadow, warm and smelling of some mixture of hers — likely an unguent to relieve the pain of the blows she had received.

It was dark, but Ewan closed his eyes anyway, as if that could stop him from seeing her struck and falling to the ground as it replayed in his mind.

"Marlie?" He didn't speak above a whisper, as his throat had gone tight. His whole body was tight. He'd spent the last few hours wishing for her presence, and now that she was beside him, he was vividly reminded of why she shouldn't be.

"Yes."

"I told you to be careful," he said. "And yet you ran right for him." The harsh words slipped out, a reprimand that he knew wasn't fair. But he couldn't stop hearing the report of the gun, and reliving the sick instant when he'd thought her gone.

He heard her breath catch, felt her body go stiff. "Are you saying I should have just let him shoot that woman? I may have to cede my home to him, but I won't let him kill an innocent if I can help it."

The displeasure in her tone was evident. His thoughtless words had wounded her again.

Ewan pressed his teeth together against his frustration. He was tired of being wrong when it came to things like this. He hadn't been the man who protected her when she'd needed him; he needed to be the man who soothed her pain instead of exacerbating it. "That was imprecise." He paused, tried to formulate the right words. "What happened wasn't your fault, and I'm sorry I implied that. And I'm sorry about what happened before that, too. I am not good at . . . things like this, but I'm here and I want to give you what you need. I can just listen."

Ewan hoped he hadn't said the wrong thing again, but then he felt her sag against his side, as if she trusted him to hold her steady. Ewan felt the import of that in the weight and pliancy of her body, and emotion surged in his chest.

"He's awful," Marlie whispered, her voice shaking. She didn't acknowledge his apology, but she didn't refuse it, either. "How can such a man exist? I know people say that there are unnatural men who walk among us, and these are unnatural times, but he's the devil's hand servant."

"Yes, he is," Ewan said. He wondered what she would say if she knew he was cut from the same cloth. He wouldn't hurt Marlie, ever, so that was at least one difference between him and the damned Reb who had hit her. "If you wish, I'll go handle things now and he won't ever bother you again.

You can pretend you have no idea who I am if I'm captured."

There. He'd as good as told her his true nature, again. He waited in the darkness for her to get up and move away from him, but she moved closer to him instead. Her forearm brushed his and Ewan exhaled sharply at the surprise of it. Her hand rested on his biceps, and Ewan was sure he could feel her heartbeat in the palm of her hand, urgently tapping out the message that she was alive and in his arms, and asking what he would do with that information.

"Thank you for the offer, but no," she said. "You forget that I could handle him, too, Socrates. With the right mixture of plant toxins, he'd die quite painfully."

There was a rough delight in her voice as she said the words. Ewan had only ever known Marlie to take care of others — she'd devoted her life to it. It shocked him, intrigued him, to know that her thoughts weren't all as saintly as he supposed.

"But I won't stain my soul for a man like him, and I don't want you to, either," she said. "I just . . . can I sit beside you for a spell?"

The roughness in her voice was gone now, and there was only uncertainty.

Tell her no.

He should have. But instead he said, "Of course. We're well past polite, remember?"

She inched next to him and rested her head on his shoulder. Her disheveled curls brushed against his ear and he shuddered; something sharp and sweet jolted down his spine.

He tried to recall her nature then, as Epictetus directed, but she was not as easily dismissed as a clay pot. Her nature most certainly didn't diminish her in his eyes. She was brilliant and thoughtful and never made him feel out of place when she most assuredly could have. She understood his humor and didn't treat him as an oddity; one could not say that of a clay pot. Clay was cool and hard, but Marlie was warm and soft and pressed against his side as if she felt safe with him. She shouldn't have.

"I was terrified," she finally said. "I've been so removed from everything. Even going to the prison didn't give me a clear picture. But seeing the Home Guard with that trussed boy was . . ." She shook her head against his arm. "Cahill would have killed Hattie simply for having dignity in the face of his callousness. He could have killed *me*. Here, on our own property where I'm supposed to be safe. But nowhere is safe.

"Your ankle has healed enough. You must go soon," she said, and then released a shaky breath. "More militiamen arrive every day and Melody is intent on letting them have the run of the place. And Stephen has left for his holdings in the North like the coward he is, leaving us with his despicable wife. That explains Cahill's bold behavior today."

Stephen? Something stirred in the back of Ewan's mind, but he could not pull it to the forefront with her against him and the truth of their situation finally spoken aloud. It was no longer safe for him to stay there. It never had been, but they'd fallen into a routine, and routines comforted Ewan.

It was more than that: Marlie comforted Ewan. The thought of leaving her was highly unpleasant, despite his knowledge that attachments were useless in this world.

"I understand," was all he said. "I should want to leave, I suppose."

"Of course." Her body pressed into his, just slightly more than it already was. He wasn't sure she was aware she had even done it. When he glanced down at her, her head was lowered, her hands folded primly in her lap. "I imagine more pleasurable diversions await you than passing notes with me in an attic."

"Marlie."

He reached out then, encircled her wrist between his thumb and forefinger because the impulse was impossible to resist. She gasped, and he felt her pulse increase where his finger bent at the knuckle. Her skin was so soft, and though her wrist was thin, it wasn't as fragile as he'd imagined. He felt the stretch of tendons as she flexed her hand in surprise — she was stronger than he'd given her credit for. Perhaps . . .

No.

He released her wrist and went to move away from her, to stop this madness before it began, but then her hand caught his shirt by the front and tugged. His face was abruptly at the same level as hers, and he stared, trying to discern its features in the darkness.

Her eyes fluttered shut and she began to lean forward toward him, so slowly that he could have dodged away as he should have, but then her lips were pressing against his, softly, tentatively. Those first few exploratory brushes nearly undid him, but it was the way her brow creased as she did it again — her eyes were closed, but Ewan didn't want to miss a moment — that sent the first tendrils of smoke up from the slow-growing fire within him. She looked . . . confused.

As if she weren't sure how to proceed.

Oh dear heavens.

Ewan was exacting in his expectations of others, but not Marlie and not this. A bolt of tenderness shot through him as he realized that she was seeking instruction. He could not push her away. If she was to remember him, it wouldn't be as the man who refused her in a moment of need. He would be the man who every other kiss had to measure up to. Ewan could allow himself that bit of baseness — the desire that she never forget him.

His hand went to the back of her neck, and when she gasped in surprise he nipped at her lower lip. He molded his lips to hers, pressing his tongue into her mouth, teasing her with long, slow licks.

His head buzzed as her arms went about his neck and her breasts pushed into his chest. Her nipples were taut and hard through her bodice, and Ewan ached to feel them in his palm, in his mouth — but no, that would be too far. His hand went to her hip instead, gripped her there hard, and she rocked up into the hold.

Marlie was adept, for she was soon matching his strokes and nipping at his mouth in turn. Her quiet sighs pierced the silence and her hands tangled in his hair, pulling him closer.

Pleasure pooled at Ewan's groin, spreading from his hardening length through his body. He'd never wanted anything so much as he wanted Marlie in that moment — he'd made sure of that — but the Fates intended to hold him to his resolve, despite his own failure.

"Oh God, Ewan," she whispered as his mouth moved to her neck, and he tasted the sweet and salty flavor of her. He scraped his teeth over her collarbone, so close to her bosom. Her hands gripped his shoulders, and she pulled him closer — and then abruptly pushed him away. Then she was up on her feet, running.

You pushed too hard. You frightened her.

That's when he heard the pounding at her door.

"Open this door right now," a woman's voice called out, sweet as a sugar drop laced with venom. "Enough is enough. After today's exploits, you'll no longer be allowed to do as you please."

Marlie looked back at Ewan, her eyes wide. Then she squeezed through the door. Ewan was up after her in a flash, shutting the door behind her as she quietly pushed the desk against it.

He heard Marlie's key in the lock, and then Cahill's voice sliced through the silence. "Now to see what this darkie has been hiding up here."

CHAPTER 12

Marlie's heart had already been beating wildly as Ewan's mouth moved against hers, and then down toward her décolletage. His grip on her had been so strong, the power of his desire imprinted against her by the press of his fingertips into the curve of her hip. She had never imagined that kissing could be like that. She had wanted more of it, so much more of it, but now her heart was beating at a dangerous rate for a different reason.

"One moment!" she called out as another round of angry knocking shook the door. "I was indisposed."

She looked over her shoulder at the high-backed desk pushed against the wall one more time, then pulled the key from around her neck and unlocked the door to danger. Cahill and Melody stood there, his face calm and hard, hers pleasant to the point of discomfort. Glee flashed in those brown eyes, and that was more frightening than Cahill's coldness.

"This is entirely unnecessary," Sarah's voice rang out from behind Cahill. "Stephen would never allow this."

Melody giggled. "Stephen would have no say in this, just as he has no say in anything of import. He can't even manage you, and you think he could stop a man like Captain Cahill, a true advocate for the Confederacy?"

She darted an admiring glance up at the man and everything fell into place for Marlie: Stephen's departure, Melody's growing boldness. Cahill was exactly the kind of man Melody had wanted for herself, and the war had provided for her. Anger surged through Marlie at the brother who'd been nothing more than a shadow for most of her life. He'd left management of the family property to Sarah and Marlie for years, and then abandoned them with his wife and her lover instead of facing his own shame.

Sarah stepped in behind them, her expression livid. "Well, fine. Search high and low and then see how foolish this is. If you think Marlie would be engaged in any subversive activity and I'd know nothing of it, you're mistaken."

Marlie's head spun. Sarah was simply trying to throw off suspicion, but Marlie was sure that Sarah also thought she was correct. It had never even occurred to her that Marlie could act on her own.

Now is not the time for such thoughts!

"This is the space where I make the tonics and teas that we sell down at the pharmacy. It's been a great source of income for the family and has eased the pain of many of your militiamen." Marlie tried to keep her voice steady, tried to keep her gaze from straining toward the desk to ensure that it was still in place.

"Don't overestimate your value," Melody said. "The Lynch coffers do just fine without your input. Stephen is good at one thing, at least." She walked over to the table that held the still and alembic and began moving things around, tossing aside precisely measured mixtures and hopelessly rearranging things.

Cahill pushed past her and went into her bedchamber, where he pulled the sheets off the bed and onto the floor and flipped the mattress aside. "What are you doing?" Marlie asked.

"I'm searching for further proof of treason," he said. "You were already a problem, but after your actions this afternoon, you've proven yourself a criminal."

"A criminal? For trying to prevent the death of an innocent woman?" Sarah cried out.

"She's been dealt with." He looked up at Marlie, his gaze so devoid of emotion that it chilled her to the bone. "Now it's your turn."

He pulled a large knife from its sheath and brought it down into the mattress, ripping a jagged line down the middle. The filling of the mattress began to fall out, and he aided it along, pulling it out in great handfuls and tossing it haphazardly onto the floor, as if delighting in the chaos. Marlie stood in mute shock, unable to take in everything that was happening. It was just a bed, but it was the thing that kept her warm and comfortable every night. It was where she passed her most intimate moments, and it was being destroyed before her eyes; the sense of foreboding she'd felt when she first spotted both Melody and Cahill overwhelmed her.

She thought of her mother, who had sent her to the Lynches because she'd thought they could keep her safe from the ills of the world.

Maman.

Something crashed behind her, and she whirled to find Melody going through books on the bookcase, flipping through them in search of correspondence and then throwing them to the floor behind her. Sarah was scrambling, trying to pick up the mess, but it was no use.

Marlie's face flushed with anger. There was no correspondence — she'd burned everything she received. The pinpricks in the books weren't detectable. Her Polybius square was safe in the hidden compartment in her desk. There was only one thing of value that Marlie hadn't hidden away.

As if reading her thoughts, Cahill strode over to the desk and began rifling through the papers. "What's this hogwash? 'The whites here seem to both relish the pain of slaves and pretend that we are happy to be subject to their whims. I wish there was a treatment for this disease of the mind.' Is this some kind of abolitionist tract?"

"No, it's no tract. A story I was copying from another source as a diversion."

She wanted to scream and cry and rip the pages from his hands. He was defiling the remnants of her mother with his coarse fingers, with his gaze upon words not meant for him. She didn't remember translating that portion, and as she drew nearer, she realized the writing was indeed not hers. The strokes were short, cribbed, as if the person writing had been in a rush but was too fastidious to let the work be sloppy. She'd seen it every time a note passed under the hidden door.

Ewan.

"Truly, truly nothing of interest," she said, reaching for them. A hand darted out and smacked her fingers, hard.

"I do enjoy a good story," Melody said, taking the papers from Cahill and adding them to the stack sitting on the desk. She turned and began opening drawers and throwing things to the floor. After a few moments of continued destruction, she sighed and turned toward Cahill. "I suppose that's that. Her outburst today was not part of some greater conspiracy among the darkies, but we'll handle it accordingly."

What more could they do? Marlie couldn't begin to conjecture.

"Marlie is a Lynch, and further abuse will not be tolerated," Sarah said, coming to stand in front of Marlie.

Cahill laughed, and Melody joined in. "Marlie is a nigger, Sarah — the Lynch name doesn't change that."

Sarah's eyes squeezed shut in frustration.

"Don't you understand? Her skin might be dark, but her soul is white!" Sarah shouted, and everything in the room went silent afterward, or perhaps it just seemed that way to Marlie. She looked at Sarah, at the conviction on her face, and realized with a horrible clarity that her sister had spoken the ridiculous words because she believed them.

It was true, the father Marlie had never met was white. But the woman who had birthed and raised her and taught her everything she knew? She wasn't, and her soul had been as pure and strong as anyone's.

Marlie wanted to grab Sarah and shake her, to make her take the words back. For half of Marlie's life, Sarah had been everything to her, both sister and, in a way, mother. She was all Marlie had. And she had just revealed that she didn't know Marlie at all. She thought Marlie's soul was white — was that the only reason she had shown her love and affection? Marlie felt a press of tears and fought at the burn behind her eyes.

Melody ignored Sarah and began to walk past her, then stopped. "Wait just a minute, now. Now I'm fairly certain Stephen said that the entire attic had been changed into rooms for the darkie, but this house is longer than these two rooms."

She turned back toward the desk and

bookcase, studying both. Marlie said nothing. Her throat was sealed by the fear that had snapped shut around her like the fly-eating plants that grew in the swamps. She was found out. She'd lost her mother's papers, she felt a thousand leagues from Sarah even as her sister defended her, and now she'd lose Ewan, too. Her life, and certainly, her soul, might be lost as well. She'd thought herself daring, but she was nothing but a fool. She wanted to sink down to the ground but, improbably, her legs kept her upright.

Cahill pushed away the bookshelf first, and, finding nothing there, then moved the desk. He saw the door, and for the first time Marlie saw some emotion in his gaze: excitement. "Well, what do we have here?"

"A room full of rodents," Marlie said. She didn't know where the lie came from, how it flowed so effortlessly from her lips. "A raccoon and her pups got loose in there, eating the plants I'd been drying, and I preferred letting them have the run of the place rather than fighting them. Cunning things. I shut the door and pushed the desk against it to keep them from finding a way into my bedroom."

"Well, if anything is living in there, it won't be for long." He unsheathed the vicious knife again and nudged the door open with his boot. Melody handed him a candle, and he stepped into the darkness.

Marlie closed her eyes, waiting for the sound of struggle, hoping that perhaps Ewan would have the element of surprise. It was the only way he could survive.

"I'll kill him if he tries to hurt you."

Marlie remembered how Ewan had said those words, as if it were an eventuality — as if he had no qualms. And he'd offered the same again, when she came to him. His eyes had gone dark and distant when he'd recalled his time in the war — in all likelihood Ewan was capable of more than she credited him with. But that wasn't something she wanted to discover that night, in that way.

She had envisioned possible discovery before, had always thought she'd be panicked or indignant, but she felt nothing. It was as if so much was going on that her mind chose to process none of it. That was perhaps the only reason she didn't rush into the room after Cahill.

She heard crates being knocked over, baskets and boxes crashing to the floor. Cahill's annoyed grunts as he searched. And then . . . nothing. Cahill came out and placed the candle on the desk.

"It seems your coons are gone," he said.

Marlie stared at him. How? How had he not seen Ewan, with his great height and his shock of red-orange hair?

"G-g-good," she said, hoping they didn't notice how her teeth suddenly chattered.

"Well, I'll just be taking this," Melody said as she pulled at the chain around Marlie's neck with the hand that wasn't holding Vivienne's papers. She pulled it up over her head, heedless when the links snagged in Marlie's curls. She tugged harder, and frowned disdainfully at the hairs caught in the clasp that she'd pulled out by the root. "Disgusting," she muttered as she undid the clasp and removed the key. She added it to her keychain.

"You'll be locked up here until further notice. Sarah. Commander."

"I'm sorry," Sarah whispered, clutching Marlie by the shoulders. Tears filled her eyes, and her expression was so pained that Marlie was almost tempted to comfort her. "I'm supposed to protect you, but Stephen has left me with few options. I will figure something out, do not fear."

She kissed Marlie on the cheek.

Marlie didn't respond. She couldn't. She felt that if she opened her mouth in that moment she'd release a shout that would shake the world.

"Come, Sarah," Melody commanded.

They filed out of the door and Marlie stood numbly in the wreckage of what had once been the last peaceful oasis in a country set against allowing her to live freely. Glass crunched as she walked, and she noticed a scrap of red — the gris-gris she'd made had been crushed underfoot.

She picked up the candle and looked about the drying room. Where had Ewan gone? For one disorienting moment, she wondered if she hadn't imagined him entirely. A figment of her imagination, conjured from her desperate loneliness. Of course, she hadn't realized how alone she'd been until she thought of being without him.

"Socrates?" she whispered.

The ceiling creaked over her head and a board lifted and moved to the side. His pale face appeared in the darkness. "One must always have a contingency plan," he said in a low voice, and she couldn't help the low giggle that burbled out of her. The giggle quickly caught on a sob, and the tears started to flow.

She felt as if the foundations of her life had been kicked out from under her, one by one, until she was left balancing precariously, like a cat chased up a pole.

"Everything is ruined," she whispered. "Everything I love has been taken from me."

Ewan said nothing, but there was the sound of shifting and scraping and then his hand lowered down from the darkness. She reached up and sighed as he caught her hand fast and held it tight. She didn't let go until her arm began to ache.

CHAPTER 13

After fighting sleep for hours, Marlie had finally dozed off — by need and not by choice. Instead of the darkness that usually greeted her, she found herself back in the house where she'd been born.

Vivienne sat cross-legged on the floor, picking through a woven basket overflowing with honeysuckle that rested in her lap. The sweet smell was mixed with rosemary, the calming scent Marlie always associated with her mother. Vivienne didn't seem to notice her as she used a pin to extract the scented droplets from the flowers and transfer them to a bottle beside her.

"Maman?"

Vivienne didn't look up at her, but she spoke and her voice seemed to emanate from the walls of the cabin.

"Put the water on, chérie," *she said. "You know what to do."*

Marlie heard a noise by the cookstove and

turned to find Ewan already there. What was he doing in their home?

Ewan lit match after match, but a cold wind blew each one out before it reached the kindling.

Then he reached for a book — her medical botany — ripped out a page, and lit that instead. It caught fast and flared and he threw it into the stove's belly before looking over his shoulder at her. He was smiling, a wide, sunny smile that looked unnatural on his face.

"They're waiting for us," he said. "Come on, we've got to go."

"I don't want to go," she said, and suddenly she was hugging her mother outside of their shack, as she had the night when she'd first left.

"You have to. Better things await you. Faites moi confiance."

The carriage was there, too, but now Ewan was at the reins. He waved her toward him, but when she took a step she crashed down into the earth. The roots of trees and plants began to bind her, holding her fast as dirt filled her mouth and nostrils. . . .

"Marlie? Hey, girl. Wake up."

She opened her eyes to find Lace and Tobias standing over her, their eyes wide with concern. She tried to capture the fading strands of her dream, the first she'd had in so long. Her mother had been there, and Ewan, but what had it meant? What was it her mother had said? Why was she breathing so hard?

It was too late; the dream was gone, erased by the stark reality of her situation.

"You hurt?" Lace asked.

Marlie shook her head, then realized her face was damp with tears. She kept her gaze on Lace and Tobias as she wiped them away, giving herself a moment of reprieve — to imagine a world in which the previous night hadn't passed — before looking at her ruined work space. At least the still hadn't been harmed too much; the other things could be replaced, eventually, but the still was her prized possession.

She shifted herself up to a sitting position and pain flared in her hip bones and back. Apparently, the pile of stuffing she'd pushed together hadn't made for a comfortable resting place, but she'd been so over-whelmed the previous night that she'd simply curled up into a ball on the first surface not covered with broken glass.

"Sarah got sent to give food at the Reb hospital," Tobias said. "Said we should check on you."

Marlie nodded, tried to stretch, and then caught herself as a wrench in her neck caught painfully.

"Marlie. Look at your hair, and your dress, and —" A tear slipped down Lace's cheek and she shook her head angrily. "This ain't right. You not supposed to get treated like this. None of us are, but especially not you."

Lace was often curt with her, although Marlie knew the woman loved her. Seeing her tears shocked Marlie.

"I'm all right, really."

"She gonna be okay," Tobias said. He rubbed one hand on Lace's back and extended the other to Marlie to help her up.

"Okay?" Lace sucked her teeth in annoyance. "Don't you see? Marlie ain't never been a slave, never been a servant. She ain't ever worked for anyone but herself. She's smarter than any of these white folk, and still she can be treated like this." She held her hands toward Marlie as if presenting some damning evidence. "What's the point of freedom if people can still do this to you and act like you deserved it?"

Lace moved away from Tobias's comfort, her mouth pressed into a line, and dragged Marlie up to a chair. Marlie felt a tug at her hair and then release — Lace had grabbed a brush from amongst the mess and was pulling it through her hair, as she had when

Marlie first arrived and Sarah had begged for help. The brush didn't feel good going through her tangled curls, but there was a comfort in the sensation of being cared for. She remembered sitting between Vivienne's legs on braiding day, and how she'd always felt beautiful afterward.

Maman. The thought of her mother's papers in Melody's hands made Marlie ill. She wrapped her arms around her stomach.

"What am I going to do?" she asked aloud, more to herself. "Melody has said I'm to be punished, Cahill has decided I need to be put in my place, and Sarah can do nothing without Stephen, who has left us again, the coward."

Marlie felt all her anger flow in his direction. He was the one who had brought this misfortune into their lives. She'd been afraid of war and bloodshed coming to their doorstep, but it was a woman in an impractical hoopskirt who had blown their lives apart.

"I wish he'd never come back. I wish Grant had captured both of them before they could make their way."

She glanced up and caught Tobias raising his brows in Lace's direction. He caught Marlie's movement and looked back over at her. "Melody been raging since this morning. She told us we weren't to help you clean up because you need to get used to the new order around here. Every servant has to take care of his own task, and she said now you're to be considered . . ."

He looked away from her.

Marlie felt dread seep into her bones. She tried not to show it, that being forced to be a servant would feel like a degradation. Why? She didn't think less of Lace or Tobias or Pearl. When she'd first arrived, she'd been reprimanded for helping them with their work. They'd been the only people she thought could understand her, but a sea of privilege separated her from them on one side and from Sarah on the other.

But she'd found a different purpose for herself, one that also wasn't considered fitting for a lady, that was largely only permissible because of the island of one she occupied in the Lynch house. Marlie imagined never experiencing the joy of the quiet concentration of mixing and macerating, of taking disparate plants and finding the right proportion to make them into healing tonics. It was magic to her, and that magic was about to be snatched away and replaced by a life of scrubbing and toil.

"Oh," she said quietly.

Marlie felt the pull on both sides of her

head as Lace began a French braid.

"Don't hold back on our account," Lace said with a rueful laugh. "It's not like I got to choose what path I took in this life. And it's not like you're some pampered debutante. You got a talent, and you use it. Melody is just jealous, when it comes down to it. She'll never be anything more than she is, and she wants you to suffer for it."

Marlie knew Lace was trying to make her feel better but she felt worse, wondering what Lace and Tobias and all the other Negroes forced into slavery or servitude might have done with their lives if given a choice. It hit her hard and all at once, this thing she had always known but never allowed herself to feel: Slavery didn't just take away a person's freedom; it took away an entire people's future. And even the freedom that Marlie had was just an illusion, if Melody and Cahill could snatch it away so easily.

She felt that scream building in her throat again, the last cry of her belief in fairness and her hope for the future.

"What happened to — ?" Tobias asked, nodding toward the open door of the still room. She'd forgotten Ewan for a moment, as impossible as that seemed. Marlie wondered how he had slept; if her body ached from the floor, she couldn't imagine what his must feel like.

"Hid away in the ceiling," she whispered. Marlie remembered what had happened before that. Her first kiss, her first sensual touch. That, too, had been tarnished. She kept her eyes averted, hoping Tobias wouldn't see where her thoughts had strayed. That was of no import now. It had been a passing whim, just another part of the fantasy world that had to come crashing down on them eventually. There was no escape from the war; the Lynch estate was not a fortress, and even if it had been, it was occupied by the enemy now.

"Marlie, we don't got much choice here," Tobias said, rubbing a hand over his short, kinky hair. He blew out a breath and then looked at her. "He gotta go tonight. If he stays here, it's when and not if we get found out."

Marlie felt every ache in her body as she thought of turning Ewan out into the Carolina wilds without a guide, but he was intelligent and resourceful. He'd make it. And she could no longer endanger the household with his presence.

"We decided the same last night," she said, rising to her feet. "Knock on the board above that pile of sassafras and you can figure things out with him. I'll start cleaning this mess."

She began picking the books up and putting them neatly in the shelves. She felt like a windup automaton as she moved, her thoughts far away from the room as if that were the only way from screaming her anger into the quiet morning of the house.

She wondered what Vivienne would have done, then recalled how her mother had described her entry to the boat that would carry her to America.

"My wrists were shackled but my spine was straight. I would not be broken by these people."

Marlie pushed her shoulders back as she picked up another book. Beneath it, a dried, shriveled thing lay on the ground. The John the Conqueror root her mother had given her when she'd sent her off with Sarah; her totem of protection. She hadn't seen it in years. She picked it up, the leathery feel of it strange on her fingertips, and then pushed it down into the bosom of her dress, close to her heart.

"You got this, Marl?" Lace asked.

Marlie nodded, tried to force a smile, and continued picking up the mess.

CHAPTER 14

Ewan had been in uncomfortable positions before, but being crammed between the joists in the attic roof for nearly twenty-four hours was nearly unbearable. He didn't mind the cramped quarters, or even the insects that brushed past every now and then. It was knowing that Marlie's sanctum from the world had been violated. It was thinking of how he had agreed to leave when Tobias had come to him, knowing that meant that Marlie would be left behind with Cahill.

Her situation was already precarious. Could he truly run into the night, knowing what would befall her? Cahill already had his sights set on punishing her, and it was the only thing the man excelled at. Worry for Marlie was about more than latent inappropriate feeling for her, Ewan assured himself. He wouldn't leave any woman to experience Cahill's idea of justice — that was solid fact, and he clung to it.

As the hours had stretched on, Ewan had reached the inevitable conclusion: He could run, but he'd have to make damned sure Cahill was dead before he did. It was what he would have done upon their first meeting if he hadn't valued scruples such as honor and morals. What were those when you'd been taught which bones to break to get a man to speak? He valued honesty, and he needed to stop lying to himself: Honor shared no part in his philosophy at this point, which was simply survival. Marlie had helped him to survive. He wouldn't repay her by leaving her to unknown terrors.

He would approach Cahill, make himself known, and then be done with this. If he survived, he'd move on. If not, he'd tried his best. But he couldn't imagine failure. Not when he thought of Marlie's innocent mouth pressing against his, at the shudder of her breath into his hair as he nipped her neck.

He could hear her moving about — she had been cleaning all day, and had come in once to sneak him food, but she hadn't tarried. He had sought out her gaze, but she kept her head down. Was she upset with him? Did she regret kissing him?

More like her entire world has been shat-

tered while you're worrying like a love-struck fool.

Other people had been in and out. Tobias and another woman. Eventually, Ewan allowed himself to fall asleep. He'd have a long night ahead of him and needed to rest.

"Let me go!"

Marlie's sudden shout startled Ewan awake; he was already lifting the board aside to jump down and run to her when he thought better of it. He needed to know what was happening — and who was causing it — before he acted. He was good at causing pain, given the opportunity, but he wasn't strong enough to run into a room and overwhelm a group of armed men by sheer force.

"No wonder you've been acting like you were better than me this whole time," a woman's voice said. Ewan recognized it from the night before — Melody. The woman seemed to take a singular pleasure in tormenting Marlie, and now she was back to inflict more suffering.

"Did you think I wouldn't find out?" Melody asked. "All that uppity behavior, all those disrespectful looks? You've been laughing at me, I bet, laughing with him and with Sarah!"

"What are you talking about?" Marlie asked. There was the sound of struggle. "Get this man off of me!"

"Do you know how long Stephen and I have been trying? For a child?" Melody asked, her voice high and thin. "Years. Year after miserable year. It never took, and Stephen always told me maybe it just wasn't God's will, but I knew it was his fault. His seed had to be weak, just like him."

Oh.

Ewan remembered a bit of what he had translated in his feverish effort to distract himself the evening before. That the Lynches' young son, Stephen, had always been so kind to Marlie's mother, and that they sometimes met in secret. . . .

Damn it.

"I demanded the truth from Sarah, and she finally told me. About him and your whore of a mother," Melody bit out. "I will not allow such an abomination in my sight for another day longer."

All the false sweetness had gone from her voice; it was pure hatred.

"I don't know what you're talking about," Marlie said. Her voice lilted in that way it did when she was working something out in her mind, like she was asking a question and answering it at the same time. "Stephen

271

isn't — I've hardly ever interacted with him. It's not as if he showers me with brotherly affection. He has nothing to do with me."

Melody laughed.

"Brotherly? He has nothing to do with you because he's ashamed," Melody spat. "You are a living reminder that he rutted with an animal, that he lowered himself enough to be ensnared by a vile darkie. And then he had the gall to ask for my hand afterward, to pollute me with his impurity."

There was a long silence, and Ewan wished he could see Marlie. Let her know that she wasn't alone although she must have felt cleft from everything she'd known.

"That cannot be true . . . Sarah is my sister. She would have told me otherwise. She would have told me if —" Marlie's voice had atrophied, was barely recognizable as her own.

"Well, he won't be reminded any longer, and neither will I," Melody said briskly. "You simply can't stay here now — I won't have it. Commander Cahill knows exactly where to put you. There's money to be made with all these soldier boys about, you see. I bet they can even charge extra for those devil eyes of yours."

Nausea roiled through Ewan's belly at Melody's horrific solution.

"You can do no such thing. I'm free — born free — you cannot sell me."

"My, Sarah really has filled your head with nonsense, hasn't she? Whatever free papers you have only hold water with someone who cares. I don't, and whoever buys you certainly won't either."

"No!" The sounds of struggle renewed, and Ewan's heart lurched at the despair in the single word.

"Oh, but I thought you were eager to bring in income to the family?" Melody's voice began to fade, as if she moved away. "You had to know this couldn't last. Sarah will have to marry eventually, old as she is, and do you think she'll keep you around then, knowing what your mama was like? All girls must give up their pets, and it's time for you to be put to pasture. Throw her in that room."

There was the sound of struggle and a man's grunts. Then Marlie landed on the floor beneath the board Ewan had pushed aside. She was bound and gagged, and tears spilled from her eyes as she looked wildly about. She screamed, but the gag muffled the sound. That didn't stop her from trying. She writhed as she fought against the restraints at her wrists. It was only when she flopped back against the floorboards, momentarily defeated, that her gaze caught his.

Ewan felt everything inside of him go still, and not because he was calm. Seeing Marlie like that — because of him, because he'd stupidly left those papers on her desk — made him want to lash out, to kick. Instead he raised a finger to his lips, and she nodded and stopped struggling. Her tears still flowed, though, and her shoulders heaved from sobs. Her anguish wrenched something inside of him; he didn't know how she felt, but he knew he would do anything to ease her pain.

The light spilling in from the workroom abruptly went dark, and the sound of the desk being pushed against the wall signaled Melody's departure.

He waited a few moments, and when there was nothing but the noise of the crickets outside, he slipped down from the cubbyhole.

He sucked in a breath as the muscles in his thighs and calves resisted their new range of motion and tightened with sharp bursts of pain. Ewan gritted his teeth against it — pain could be overlooked. It was just a temporary reaction of his body, and his body was one thing Ewan could control.

He limped the few steps that got him to Marlie and undid the band around her mouth and then the knots at her wrists. She took in great heaving breaths, but he could see they did her no good because she started to take them more quickly, hiccupping gulps as her eyes went wide.

He placed his hand flat over her chest, feeling her heart race against his palm like a trapped rabbit's. "Breathe in, Marlie. Breathe in, and breathe out. Slowly." He modeled it for her, taking several exaggerated breaths. "I know you're frightened right now. But I won't let anything happen to you."

"How's that, Socrates?" Her hands clasped over his on her chest, but didn't pull it away. "Melody has decided my fate. She's already taken everything: Maman's writing, my life as I knew it. She decided I shouldn't have anything, and she's made it happen."

Ewan tilted his head, then stood and reached up into the cubbyhole. "I can't return your life to you as it was, but I can give you this." He handed her the sheaf of papers, tucked into the leather portfolio she'd kept them in, and she looked up at him in disbelief.

"Is this what I think it is?" she asked.

Ewan ran a hand through his hair, hesitating. "I left this room yesterday when I was . . . upset about your predicament. While I was at your desk, I thought that, if something had happened to you, perhaps you wouldn't want anyone to have your mother's words. So I brought the original in here with me."

He didn't tell her how in that moment of panic he'd thought the papers might be all he would have left of her. She didn't need to know that, and he didn't need to feel it.

"I was going to tell you last night but —"

I was too busy kissing you.

"So what did she take?"

"I believe that was just the portion I translated yesterday, and perhaps some of your notes. Unfortunately, it contained something that I gather came as quite a shock to you."

Her frown deepened, and she nodded.

"Stephen . . . is he truly what she said he is?" It seemed she couldn't bring herself to say the word *father,* something Ewan understood all too well.

"In the portion I translated, your mother stated that he seemed to be captivated by her, had shown her kindness, and they'd begun to meet in secret. She didn't discuss it in detail but in the last section I translated,

276

she'd dreamed she was pregnant with a beautiful baby girl."

Marlie stared down at the portfolio.

"Thank you. I don't want to discuss this any further," she said. It felt like a slap, and he realized it was the first time she'd closed part of herself off from him. It was ridiculous for him to feel that way; he kept his emotions and impulses in check at all times. He thought he hadn't succeeded in doing that very well with Marlie, then realized that wasn't true. If it was, he would have kissed her days ago. At the prison, perhaps.

Ewan was adept at getting what he wanted from people. He told himself that wasn't what prompted his new course of action.

"This changes my plans quite a bit," he said. He stood carefully — the last thing he needed was a setback with his ankle hampering him. Them, as it were. He moved to the pile of fabric and pulled out a small knife from his pants pocket, thinking over his plans to kill Cahill. He could finally be done with the man, but it would no longer be in the service of keeping her safe. Not unless he planned to kill Melody, too. Harming women was one line Ewan had yet to cross, and though he'd do it to keep Marlie from harm, there was another way to keep her safe.

"I'll still be departing tonight, but you'll be leaving with me." He began cutting the first strip of fabric from his bedding. He tried to keep his proclivity toward donnishness in check, but he didn't see this as a topic up for rational discussion.

He expected some resistance. But when he looked at her, she clutched the portfolio to her chest and stared at him with a blank expression that made her look like someone else entirely, someone who was hurting very badly.

"However you got out there yesterday. Can you do it again?" She nodded her head in the direction of the door.

"Yes."

"I have to get some things for the journey. Then . . . then we'll leave Lynchwood."

CHAPTER 15

Marlie couldn't think of the immensity of what she was undertaking. She couldn't, or it would freeze her in her tracks. Many people escaping enslavement had passed a night at Lynchwood, but she'd only seen the glory of what they were undertaking. Their hope for the future. It had seemed frightening in theory — like the stories about battles that she read in the paper, which upset her but seemed far removed from her everyday life. She had never truly empathized until she slipped into her own room on stocking feet and tried to figure out what the most important items were — just as she had when she was a girl. But this time, she wasn't heading to a more comfortable life; she was heading out into the wilds of the Carolina Piedmont. This time, she was running for her life.

She took a deep breath and commenced the unpleasant task. She tried to be practical. A change of clothing wouldn't do, but she grabbed a couple of pairs of drawers. The scented hair oil she used, because she refused to give up that one vanity. Her brush. She threw together the same materials she grabbed when passengers showed up at their station, except this time she'd likely have to use the things for herself or Ewan. Some biscuits Lace had brought up for her, wrapped up in a cloth napkin. She picked up her *Illustrated American Botany,* which had served her so well, but that was impractical. She'd get another copy someday, if she survived the journey.

There's a chance I won't. Fear froze her then, with the heavy book in her hand and her heart jumping about in her chest like a chipmunk in the underbrush. She slowly put the book down. *But if I stay here, I'll learn that surviving might be worse.*

She pulled out the drawer in her desk and popped open the false bottom, from which she removed the greenbacks she'd saved from her sales at the pharmacy. Her free papers, in case they were stopped, though they might not be worth much given the current climate. She snatched up the letters Ewan had slipped beneath her door, too. She hadn't been able to burn those along with the Loyal League correspondence, although in retrospect it was an unforgivable omission. But if they made it to Tennessee, they'd be all she had of him when they went their separate ways. A few days of companionship and one kiss hadn't given her any illusions they could have more than that. And even if they had, his comments on her mother's beliefs had dashed them.

She couldn't give herself to someone who could hurt her so easily. Sarah had lied, her father had lived under the same roof and treated her like the merest acquaintance. Even her mother had denied her the truth of her lineage and a choice in her life's path. Ewan had managed to scald her with a mere sentence — she couldn't let it progress any further. They would travel to Tennessee, and then she would bid him adieu.

She patted at her chest to make sure the John the Conqueror was still tucked against her bosom, and then she pushed aside the pile of stuffing from her mattress and grabbed Ewan's haversack, which Tobias had filled earlier. They'd need all the provisions they could safely carry. She gave one last look at her laboratory. It was when she ran a hand over the stout metal body of her still that she felt sadness erupt in her like an abscess: a sudden, blinding pain that rocked her back on her feet. She sucked in a breath and swallowed against the roughness in her throat.

Must I really lose all that I have gained?

Yes.

She turned away and silently climbed through the door behind the desk, pretending it didn't feel as if a part of her was being cleaved away. She'd always thought of Lynchwood as her second home, but really it was her only one, and she was losing that, too.

"You deserve a better life," she remembered her mother saying. She did. She refused to be forced into sex with men who saw her as a taboo with whom they could slake their dark desires before returning home to their blushing brides. She didn't know much, but she knew why women like her fetched a good price: White men saw them as a novelty to be tried at least once in life.

Is that what Maman was to Stephen? The thought cut deeply, and was immediately followed by something even more painful. *Is that what I am to Ewan?*

Marlie couldn't think on that. She couldn't conjecture what it meant that he wanted to kill for her, to save her, and to kiss her like he needed it to keep living. None of those things was important anymore. Only getting to Tennessee.

"Ready?" The whisper was followed by a grunt from across the drying room. Ewan's sleeves were rolled up and the veins on his forearms flexed as he pulled at something with both his hands. He'd tied the strips of fabric together and was testing the knots. That meant . . .

"We're leaving by the window," she said. Her stomach lurched and wild fear galloped through her veins.

I can't. I can't. I should give up now. How can this succeed?

"I told you I've done my fair share of escaping," he said, and then had the audacity to smile. "I don't think it would be incorrect to call myself an expert. Trust me, Marlie."

She wanted to, but this was more than a kiss. It was her life.

"We have to go now, before Cahill arrives," he said calmly as he tied one end of the rope to a solid support beam. He tested that it could hold their weight by planting one foot on the beam and tugging at the makeshift rope with all his might.

"Sturdy as an oak. All right. Remember something, now." Marlie looked up at him, tearing her gaze from the window and the forest beyond. "Two things: First, don't look down. I'll go before you, and direct you if need be. Second: You're in control here."

"Excuse me?" She didn't hide the agitation in her tone. This wasn't the time for a philosophy lesson.

"Melody wishes to master you, and in this house she has that power. But this?" He walked over to the window and opened it. "Climbing out of this window, down this rope, and heading into the woods? This is in your control."

"What about when we get outside?" she asked, taking a step toward the window and faltering.

"I will never make you do something you don't want to do, Marlie."

Marlie looked at him, then past him at the stars studding the night sky and the full moon that glowed bright amongst them.

Full moon means a parting of ways.

She didn't know where Sarah was, and trying to reach her would lose valuable time. She blinked against the tears in her eyes and bit back the sob rising up in her. Sarah was her aunt, not her sister. Sarah had withheld the truth for years. But that didn't mean Marlie didn't love her.

"Let's depart at once," she said. Ewan hung his sack around his neck and shoulders, tested the give on the tied-together fabric one last time, and shimmied through

284

the window. The rope was pulled taut over the sash, and bounced with his movement as he climbed down. Then he was gone.

Marlie took a breath and stepped forward, and Ewan's ginger head popped up above the sash again. "Remember, don't look down!" And then he was off.

Marlie took hold of the rope.

Ancestors, help me.

She threw her legs over the sash, planted her feet against the wall, and let the rope take all her weight. The wind whipped about, blowing her hair into her face and tugging at her skirts. At her back she felt the awful press of nothingness. She closed her eyes tightly.

She carefully slid one foot down, and cringed at the noise she made. She fought against the cry of fear rising in her throat, lifted a foot, and placed it firmly but quietly down. She needed her hands to follow suit, but they held on to the rope and refused to budge as if they had their own free will.

You are in control. You are in control.

She thought of Melody walking around the house and finding her frozen with fear, of the way the woman would laugh and sneer. Marlie's hands loosened one at a time and she began to move. After a few steps she had a rhythm. Left hand, right foot;

right hand, left foot. She focused only on finding a stable place with her foot, and on the reverberation of the rope that transmitted Ewan's own climbing rhythm to her. His words echoed in her head with each sure jerk of the rope.

You are in control.

It was when they were halfway down the house that another sound filtered in: hoofbeats. She glanced back over her shoulder and saw scattered torchlights jumping down the road in the distance, moving at a good clip. Cahill and his men were returning from their marauding. They had no care for the upkeep of the lawn, and would sally up to the area of the yard where Ewan and Marlie were descending.

The rope gave a violent jolt. "Hurry!" Ewan's agitated whisper pulled her senses back to her. She was no great adventurer, but she was certainly not going to allow herself to be caught if she could help it. She began climbing down again, trying to recapture the rhythm she'd had, and then increasing the pace.

Her breath came as a rasp in her ears and throat, the sound unbearably loud to her, but less disquieting than the approaching hooves. Now she could hear the yells of the men, the snorts of their horses.

God, God, God. I won't make it.

Marlie broke a cardinal rule and looked down. Ewan was already on the ground, his gaze pulled in the direction of the arriving militiamen. His fists were balled, his stance solid — he was unarmed, but prepared to fight instead of flee.

He looked up at her, and the truth of their situation was clear: She wouldn't make it at her current rate. Despite that, Marlie no longer felt afraid. Calmness overtook her, and she felt the sensation of rightness that always came to her when she got the measurements for a tincture just right by sight alone.

She closed her eyes and released her grip on the rope.

CHAPTER 16

The situation was decidedly not good. The Home Guard was closing in, and if Ewan could see them, they would soon see him — and Marlie, who dangled halfway down the entirely too large Lynch home. He looked up at her, expecting to see her scrambling or showing some other sign of fear. Instead she released her grip on the rope and began plummeting down. For a moment he thought she would simply crash to the ground, but then she slowed. He realized she hadn't released the fabric completely, but was letting it pass through her hands and holding tight when she began to lose control.

She wore no gloves, and Ewan could only imagine how painful it was — the friction of the rough fabric would be tearing at her skin. But then she was on the ground before him, her objective attained.

She stood still for a second, as if adjusting

to solid ground beneath her feet, then looked up at him with a wild-eyed grin of success that dashed away his fear like summer rain on dusty stones. But they had no time to dawdle.

He eyed the telltale rope hanging from the house. If he left it, the soldiers would be able to tell something was amiss as soon as they arrived. He grabbed a fair-sized rock along the side of the house and wrapped the end of the fabric around it, then lobbed it up into a nearby tree. The fabric could be noticed if anyone looked up, but he'd have to hope that the men wouldn't. He didn't put much truck in hope, but it would suffice just then.

"Are you all right?" he whispered.

She winced as she attempted to curl her palms, and her shoulders hunched as if she fought the urge to cry out. That was an expression Ewan knew all too well. "Yes."

"Then let us make haste," he said, accepting her lie.

He started to move forward but Marlie surprised him. "Follow me." She adjusted the bag over her shoulder and took off at surprising speed for someone who had skirts to contend with. She stopped at the corner of the house, peering around to make sure no one was about. After looking back to check that he was following, she moved, keeping close to the house, where shadows lurked and no one looking through a window would catch sight of them. They passed under the kitchen window, where a woman was singing a doleful song. Marlie paused and looked up, but then kept moving forward. She crouched now and again as she walked, and he realized she was snatching up leaves from the garden plants growing behind the house, tucking them away into her apron pockets.

When they got to the edge of the next corner, she looked back. "We have to run that way." She held bunches of leaves between her fingers, but they didn't obscure the direction in which she pointed. It was the same direction he'd arrived from — or there was a shed similar to the one he had stayed in. But other than that, there wasn't much cover. Anyone looking from the house or who walked around it would see them.

The shouts of the men grew louder, the clap of their hooves announcing their arrival on the property.

Marlie's and Ewan's gazes met and held for a long moment.

"Now."

They took off, Marlie ungainly as she held up her skirts with her fingertips, Ewan's long legs outpacing her by double, even with his tender ankle. He slowed and tried to take her hand but she snatched it away before he could, stretching her legs farther and trying to keep pace. Behind them there were whoops and shouts, but Ewan couldn't stop to see what the racket was about. They ran, the woods getting closer, their path to freedom almost secured.

Joy surged through Ewan as they entered the copse of trees, but diminished when a shadow stepped toward them, metal glinting off the weapon in its hand.

Marlie gasped and Ewan stepped in front of her.

"Marl?"

"Tobias!" She breathed his name in relief.

"What you doin'?" His gaze latched on to Ewan, and instead of *Get in line, son,* there was something much more menacing.

"You don't know?" Marlie gasped, still trying to catch her breath.

"Been out at the farm," Tobias said. "Got held up helping birth a calf."

"Melody discovered that Marlie is Stephen's daughter and intends to sell her into prostitution with the help of Cahill. To avoid that unfortunate outcome we must flee. Now." Ewan looked back over his shoulder. "Forgive me for not being more polite, but the militia just arrived and her absence could be discovered at any moment."

Tobias's expression was sober. "You leaving us?" he asked.

"I have to," Marlie said. "I'd die before letting Cahill sell me off."

Marlie spoke the words with a vehemence that rocked Ewan. After seeing her defy Cahill, a man whom he knew to be intimidating in the extreme, he didn't think her soft, but to hear her speak so fiercely reminded him that Marlie contained depths that were still unknown to him.

Tobias looked at Ewan again, and then extended the butt of his rifle in Marlie's direction. "Take this."

"I can't," she said.

"You need protection," Tobias insisted.

"I do, but my hands aren't quite up to the task. Please give it to him."

She held up her hands and Ewan could see the bloody pink of her palms now.

"We have to go. Tobias, tell Sarah . . ." Her voice broke then, and the tears spilled down her cheeks.

"I will," he said, wiping away the tears. He handed the gun to Ewan. "Keep her safe. And if you have any designs, redraw them."

"Tobias! Enough."

The man pulled her into a gruff hug. "I'll hold 'em off from getting to your room for as long as I can. Go on, now."

And then they were running into the night again. Beneath the cricket song that filled the night air, Marlie's breathing occasionally hitched with a sob. She didn't stop running, though.

They slowed as they moved deeper into the forest, the undergrowth making a faster pace impossible.

"Do you know where we're going?" he asked. He looked about at the kudzu-covered trees looming like ancient giants around them. Everything was dark shadows and leaves rustling in the wind — there was no sign of what direction they should turn.

"I have a general idea," she said. "The road is running alongside us over through those trees, and that's the road I take to get to the small farms every few months. I'm usually in a carriage, but the road runs northwest."

The smell of something fragrant and savory hit Ewan's nose, and he looked in her direction to find her running her teeth over a bundle of leaves before clasping them in her fists. "Sage. Good for cleaning wounds."

"And parsley?" He nodded at the curly

leaves that peeked out from the pocket of her apron.

She nodded. "Helps with swelling."

They walked in silence, the kind that Ewan hated. He grasped about for some subject to engage her in, but could find none, and the silence stretched taut between them. The easy conversation of days past had left them, in part because of his careless words. He hadn't thought past getting her out of Lynchwood. Now she was by his side, but may as well have been back in her rooms, as she seemed entirely unreachable. Ewan felt an uncomfortable tightness at his neck.

Is there any way to make things right?

"I can't believe no one told me," she finally said. "Now I look back at all those interactions and realize that everyone in the household knew who my father was but me. He sat in the same room with me, and said nothing. He watched Melody — his wife! — make me feel unwanted in my own home, and allowed it."

Ewan realized that while he was fixated on her silence, she had been mourning her life. He chastised himself. His perspective had narrowed to a tiny window when he needed to be surveying the wide vista of what Marlie might need from him.

"Surely everyone wasn't aware," Ewan said, and Marlie cut her gaze in his direction.

"Tobias didn't even blink when you told him," she said.

"Ah. Correct." They walked on. "Do you think you would have preferred knowing?"

Marlie chewed on her parsley a bit and then mashed that in her fists as well. "I'm not sure. But anything would have been better than finding out like this."

Ewan heard her breath hitch, and couldn't tell if it was anger or sadness or both.

"I have to say that if Stephen is your father, which appears to be the case, and he allowed you to be treated in this way, he was not worth your mother or you."

"That's easy for you to say." She stopped and faced him. "You may not have liked your father, but he was there! He claimed you!"

Ewan couldn't help the laugh that escaped his lips. "You think I merely didn't like my father? I hated him. I wished him gone, and the best thing that ever happened to my family was the day he took his own life."

Marlie gasped. "You can't mean that," she said.

"I've had the good part of a lifetime to reflect upon it and my opinion hasn't changed," he said. He understood most people valued blood relations, as if that link magically allowed for all types of transgressions. That was not a part of his philosophy. "I do not say this to diminish your pain and anger, but to remind you that Stephen is weak, as was my father. You have already been made to suffer for his weakness — you are here with me right now, driven from your home, because of it."

"How could he pretend I wasn't his daughter? All these years of him barely speaking to me. I thought it was because I reminded him of his father's misdeeds . . . I feel like such a fool." Marlie bit her lip, but that didn't stop the tears from spilling from her eyes. This time Ewan didn't restrain himself. He brought his hands to her face and brushed his thumbs over her cheeks, wiping the tears away.

"Don't you wish your father had been kind to you?" she asked.

"Wishing is for fools," he responded reflexively, and for some reason that made her laugh.

"So my point stands," she said. "I am a fool."

He'd never met a person the term applied to less, and in that moment he added Stephen to the list of men he wanted five minutes alone with.

"Mourn your father. Or hate him. But be sure that you know *he* is the one who should be ashamed and feel foolish, and not on account of your mother or you. You are perfect, despite his part in creating you, which means your mother must have been magnificent. His shame lies only with himself."

She stared back at him for a long time, silent as the hot tears ran over his fingers.

"We have to go," she finally said. She patted his hand, then turned and began walking.

They walked, resting every now and then, and Ewan began to worry about where they would pass the day. Spending the daylight hours unprotected with the Home Guard around would be asking for trouble. There was also the risk of Rebel pickets and Secesh neighbors who would turn them in as easily as breathing.

"We're almost there," Marlie said as if reading his thoughts.

The trees began to thin, and a small, fallow field opened up before them. On the other side of it was a less than modest home. Even in the predawn darkness, Ewan could see that it was in need of serious repair.

"Will we be welcome here?"

"There's only one way to find out." Marlie marched up to the porch and Ewan followed.

CHAPTER 17

Marlie told herself that she was not afraid as she approached Hattie's door. That was partially true; the flight from her home had left her too tired and sore for fear. She was mostly angry and disappointed, the feelings mixing into a toxin that seeped into her veins, willing her to give up. Those feelings should have been familiar to her, given her race and sex, but she'd been shielded from so many of the ugly truths of the world. Every shield has its breaking point, and the fragments of the lies that had been protecting her had been raining down since Melody had arrived. A shield, once broken, was only so many splinters, and Marlie was discovering just how sharp those splinters could be.

She felt Ewan's rangy presence next to her, and took some comfort in that, even though she shouldn't have. She harbored no fantasies of protection, but Ewan was reliable, and that was one thing she needed just then. And he was honest, to a fault. He said what he was thinking, even if it was rude, as she'd learned. She didn't always like it, but she'd take his lack of etiquette over the polite lie she'd been living for so many years.

They stepped onto the rickety porch and Marlie took a deep breath, then rapped lightly on the door. She winced against the pain of closing her hand into a fist. In the trees, the birds that signaled the first stirrings of dawn began to tweet. She knocked again, a bit more urgently.

There was movement, shuffling about, and then a trembling voice asked, "Who is it?"

"A friend in search of shelter," Marlie said. "A friend who needs a hero."

Marlie hoped she'd said the right thing. She wasn't sure what passcodes the Heroes of America were using now, but that was a close enough approximation, it seemed. The door creaked open and a sallow face peeked out: Penny, Hattie's daughter.

"Miss Marlie?" She looked back over her shoulder, then opened the door wider. "Get in, now."

She closed and latched the door after Marlie and Ewan had entered.

Hattie stood in the small parlor space, a blanket wrapped around her shoulders. Her gaze slid to Ewan. "You conducting now?" The question was asked with the same skepticism Lace had shared at Marlie's attempt at serving.

"I'm running," she answered. "From Cahill."

She didn't add the why. Hattie had seen Marlie push the gun away. She didn't need to know about Stephen and Vivienne.

Hattie looked at her hard. "You're rich and giving him aid, and he still after you?"

Marlie dropped her gaze to the floor. "The Lynches are rich. The white ones. The Negro one is disposable, it seems." She felt her anger well up again. She wasn't being fair. Sarah hadn't known what Melody was planning. She had to give her sister — her *aunt* — that much credit. And Sarah would be devastated when she learned what had passed.

"But her soul is white!"

Why were those words more painful than Cahill's blows? Than Ewan's tactlessness? Marlie shook the memory away.

"And you think I should help you, huh?"

Marlie thought of all the free care she'd provided over the years. She had done that because she wanted to, not to leverage favors, but the bond she had built with these people had to count for something, didn't it?

"I thought it wouldn't hurt to ask. Just a place to stay and figure out our next step. Day is breaking soon and between the militiamen and those fighting them, it's not safe."

Some of the anti-secessionists were honorable men fighting against oppression, and some thought that war meant that the rules of society no longer applied. They'd have no qualms about robbing her and Ewan, or worse.

Hattie stared for a while. "We can barter. You do some healing and I'll put you up."

She moved aside the blankets and held her hands out and Marlie could see her thumbs were swollen and gnarled, inflamed so that they no longer looked like human digits but that of some strange creature.

"Oh, sweet Jesus," she gasped, rushing to cup Hattie's hands and then remembering her own injuries.

"Bad, ain't it?" Hattie shook her head. "I can't afford the doc, and he's secesh through and through. He barely showed his face around here before, and ain't been back in months."

"What happened?" Ewan asked, but they both already knew it wasn't any malady

302

found in nature. This was the work of men.

"Cahill and his guardsmen came after me. Slung a rope over a tree branch, tied it around my thumbs, and pulled until I was hanging with my toes just above the ground."

Hattie wasn't a large woman, but supporting the weight of her body with two bound fingers must have been excruciating. Marlie's stomach turned.

"They said if I told them where the skulkers were, they'd let me down and let David go. They wanted me to go to a meeting spot and lure some of 'em out. I didn't say nothin'."

Hattie's expression was hard, like many of the poor women in the region, but a proud smile tugged at her lips. It wasn't one of joy, but of defiance, and it went through Marlie like an infusion of fire, burning up the remnants of her naiveté. Hattie wasn't sad or scared. She was proud, just as she had been when she'd stared down Cahill.

She was willing to die for what she believed in.

Marlie had thought herself in danger before, but she'd had the protection of the Lynch name, despite the threats of those who suspected Sarah's Unionist leanings. Hattie and the other women in the region had nothing to protect them, and the enslaved population even less.

"I'll see what I can do," Marlie said, trying to hide the shake in her voice. "Come sit over here. Ewan, can you get that fire going? Penny, can you put some water to boil? And have you got any thyme?"

"Marlie, perhaps you should see to your injuries first," Ewan said. His words were phrased gently, but that didn't hide the fact that they were an order. He was staring intently at her hands, his brow creased.

Marlie looked down at the abraded flesh of her palms. They still hurt something awful, but seeking shelter had been at the forefront of her mind. Funny how one could ignore something painful when necessary. "Ah, yes."

She took a moment and recalled the area around her. She had carried some of her tonics with her, but it was best to forage from the land if they could. It would be an arduous journey, and the injuries encountered now were minor in terms of what could happen to them. She'd also need to think about bartering.

"Penny, can you bring me a branch from one of the pine trees out back, if it's not too much trouble?" She smiled in Hattie's direction. "That will be useful to both of us."

Penny nodded and ran off. Ewan was already at work at the hearth, setting the twigs and kindling just so, which wasn't surprising in the least. He gave it the same amount of attention he dedicated to all he did, including kissing her.

See, it was nothing special. He'd kiss any woman just as thoroughly because Ewan isn't a man who does things in half measures.

He had called her perfect, too. Had that been true, or just a platitude to ease her pain? She couldn't begin to conjecture.

As the flames sparked to life, more of the small, dark house came into view. It was a wreck. Objects were strewn all about, and a fine white powder that was likely flour covered the kitchen area in a thin layer.

"Cahill," was all Hattie said when she tracked Marlie's gaze. She took a seat in a chair that looked old and rickety enough to have belonged to Washington's grandfather and stared into the fire. "They tell us this war is what's right, it's what's best, but they tell us as they rip apart everything we got that they don't steal."

"While force is sometimes necessary, in this case it's being used in place of persuasion," Ewan said as he fed sticks into the

305

fire. "None of these men can provide a coherent argument for this war, one that has nothing to do with profit or pride. Neither of those things are an honorable reason for secession. So they resort to fear, and when that doesn't work, to force."

Hattie gave a bitter laugh. "I seen so many slaves pass through here over the years, heading North to freedom. Been seeing whites on this road, too, last two years, all running up North like the devil's bloodhounds were after 'em. Men like Davis and Vance and Cahill think you beat a man into doing what you want once, and that'll keep him down forever. World don't work like that, though. A man can be compelled to do something he don't want, but he can't be forced to believe in it, or to keep doing it. They gonna find that out one of these days."

Penny arrived then, and Marlie took the branch from her in lieu of responding to Hattie. She winced a bit as she began to strip the pine needles, and then a hand rested atop hers, stopping the motion. She looked up into his eyes, both the same piercing blue but somehow stranger than her own. Strange and mesmerizing.

"Tell me what to do, and I'll do it," Ewan said.

She didn't know why those words caused emotion to surge into her chest, or why her eyes were suddenly stinging. Ewan was only being helpful, but the way he said the words . . .

"I'll kill him if he tries to hurt you."

Marlie pushed the memory away, and blinked back the sudden press of tears. They were no longer tucked away in her attic rooms and anything she had imagined then could no longer come to pass. The way Hattie was looking at them, brows raised in curiosity and mouth flat with judgment, assured her of that.

She pulled her hand away.

"Thank you. If you could get these pine needles into that water to make a tisane, that would be wonderful."

Marlie reached for some of the sage she had stuffed into her apron pocket, and for the small folding knife she used for collecting cuttings. She tried to unfold it but Ewan was there again, pulling it gently from her fingertips to open it for her and then handing it back. He went back to stripping the pine bough.

Marlie swallowed deeply and then began cutting quick and light across the surface of each leaf. She glanced at the pot of pine tea and leaned forward to drop the thyme in.

The clean, strong scent of pine sap filled the air.

"Should I get some cloth to strain this through?" he asked as he stirred, and she again felt that strange prickly feeling in her eyes. They worked well together, just as they had in her work space. She wondered if her mother had thought the same of Stephen.

"That's all right, we won't be drinking it," Marlie said, and kept at her work just so she wouldn't have to look at him. Her face was hot and her eyes hurt and she wished she were back home in her bed — except her bed had been destroyed. Her life had been destroyed. There was no going home.

She pulled the pot from the flames and used a tin cup to scoop some of the liquid into a bowl. She placed that aside and then took up another cupful. When both had cooled, she placed the bowl in Hattie's lap and had her soak her mangled thumbs in the warm liquid. Then she cupped her hands together over the edge of the fireplace, where anything spilled would soon dry.

"Can you?" She nodded toward the cup and Ewan picked it up and poured the warm liquid into her hands. Marlie blinked against the sting, but didn't move as the liquid slowly sieved through her fingers.

What pooled in her palms cleaned her wounds, and helped fight against festering. After a few moments, she released it from her hands and began taking up the macerated sage leaves. She dipped one into the steaming liquid, then placed it over her wound.

Ewan grabbed the next leaf from her and took over the job. "Faster this way," he said, but his touch wasn't rushed at all. He took his time plastering each leaf over the wound, spreading it flat with his fingertips. He was careful not to cause her harm, but his gentleness was stirring the direct opposite of pain in her. It was a stroke of sweet pleasure that licked through her at each caress of his fingertips. She trained her eyes impassively toward the fireplace, then forced herself to look at Hattie, who was staring resolutely at her own hands. Did Ewan's touch look as intimate as it felt?

"Is that helping with the pain at all?" Marlie asked. "In a bit, we'll wrap them up how I'm wrapping my hands, but with a poultice made to keep the swelling down."

Hattie nodded, pulling her hands from the liquid to see if there was any difference. "I'd heard that they was doing awful stuff to women. But you hear all kinds of things. I didn't think a Southern man, dashing about in a fine uniform, would hurt a lady like that. Though I guess men like Cahill don't consider me good enough to call a lady, let alone treat as one."

"All of the men who followed his orders, who didn't stand up to him, are barbarous," Marlie said. "War is one thing, but torture? I will never understand how someone could do that and still call themselves human. Ouch!"

"Sorry. Didn't mean to hurt you." Ewan's mouth was drawn, and she noticed his hands trembled slightly. He must have been exhausted from their journey, too.

He laid the last leaf down and then wrapped her hands with the strip of sheet they were using as a bandage, but didn't meet her eye. She'd seen this look of agitation before when Cahill's name came up. What was it that bothered him so?

With her hands bound, she moved to Hattie to finish cleaning her up. Ewan got to work cleaning the house, ever of service, but didn't look her in the eye even as they were shuffled into the root cellar an hour later. She glanced at him before the door closed, and his face was blank as he stared down at the ground. They were confined together once more, but Ewan's attentiveness was gone. There was only darkness and silence.

As exhaustion blanketed her, a vision of the crushed gris-gris filtered into her mind.

"Deliver me from Melody's presence," she had written. This was why Maman had always warned her not to throw: When you gave your intentions over to a power like that, you might get what you wanted, but not without paying for it.

CHAPTER 18

It had been dark in Ewan's dreams, and he opened his eyes to a different shade of black. For the briefest of moments he was hit with a fierce longing for home. He didn't think himself the nostalgic type, but the desire for his own bed and the familiar smells of his mother's cooking welled up in him. It was hard not to miss the comforts of home when one had been sleeping in trenches, prisons, attic ceilings, and cellars for months on end.

His body ached, but he couldn't remember the last time it hadn't. He tried to move to a more comfortable position, but something weighed him down. He was about to shove the weight away when he caught a hint of wisteria. Marlie's hair oil. That was when he realized the weight against him was warm, beneath layers of clothing, and breathing. His arm was wrapped around her, pulling her close, and her skirts pushed against his legs where she rested her thigh atop his.

Ewan thought of the disgust on her face when she'd talked about Cahill and his militia. It had been like a slap to the face, waking him from a foolish dream; yet another reminder that what they'd shared when she'd provided him with sanctuary had been nothing more than brief respite from too harsh reality.

Her bandaged hand rested on his chest, and Ewan picked it up gently by the fingertips to move it away, but found he was remiss to let it go. He'd never been so intimate with a woman, never felt the push of soft breasts against his side as he slumbered or awoken holding someone in his arms. Ewan had certainly never been called a romantic, and his relations with women had been perfunctory, though pleasurable. Army life meant he was no stranger to bedmates, but they were usually smelly, hairy, and of the platonic sort, give or take a few overtures for more. And although Marlie was only pressed against him due to her exhaustion and the small space they shared, Ewan found he quite liked it. He wished . . .

"Don't demand that things happen as you wish, but wish that they happen as they do happen, and you will go on well."

313

Right. There was no room for wishing. They would depart for the Tennessee line, and try to make it there as quickly as possible. Once they arrived, they would part ways. That was the sum and total of what could pass between them.

Something sharp and uncomfortable radiated in his chest at that thought. What would she do? Where would she go? She was leaving everything she knew behind. She had grown accustomed to a life with certain luxuries, but in the North, would anyone care about her skill? Her intelligence and wit? The war was to end slavery, but the sentiments in the North weren't vastly better when it came to Negroes, free or enslaved. He had no say, no control, over her fate, but his mind held fast to the problem as if it were a riddle that could be solved.

She shifted against him in a way that let him know she had awoken, even if he couldn't see her. Her fingers flexed in his, reminding him that he was still holding her hand. He froze, caught in the act, waiting for her to pull away. Instead, her fingers began to close slowly around his. He felt the wince go through her and knew she had only stopped because of her injured palm.

"Still paining you?" he murmured.

She nodded against his chest. Ewan marveled at that silent form of communication: her hair shifting against the fabric of his shirt and her chin pressing into his rib cage. They could probably communicate a great many things without speaking, there in the dark. If her thigh moved up a few inches more, she'd receive the rousing message that had been telegraphed to his nether regions as her fingertips brushed against the sensitive skin on the back of his hand.

Heat spread over his skin at the thought. Beads of sweat formed on his upper lip, even though the root cellar was cool and dry. He'd broken men's wrists and fingers and calmly told them what else he'd break if they didn't talk without perspiring at all, but Marlie settled against him, as if she were his, was all it took to make his palms go clammy.

"It's the least of my worries right now," she whispered in a husky morning voice. "Ewan, when you were upset before —"

"I wasn't upset."

"When you appeared to be upset, then. I know Cahill was often at Randolph. Did he do something to you? Is that why you escaped? Were you tortured?"

She sounded so concerned for him, and the naiveté of her question made him burn

315

for her and want to push her away at the same time. Ewan held his breath to keep his chest from shaking with the rueful laughter that built up in him. If Marlie knew what had truly passed between him and Cahill . . .

"No," he answered. "Do you know where to go once we leave here? We should have some kind of plan."

She sat up, moving away from him. "I have a general idea. I'm sure Hattie will assist us with the specifics. I still can't believe this is happening." She sighed. "Even after seeing all those people running over the years, those people who looked like me, it never occurred to me that I could be in their shoes one day." She sighed deeply.

"Marlie, I don't think anyone could have envisioned what came to pass with Melody and Cahill."

In the darkness he heard a trembling sigh. "Maybe not. But that's just it. I felt that something awful was going to happen, but —" She paused, shifted against him some more. "I thought I saw the runaways I helped as people, but I think I was still see-ing them as slaves. I should have known something like this could happen, but I thought my free papers had given me some kind of immunity. I never thought of myself as a slave because I was born free, but now

I understand. Those people didn't think of themselves as slaves, either."

Ewan tried to wrap his mind around the immensity of her words.

There was a scraping sound, and then the door to the root cellar opened. "Y'all can come out now."

Ewan helped Marlie move through the door and then climbed out into the room. Two plates sat on the sad excuse for a table, the corn cakes and poke salad showing just how lacking the pantry was.

He and Marlie sat down to eat on chairs so rickety it was probably safer to sit on the floor. Ewan's eye kept catching on the mess Cahill and his men had made of the place that he hadn't gotten to the night before: broken cabinet doors, supplies left in disarray. Mess always bothered him, and knowing how it had come to pass made this particular mess even worse.

After the hurried meal, Marlie sat beside Hattie and checked on the progress of her thumbs.

"They look better already. You'll be back to giving the Home Guard hell in no time," she said with a smile so bright it coaxed one out of stern Hattie. Ewan didn't realize he was staring until the girl beside him cleared her throat.

"Do you have a hammer and nails, or any other tools?" he asked, tearing his gaze away from Marlie.

Penny got up obediently and ran behind a curtained-off area of the house, returning a moment later with a small box.

"Papa's tool kit. The Home Guard took the things we couldn't hide."

Ewan nodded and got to work. An hour later, the table and chairs were as level and sturdy as was possible, the cabinet doors were rehung, and the shelves put into some semblance of order. Ewan then headed out behind the house and took up the axe, breaking down the large pieces of trees into firewood.

When he came back in, sweaty but clear-headed, he saw Marlie with her arm wrapped around Hattie's shoulders. "So it's the root, ya say?" Hattie asked quietly. Her mouth was tight.

Marlie's expression was somber as she nodded. "Yes. If your courses don't come, you take the root of the young cotton plant and boil it up, then drink that tea every day for three days. That'll . . . take care of things."

Hattie nodded sharply, then glanced at Ewan. "Time for y'all to get moving."

When they left, Penny was holding a

bundle that she handed off to Marlie. "We ain't got much. Here are more of the corn cakes." She glanced at Ewan and her cheeks went rosy.

"Thank you for your kindness," Marlie said as she tucked the food into her bag. She pulled something out and handed it to Hattie, and Ewan realized it was money. Greenbacks, not the devalued Confederate money floating around.

"It's dangerous out there, girl. You got a good heart, but I don't think you know from danger." Her gaze skated to Ewan. "You though? I think you know a thing or two. You best keep her safe."

Marlie looked confused, but Ewan nodded. "I'll do that."

"Head on back into the woods past the outhouse. Once you get into them woods, you likely to meet some men who can let you know if you're headed the right way. Penny, get that ribbon."

Penny came forward with a strip of red ribbon in her hands. She tugged it taut between the index finger and thumb of each hand, and from the way she started blushing again, Ewan knew he should stick his arm out. She tied the string about his wrist.

"That's one of the signs the resisters use to show they're on the same side," Marlie explained. "In the Bible, Rahab hid spies sent by the Israelites within Jericho, and helped them escape by lowering a red rope over the city walls."

"Yep," Hattie said. "Those men laid out in the hills for three days to escape capture. It's been a sight longer than three days for our boys, but they'll help bring this infernal war to an end."

There was nothing left to say. Marlie and Ewan headed out into the night, the playful spring breeze at odds with the solemn journey they were setting out on. Ewan looked about as they walked, the still-bright moon illuminating the clearing around the house more than he would like. The woods were full of the usual night sounds — insects, birds, and the scuttling of small animals — but then the sound of footsteps stomping through the pine needles and fallen leaves that blanketed the undergrowth caught Ewan's attention. A person couldn't be that loud unless they wanted to signal they were coming, but that by no means meant they were friendly.

"Miss Hattie?" a male voice called out. The tone was neutral — it could have been a Hero of America looking for food as surely as it might have been a Reb unsatisfied by the previous interrogations. They were too far from the forest to make a run for it, and could not make it back to the house and into the root cellar in time.

"Come," he said, and pulled Marlie into the small wooden receptacle that was their closest source of shelter. It seemed Fortune was laughing at him again: In the course of twenty-four hours he'd gone from an attic, to a cellar, and now an outhouse.

The smell of the enclosed place assaulted his nostrils.

Marlie made a low sound of distress, so he cupped the back of her head and pulled her close. "I'm sure I don't smell much better, but . . ."

She followed his lead, settling her head into the crook of his neck and inhaling.

He felt her lips curve into a smile against his collarbone and the tickle of her warm breath as she exhaled. "You smell fine," she whispered, and inhaled again. "Comparatively."

Her lips brushed against his collarbone as she spoke, and Ewan tried to ignore how the sensation rippled pleasantly through him.

"This rancid air beats the smell of prison. Or sulfur, if it comes down to a fight and I lose. We'll wait here until whoever it is passes."

Unless Hattie has need of us.

Ewan allowed himself to lower his head so that his chin rested against Marlie's head and his nose hovered close to her hair. If he had to be inundated with scent, he wanted it to be wisteria and woman. He told himself that it was simply common sense, but despite the fact that they were in great danger and crammed into as disgusting a place as Ewan could think of, his body stirred.

"Sulfur?" she whispered. "Do you assume that you'll go to hell?"

"Assumptions are for men who lack facts."

"Ewan," she whispered. Her head pulled away from him.

He looked down at her. Moonlight crept in through the warped slats, and a band across her face illuminated the censure in her eyes.

"Don't worry for me," he said. "I've a taste of heaven right now, and a taste is more than one man should ever ask for."

Ewan didn't know where the words came from. He didn't know why his arms tightened around her, or why he wanted nothing more than to kiss her in the reeking enclosure they were stuck in. It was utterly illogical. He did know that her pupils grew wide, overwhelming the brown and green of her eyes so that they looked like a matched pair. He did know that her body pressed against his instead of away.

There was a sound outside the outhouse then, and Ewan dropped his arms from around Marlie and picked up the rifle Tobias had given them. He held it by the muzzle, ready to jab out the butt into nose or throat or some other vulnerable body part of anyone who dared intrude.

There was a creak as the door was tugged and the warped edges resisted. Marlie's breath was audible now, a side effect of her distress.

He would let no harm come to her.

The door opened completely and a man stood with his hand at the fastening of his trousers, gaze toward the ground. His garb was Confederate gray, or something close enough; it was obvious that the fabric was roughly hewn and hastily assembled, like many of the poorer recruits' uniforms were.

Ewan wasn't panicked, though he could feel Marlie's heart fluttering against his torso like a bird beating against a window. He would have to fight this man, was the simple fact. The man looked up and stumbled back as he caught sight of them. He stared at them for a long moment, and Ewan could see the resemblance to Hattie

323

in his widow's peak and thin lips.

The man stepped forward and Ewan positioned his hand against Marlie, ready to push her behind him. Then the man reached for the door and slammed it shut.

His voice came through the warped wood, altogether too friendly for a Rebel. "Apologies for the disturbance. Should have knocked."

His footsteps moved away, and then stomped onto the boards of Hattie's back steps. The door closed loudly. He was making it clear that he was turning his back, just as he had announced his arrival.

Marlie was shaking against him, "Maybe wishing isn't for fools after all. Let us go now before he comes back."

They eased out of the outhouse and dashed into the woods. When no one showed up in pursuit after several miles, they slowed their pace and continued on toward Tennessee.

CHAPTER 19

Marlie was exhausted. They had stopped to eat the corn cakes hours ago and then continued walking through the night. It had rained, cold and hard, and they passed through mud that went up to her shins and threatened to suck her boots right off her feet. Both of them had fallen into rain-filled ditches, leaving their clothes soaked through and coated in a layer of grime. The moon gave them some light, but even the brightest patches of forest left them prey to gnarled roots that caught at their feet and threatened to snag their ankles and branches that seemed designed to poke out their eyes and scratch at their faces. Her feet ached, her body was exhausted, and she was facing the possibility that they were utterly lost.

"I think we should have passed into Guilford County by now, or maybe Forsyth if we're heading west like we were supposed to," she said as she lifted her skirt for the thousandth time that night. It snagged onto a bramble despite her attempt, and she found herself suddenly on the ground. She was so exhausted that the resistance of the skirt had dragged her down. She tried to pull the skirt away, but her hands were clumsy and ineffective with fatigue.

Helplessness enveloped her. Had she always been this weak, or had her life of luxury with Sarah reduced her to this? She had always felt strong when she was with her maman, but her strength in the Lynch household had been based in a sedentary life of reading and experimenting. She pressed her knuckles to her eyes, and did not remove them even when she felt Ewan gently pulling her skirts away from the bushes. Tears squeezed through spaces between her fingers, their salty warmth stinging at her healing wounds.

"It will be day soon and we haven't seen anyone who can pilot us or provide some other assistance," Ewan said. "Perhaps there's a house nearby, or a barn we can hide in. At worst, we'll have to find cover in a pinery and hope no one happens upon us, but I'd prefer to get you somewhere safer than that."

Marlie wiped at her eyes and looked about. She had seen nothing but trees for miles. She wondered if perhaps she was stuck in some kind of purgatory, where she'd walk endlessly through the Carolina woods. She stood and felt the jostling of something against her bosom. Her John the Conqueror root. She placed her hand over it, closed her eyes, and wished like a child who still believed in such things.

Please help us to find shelter soon.

When she opened her eyes, Ewan was staring at her again. She wondered what he was thinking. He'd be judging her for her tiresome behavior if he knew what she had been asking of an inanimate object, but that no longer mattered. In any case, she'd often felt his gaze on her as they moved through the forest. One might have imagined that he was reluctant to look away from her, if one wanted to think dangerously.

She tried not to think of how she'd awoken in the root cellar, with her hand in his, or how he'd pulled her close in the outhouse. She hated that she still felt this strange pull toward him, and she hated that when he looked at her now she wondered if Stephen had looked at her mother the same way. Vivienne was so much stronger than Marlie. If she could be taken advantage of, how could Marlie trust herself?

"Can you manage?" he asked, rubbing his

hands against his trousers.

"I'll have to," Marlie said. She pushed ahead through the bushes, not waiting for him. They walked on in monotonous silence, searching for shelter as Marlie tried to hide her ever-growing panic. They passed into a heavily wooded area that required every ounce of concentration to avoid falling, and only her fatigue delayed her realizing that her feet were on solid ground one moment and then weren't the next. The ground had given way and Marlie was sure she was falling to her death, but instead she landed a short distance below, unharmed.

"Marlie? Marlie!"

"The ground gave way!" she called out, surprised at the fear in Ewan's voice. "I'm all right."

"Where are you?" he demanded.

"Can you follow the sound of my voice? I didn't fall very far." A moment later Ewan clambered into the dark space and lit a match, revealing what Marlie had suspected.

"It's a skulker's cave," she said as he lit a candle that had been left behind. He picked it up, illuminating more of the small space. It certainly couldn't be called roomy, but there was enough space for them to sleep and a small fire pit to warm the coolness retained by the earthen walls, if they kept it low and smokeless.

"I'll head up and repair the foliage that you fell through," Ewan said, and then he sprang into action doing what he did best: being of service. The man couldn't sit still knowing that there was work to be done, and when there was no physical work . . .

Well, then there's you.

Marlie sighed. She was a pastime, something to keep his mind occupied when there was no wood to be chopped or plants to be organized. Reminding herself of that was the only way she'd survive their journey with her heart intact. She couldn't repeat her mother's mistake.

The knowledge that that's what she was, essentially, a mistake born of trickery, hit Marlie with a fresh wave of sadness. Had her mother thought of Stephen every time she saw her strange eyes? Had she regretted that Marlie had ever been born? She thought of the day Vivienne had sent her away, and how rarely she had seen her after. Marlie had convinced herself that her mother had sent her away out of love, but that was before she had known the truth.

The pain of the thought started her tears anew. Marlie sank to the ground, wrapped her arms around her knees, and wept. She had escaped Lynchwood, but Melody had truly won. She'd taken her home, her sense of self, and now — most unforgivably — Melody had taken away her mother. Marlie had nothing at all, and she realized that she never had. Like her time with Ewan in her rooms, it had all been an illusion that couldn't survive the light of the truth.

Marlie awoke to the smell of peaty smoke. She stretched, and found that her bare toes dug into the earth. When had she removed her shoes? Something shifted and she glanced up to find Ewan staring down at her. His face was expressionless, his gaze piercing. Marlie wondered what she must look like: caked in mud, hair snarled from being caught on low branches.

"I started a fire to dry our things." Wood popped and crackled out of her line of sight, as if verifying his claim. "There's warm water if you want to clean up. And maybe . . . I dried my clothes and our shoes. I wasn't sure if you wanted . . . your dress is still rather damp from your tumble into the ditch."

A flush spread across his sharp cheekbones, erasing the years so she could imagine what he'd looked like as a boy. Not childlike — she was certain he'd always been quite serious — but softer, less hard-set. She wanted to trace the rosy path with her fingertips up into that auburn hair of his, but she pulled herself to her feet instead.

She walked over to the fire, where he'd set up a few sticks in the ground at an angle from which to hang their clothes.

"I'll turn away," he said, and when she looked over her shoulder he was facing the wall. Her bag was beside him, and atop it, the ledger in which she kept her mother's papers.

Her fingers froze on her buttons. "You went into my bag?"

"I wanted to keep watch for a bit, in case we were encroaching on someone's daytime hideaway." She saw his shoulders rise and fall.

"And you thought that my private papers would serve as entertainment while you waited?" The anger and despair that she'd felt before crying herself to sleep returned twofold. Marlie had never been quick to anger, but she felt an evisceration on the tip of her tongue waiting to fly forth.

"I was ensuring they hadn't gotten wet during our journey," he said in a dry tone that spoke to how offended he was. "And as I looked the papers over, I realized that you've been given an emotional shock without even the benefit of hearing it from your mother herself. I thought perhaps it might comfort you to read for yourself, and to know something more than the invective Melody threw at you. Because this is now more than your mother's story. It's yours. You deserve to know."

Marlie sucked in a breath. She thought about Ewan's penetrating gaze and how it sometimes saw into her thoughts. Perhaps he had the gift others often credited her with? She resumed unbuttoning the heavy dress.

"What if I don't wish to know?" she asked quietly. "What if I don't wish to find out that my mother didn't want me at all?"

Ewan laughed, and the sound raised her pique again.

"Perhaps I've failed in my job as a translator. As I've said, my French is subpar. But if we've been reading the same thing, the only logical deduction is that it was written by someone who loved you very much."

Marlie didn't say anything as she tugged her sleeves down. She stared at Ewan's back, watched the movement of his elbow as he scribbled down a few words.

"My mother was attacked before we came to the US." He was still writing. *"During the Clearances, when they forced us off our land. She had never been on a boat before the*

weeks-long voyage and thought her sickness was caused by the tempestuous sea. It was only after she arrived that she realized she was pregnant. My sister Donella looks like no one in my family. She was the product of the most horrific moment of my mother's life. And damned if she's not Mum's favorite child, exasperating as she is."

Marlie struggled to get her sleeves over her hands, to free them so she could wipe away the hot tears coursing down her face, but she was hopelessly immobilized by the bunched wet cloth at her wrists. She let out a sob and Ewan turned.

"I'm in need of assistance," she managed before gasping another sob.

Ewan placed the papers carefully back into the ledger and came to her. He pulled her sleeves back up to her shoulders, then pulled them down again from the cuffs, carefully, methodically, avoiding the mess she had made of things. He pulled one hand through, then the other.

"I don't know the circumstances of your conception," he said as he turned her. There was a tug at the string of the apron she had tied over her skirts, then another at the dress itself. Both pooled at her feet, leaving her in her chemise. "The only thing I know is you. No matter how you came to be here, you are beautiful, intelligent, and brave, and I'm sure your mother saw that, too."

"Why are you telling me this?" she asked. His gaze was trained on her face, despite her state of undress. Her heart was beating wildly, and she wished she could breathe properly but she seemed to have forgotten how.

Her anger and sadness weren't forgotten, but something sweet and warm was pushing its way to the fore, crowding out all her anger and suspicion. Something that made her want to press a kiss to the freckles on the bridge of his nose. Something that didn't care that they were both in various states of undress, but was very much aware of what could pass between two willing adults in such a state. She was suddenly feeling quite willful.

"I don't know," he said, his voice strained. "I must admit, I haven't quite been myself since I met you."

"Likewise," Marlie said, and was surprised to find herself smiling. "To be certain, I hadn't made a habit of kissing strange men, no matter how handsome I found them."

Now Ewan was smiling, too, a harsh upturn of the corners of his mouth that spoke to something more than amusement.

"And I'm not in the habit of taking liberties with beautiful women, no matter how competent I find them."

"Liberties?"

Ewan's only answer was to take a step forward, cup her face in his calloused hands, and press his mouth against hers. Marlie made a noise of surprise, Ewan groaned, and the sound of both noises together thoroughly scandalized her. Marlie already knew he was more than proficient at kissing, but when his tongue curled into her mouth it sent a stab of pleasure through her core.

His knee bumped against hers and she realized he was walking her back across the small space.

"What are you doing, Ewan?"

"Straying far, far from my ship," he replied as the hard-packed earth hit her back. His hands moved down from her face, his thumbs leaving trails of sensation on her neck as they traveled down to brush over her nipples as he cupped her breasts.

Marlie had touched herself before — had even imagined Ewan touching her while doing so — but perhaps her creativity only lent itself to matters of science. She could never have imagined the brazen insistence of his calloused thumb against the taut tips of her breasts, nor the way the friction of his fingertip and the fabric of her chemise against her sensitive skin would multiply by a hundredfold, a thousandfold, the pleasure that trembled between her legs and in her womb and then spread everywhere in her body. His tongue lashed hers as his hands worked her breasts, and she moaned and sighed like a wanton woman.

One hand slid down and squeezed her at her hip as something hard and hot pressed against her belly. That was Ewan. All of that.

"May I touch you?" he asked.

"You are touching me," she said through the haze of pleasure.

"May I touch you between your legs? Please?"

Marlie let out a shocked laugh into his mouth. Trust it to Ewan to manage to be both polite and forward in the same sentence.

"Yes, you may," she whispered.

His hand stayed at her waist but his fingers began to stretch and curl, stretch and curl, pulling the fabric of the chemise upward, gathering it. When his fingertips pressed into the bare skin of her waist, her hips thrust forward of their own accord. She closed her eyes in embarrassment.

"I don't have much experience," she said. "And by much, I mean any."

A gentle kiss brushed over one eyelid and then the other. She opened them to find him staring. "Well, I don't have much, either, but I'm hoping my ingenuity suffices, as ever."

Marlie's gaze swept over his face; he was a beautiful man.

"But you're so . . ."

"Easy to get along with?" he ventured as his hands worked the tie of her drawers. "Friendly? Nonjudgmental?"

Marlie laughed but that was short-lived. Ewan's long fingers were stroking the hair at her mound, petting her, sliding down farther with each stroke. Her breath came fast and heat sparked through her, but however wonderful his touch was, it wasn't enough.

"You've pleasured yourself before?" he asked.

She nodded, and then his teeth were nipping at her ear, his tongue tracing the shell of it. His hand cupped her and stopped moving. "Show me how to please you."

Her hand left her side and covered his to find that she wasn't the only one shaking. She pressed down on his fingers, showing him the right amount of pressure. She gasped and bucked a bit, tantalized by the difference in size and strength in the feel of his hand and hers. She moved her fingers in a circle, keeping up the pressure, and he took up the motion. Then Marlie's hands fell away and her head dropped back because, of course, Ewan was touching her exactly right.

"Oh, yes," she whispered.

His head dropped to her breast and his teeth grazed at her nipple through the material as he changed the pressure of his fingers just a bit, pushing harder at her slick center, circling relentlessly as pleasure built in her toes and fingers, slowly wending its way through her body to the source of her bliss.

"Ewan." She reached out and caressed the length of him through his pants with her fingertips and he groaned. She didn't know what compelled her to do it, other than a curiosity to see if she could have the same effect on him that he did on her. Apparently, her hypothesis was correct. He shuddered and his hips bucked forward. His free hand fumbled at the fasts of his pants and then instead of rubbing the rough fabric of his trousers, she had the hard, hot length of him under the loose curve of her fingers. Her bandaged hands wouldn't allow for more.

Marlie's eyes squeezed shut against the sensation building in her, and then she opened them to meet his gaze. "I've imagined touching you," she admitted.

"Oh."

"I want . . . to do that. Touch you. How you're touching me. But my hands . . ."

"Oh."

Marlie had expected more of a reaction, but then he stepped closer to her. His hand moved from between her legs and the length of him slid between her folds. Marlie froze for a second and then realized he hadn't penetrated her, that he wasn't even trying to.

"I have found some useful things in all of those dusty old Greek books," he said. "Is this all right?"

He was thrusting his hips slowly, the angle as they stood meaning the rigid length of him slid up and against her sensitive nub as he moved. The moisture of her own pleasure coated his penis, easing his path. The pressure was even more intense, more erotic, than his hand had been.

"Yes. That's perfect, Socrates."

"Ewan," he said roughly.

"Ewan," she repeated, on a moan.

He kept thrusting. His mouth covered hers again but his eyes stayed open and she followed suit. She pressed her thighs together harder and he huffed against her lips, dropping his forehead to hers.

"God, Marlie, I — I —" He shook his head then and kissed her instead. His thrusts were rough now, uncontrolled, and his eyes slammed shut as his body shook with need. Marlie's entire body throbbed on the precipice of release, and seeing the ever-reserved Ewan falling to pieces . . .

Lightning or some other natural phenomenon struck Marlie then. Her back arched, her hands clutched Ewan's arms, and she bit into his shoulder to muffle her cries. Then his back hunched, his hips jerked, and warmth slid down her thighs.

They both stood shaking in the aftermath, Ewan's weight pressing Marlie into the earthen wall.

"Are you all right?" he asked.

"Quite," she answered, but she was definitively not.

She pressed her face into his chest for just a moment, listened to his heart thudding heavily, and reminded herself that he had just rendered her a service — a pleasurable one, but one that he'd benefited from as well.

"Taking is different from loving. Problem is, it feels a lot like loving 'til you find out otherwise."

She moved away from him, toward the

water warming near the fire. She reached into her bag for the soap she had shoved in with her other belongings, holding it between her fingertips for a moment as she stared into the flames.

Yes, best to remember. Service was all it was, and all it could be, with Ewan McCall.

CHAPTER 20

Ewan had made a grave error. He'd realized this as soon as he felt Marlie's thighs squeeze around his member, as he felt the warmth of her sex encompass him and the friction of the hair between her legs. More so, he'd known when he looked into her eyes.

Ewan's previous experiences with women had been distant. Impersonal. He was fine with that — had ensured that it stayed that way. No amount of ribbing from fellow soldiers on their way to brothels had changed that. To Ewan, sex lacking emotion had been pointless, and sex with emotion had been something he wouldn't allow himself. He'd been a fool to think he could come away from such an interaction with Marlie with his principles intact.

He'd felt something give way in him as she'd cried out in his embrace, like a retaining wall had crumbled down and every pent-up emotion he held for her had come rushing in, engulfing him. Now he was drowning and Marlie seemed content to stand on the riverbank and watch.

"Are you sure you know where we're going?" he asked as they tramped through the underbrush. The question was peevish, but Marlie hadn't spoken to him in three hours. She had retreated into herself, and Ewan had let her be — he was sure their encounter was as emotionally taxing for her as it was for him, and she was still dealing with the shocking news she'd received. Before they'd set out, he'd worked on retranslating the pages of the memoir that Melody had taken, this time paying attention to every word; it had taken all of his principle to translate faithfully and to the best of his ability.

Stephen Lynch had appeared to love Marlie's mother, if a man could truly love a woman he owned. He had told her he would free her, and when she became pregnant, that he would start a life with her. That they would be a family. When his father caught wind of the plan, he sent the heavily pregnant Vivienne away. She was given her freedom, and Stephen had told her he would join her soon.

Ewan had handed Marlie the pages and watched her read them, squinting in the firelight. He'd expected her to have some reaction, but she had rolled onto her side, her back to him. She'd remained silent after getting up, and remained so as they marched through the night, seemingly without purpose and definitively without connection.

Marlie stopped and looked at him. "Aren't you the expert at escape? You can lead the way, if you know better than me."

"I was simply trying to ascertain —"

"You were simply trying to tell me that I'm wrong," she said. "Well, I know I'm wrong. I know that! I may have been good enough to scratch your itch, but you shouldn't expect anything else of me. I don't know where we are or where we're going and . . ."

To his horror, her eyes filled with tears.

"Oh, I'm useless," she muttered, angrily wiping at her face.

Ewan was poleaxed. Marlie was sheltered, for certain, but she had never seemed to lack self-assurance. But now she was crying, great heaving sobs that triggered a sort of panic in Ewan as he scrambled to make things right.

"Marlie," he said, reaching for her in the shadowy darkness of the forest and getting a hold of her arm. "Don't cry. You're far from useless."

"Yes, of course you don't find me useless," she said. "Men like you will always have a use for women like me."

"Men like me?"

"Never mind." She pulled her arm away. "We must keep moving."

She looked up at the cloudy night sky as if it would point her in the right direction.

"We do, but if I've done something to hurt you, you need to tell me right now." Ewan felt the first throbs of a headache pulse between his eyes.

"I don't want to talk about it," she said quietly. She no longer pulled against his grip — her arm had gone limp in his hold.

"How can I make things right?" he asked.

"You can let go of me right now, and never touch me again," she said. Her voice trembled, but that didn't dull its edge.

"What?" Ewan had not been expecting quite so definitive a statement. In fact, he'd thought perhaps he could just kiss her. That's what women wanted when they were upset, he'd been told. That's what she had wanted from him before. He was out of his depths.

"I am asking you to relinquish your hold on me. For the remainder of our trip, I ask that you make no assumptions about what passed between us and to not touch me so boldly again."

Ewan let go of her, the headache flaring to life in his skull. "May I ask why?" There was no logic to her behavior, or if there was, it was lost to him.

"Because if I learned one thing from what I read today, it's that I cannot trust you, or myself." Her voice shook a little but she kept her head high.

"It's not fair of you to punish me for your father's cowardice," he said. He didn't know why he debated. He didn't *want* anything more. Wasn't that the case?

"And it is not fair of you to ask me not to," she retorted. "My entire life has been based on one lie after another, and those from people who knew and cared for me. And I should expect more from you, who I barely know? Surely you know that when we reach Tennessee you will go back to your life and I will have to start mine from scratch. There is nothing to be gained from pretending anything can come of . . . *this,* and I am too tired to pretend otherwise."

"But —"

"But what?" She stepped toward him in challenge, the moonlight reflected in her eyes.

She stared at him, and none of his words came to him. She was correct; he had spent the last several weeks reminding himself that his feelings for her were something to be repressed and ignored. Even if the thought of parting from her made him feel hollowed out, he was not the kind of man she needed or deserved. Best to cauterize whatever feelings he had now, before she discovered who he really was.

For another will not hurt you unless you please. You will be hurt only if you think you are hurt. Epictetus's words didn't explain the numbness that fell over him, because it wasn't a numbness in which one felt nothing. It was the burning, impotent pain of a limb that has been slept upon and then called into quick usage.

"Well?" Her voice was both hard and fragile, an eggshell containing emotions that would remain a mystery to Ewan unless he applied enough pressure to crack it.

"Nothing," he said stiffly. "I'm a stranger to you, and you do not owe me anything. I will refrain from further contact for the duration of our journey."

"Of course you will," she bit out, and then spun on her heel and stormed off. Ewan was completely confused. He had conceded to her wish and yet that seemed to make her *more* angry. He had a mind to catch up to her, to demand what exactly she was playing at, but what would that gain him? Or her, for that matter?

Instead, he kept a few yards behind her, following the sounds of her footsteps. The night wore on, and she was stumbling more than walking after a certain point, but Ewan fought the urge to go to her. Eventually the stumbling stopped, and he realized it was because they were walking on a well-worn path. He jogged to catch up to her, and she didn't turn even when he was at her side.

"Do you think it wise to follow this path?" he asked.

"Do you think it wise not to?" she retorted. "We must find a place to hide ourselves. Listen."

Ewan strained and heard nothing for a moment, and then a low murmur carried on the early morning wind. The sun had not yet risen, but he heard the low sound of singing, as if a church service was going on. They headed toward it, walking for a few moments before they came upon a small clearing, where a circle of people were standing around a fire. They were gathering up their things, as if making ready to leave.

Ewan looked over the group: their dark skin and ragged clothing. For a moment he took them for runaways; then he saw the large metal pots on the ground — he'd heard they were held up during secret gatherings to prevent sound from traveling. The group turned to them, one woman's eyes large with fear, several faces creased with confusion when they saw both Marlie and Ewan and realized they were together.

"Hello," Marlie said calmly, as if they were all gathered in front of the general store and not in the middle of the woods.

" 'Lo," one of the men replied, and several others echoed him.

"Do you know any place around here we could take shelter until nightfall?" she asked. "We're heading to Tennessee."

The group shared another look, one that involved raised brows and pensive frowns.

"Ya'll can come with me," an older woman said with a sigh. "There's space in the hayloft, and massa don't never go up there. I hid a few Yanks up there week before last and it was fine."

"You sure, Sallie?" one of the men asked. "There's that empty house down by the plantation, too."

"Naw, that place ain't safe. Slave catchers been lying in, waiting to catch folks. Man met his wife there for some private time and got the lash 'cause they said he was trying to 'scape."

An older man with his hands shoved in

his pockets piped up. "I would take them, but massa got suspicious after the last Yanks what came through ran off with one of his pigs. He checks the grounds every night, and been keeping an eye on me."

He looked pointedly at Ewan.

"I won't steal any livestock."

The man continued to stare at him.

"Or anything else," Ewan said. "I wouldn't take advantage of kindness bestowed upon me in that way."

He pointedly didn't look at Marlie; he wasn't sure she'd vouch for that as a statement of fact. He felt a pressure in his skull as he recalled what she had said to him, but there was nothing further to discuss. He wanted her, he couldn't have her, and trying to convince her of the former while knowing the latter would have been as unkind as she suspected him of being.

"My place got some Rebs hanging about, looking for skulkers," a younger woman said. She glanced at Marlie, then quickly down at the ground. "Besides, you sure you trust them eyes of hers?"

"I said I'd take 'em, and I'll take 'em," Sallie said. She shook her head, then turned to Marlie and Ewan. "Come on now."

She hefted up one of the heavy pots and waved good-bye to the group, and Ewan came up beside her.

"I can carry that," Ewan said.

"Mm-hmm," she responded, and handed it over.

"Thank you for helping us," Marlie said.

"Mm-hmm," Sallie replied again.

They walked on in silence. Ewan couldn't tell if the woman was annoyed or fatigued or simply the silent type, so he kept his mouth shut.

"I need ya'll to be straight with me: Why you traveling together?"

Marlie drew in a deep breath.

"I ain't trying to be in your business," the woman said, then chuckled a bit. "Okay, that ain't true — I'm nosy. But I also need to know I'm not putting my family and friends at risk because massa's son got a little bold and decided to run off with his lady love. I'll still help you, but I need to know what you running from and how close it is behind you."

Ewan appreciated her straightforwardness and decided to reply in kind. "I'm a Union soldier running from prison, trying to make it back North. She's free and running to escape being sold to a fancy house. We have an enemy in common, and that's it."

"Yes, that's it," Marlie echoed. "It's a mutually beneficial arrangement."

"Mm-hmm," Sallie said again.

"It seemed from the conversation you had that your group helps a lot of people who pass through on their way North," he noted.

"That's right," Sallie said.

"Do any of you ever join them?" Ewan asked. There was a sting at his arm as Marlie whacked him. He turned to face her with raised brows, able to make out the censure in her expression in the faint glow of the early morning sun.

"A couple of us done run off, on our own. Some made it. Most didn't," Sallie answered.

"You can come with us, if you'd like," Ewan said. "Do you have family you'd like to bring? Friends?"

He didn't see why it should be a problem. If there were too many they could break into smaller groups. He could be at the fore, scouting.

Sallie stopped to look up at him. Her dark eyes were inscrutable. "If it was that easy, you think we'd still be here? Too many to run off with. Too many lives to risk." She shook her head. "You know you the first Yank who ever asked that?"

She started walking again, and Ewan and Marlie followed along. "Sometimes it's like they think we just haints who wander the forest, looking to do some good for them, like we ain't got our own kin to do good for. Half the time they don't even say 'please' or 'thank you.' Sometimes they talk past us, like we not even really there."

"And you still offer to help without hesitation?" Marlie asked.

"The Lord didn't specify you had to like a body to help 'em," Sallie said. "I'm just doing the little bit I can do from where I am. And counting on Lincoln and his Yanks to do what they can to win this war."

Ewan felt a peculiar sensation in his throat. He knew very well how Sallie and her friends would have been treated; most of his fellow soldiers weren't abolitionists. They told awful jokes about contraband and took offense when chided. They made lewd remarks about the colored women working in the prisons and army camps, and even when they were kind, often treated Negroes as children instead of people with lives and dreams of their own.

"I will do everything I can, Sallie," he said. "It might not be much, but I'll do my little bit."

Sallie glanced from him to Marlie and back to him. "I'm gonna take your word on that."

She didn't know that for Ewan, *everything*

entailed causing others pain. Since he'd been imprisoned, he had often overlooked what reaching North would mean for him. Breaking bones. Making grown men cry out to God and their mamas and sometimes their grandmamas, too. Perhaps he'd secretly hoped that things would work themselves out while he was locked away, that he could have emerged to a reunified nation in which the only thing he cracked was the spine of a book.

Guilt tugged at him. He should have escaped Randolph earlier. He should have been out there helping instead of indulging his own fantasies of a quiet life spent conversing with Marlie and helping her with her work.

When he glanced at her, she was staring down at the ground before her, her fingertips holding up her skirts as she walked.

He had been a man of his word once, and he would be again. He'd vowed to fight the Confederacy, and to never touch Marlie again, and he'd stick to both, no matter what it cost his soul.

CHAPTER 21

They passed through a cluster of small wooden shacks on the midsize plantation and made their way to a barn. The few cows lowed and swished their tails as Sallie led them toward the rickety ladder and up into the hayloft. She quietly descended, and the rhythmic sound of milk splashing into a metal pail broke the silence that hung between Marlie and Ewan. He wanted to say something, but perhaps silence was for the best. His silence couldn't hurt her like the ill-chosen words could.

A few moments later, the ladder creaked and Sallie appeared in the opening. She handed up a bucket containing a bottle of milk, sandwiches, and a bit of cake. Marlie picked up the stale cake — dried out frosting and who knew how old — and tears stood in her eyes.

"If anyone is sick I can help them," she said. "Or try to."

"You got the gift?" Sallie asked, eyebrows raised.

"I can help," was all Marlie answered, but Ewan noticed it wasn't a denial.

"She comes from a long line of conjure women," he said. "And she's read as many books as any doctor. She's got a gift."

Sallie looked between them. "Don't get into any foolishness up here, gift or no."

Ewan drew himself up. "It's simply a mutually bene—"

"Yeah, yeah. We got us a few sick folk, since they sold our root woman off after massa near died a few months back. Mistress was sure someone had laid a trick on him, instead of asking if maybe the Lord was punishing him for his sins." Sallie shrugged. "You can tend to them before you go."

She headed back down the ladder, leaving them alone. Silence fell in the loft again and Ewan wished he could think of words he was sure were the right ones, though conversation shouldn't have been a priority given their predicament. It didn't make him want to hear her voice any less.

"Suddenly you're not tired of hoodoo talk?" Marlie asked as she settled into the hay a few feet away from him.

Ewan regretted his desire to break the silence.

"It was mean-spirited to say what I did that day." Ewan picked some hay from his shirt. "If you want the truth, I said the first foolish thing that came into my head because if I didn't, I would have kissed you."

She moved a bit, producing a low rustle in the hay.

"So insulting my mother and my background was preferable to kissing me? Excellent."

Ewan exhaled deeply.

"No, it was hurtful and wrong. Although I must point out that you were the one who said you no longer believed in those things."

"Would you like it if I impugned one of your family members, Socrates? Because I thought you might agree with me?"

He didn't like that she was calling him Socrates again. Before it had been something that joined them together, but now it was being used as a wedge.

"No. I shouldn't have said anything. I have a tendency to say the wrong thing, often in service of doing the right one."

She didn't say anything for a long while. "I tried to go back home, when I first got to Lynchwood. First they found me down the road with one of the horses. Then I tried . . .

I tried to lay a trick. I'd brought some dirt with me, from my mother's house. I did everything I was supposed to do."

He imagined Marlie as a girl, placing all her love and hope into a palmful of dirt.

"It didn't work. And I felt so betrayed by that. Like my mother had sent me off with a knife that crumbled when I tried to cut the ropes binding me. But if you think science is any different, it's only because it's a white man with a fancy title giving it import." There was more restless shuffling in the hay. "You have an idea. You decide to test it out. Sometimes it works, and then you have to figure out why exactly it did. Whether you think it's the power of nature or the power of some higher being doesn't change the outcome."

"I can't say that I'm a wholehearted believer, but I will check my presumptuousness in the future."

"Good," Marlie said. Then, more quietly: "Think about what my maman could have done if this country would have let her."

He was going to answer that Marlie was an example of that, but that wasn't true. Marlie had received more advantages, but in the end she was subject to the rules of the same society. Despite her name, and money, and skill, she was up in a hayloft running for her life because she could be sold on the basis of the color of her skin.

Later that evening, Ewan helped Marlie as she treated a baby who wouldn't take its mother's milk, a girl with a rash that covered her face and neck, and several older people with aching joints. Some people in the North assumed slave owners treated their slaves as they would any investment; they would have been surprised to see the sad state of these people who worked their lives away.

He wondered at the food Sallie had given them; his belly was full, and it had cost some of the people who gathered in the shack where Marlie tended to them. The fact that he'd been gone from the war so long had cost them, too. Ewan knew rationally that the War Between the States wasn't contingent upon his participation, but he also knew that he'd gathered valuable intelligence before his run-in with Cahill and his time in the prisons. Any intelligence the North gathered brought them closer to victory — brought Sallie and her family and the other slaves closer to freedom.

"That's it for now. Anything more and people will get suspicious," Sallie said, handing them a few more pieces of chicken.

"You should get on your way."

"Thank you for your kindness," Ewan said. He looked at the people around him. "We have food, if you need this here."

"Consider it a loan," Sallie said with a wink. "When you Yanks come riding in, you can pay me back then."

Ewan nodded.

She kept pace with Marlie as they walked toward the forest. "I don't know what you looking for when you get to Tennessee but I hope you find it."

"I do too," Marlie said. "I've never been so far away from home before."

"The first thing I want to do after this war is won is go see things," Sallie said. "Just walk out across this country and see everything I heard of and never got to see with my own eyes."

"You sound so sure the North will win," Marlie said.

"You the one with eyes like you can see the past and the future," Sallie said. "You really think the South will win? You *feel* that they will?"

Marlie closed her eyes, inhaled, and then shook her head. "No."

"Then I need to start planning. Think I might go out West and find me some gold." She laughed softly. "Good luck."

Ewan and Marlie walked off into the night once more.

"She said to just follow this star until we hit the railroad tracks, then we could follow those west," Marlie said.

"Do you have any idea what you're going to do when you get to Tennessee?" Ewan asked. Sallie's words had brought to the fore the question that had been pressing at Ewan since he'd told Marlie she was coming with him. What would become of her?

"I'll write to some acquaintances and see if there's some way I can continue aiding them in the war effort," she said.

"Continue?"

"It's none of your concern," she said.

Ewan took a deep breath.

"I have agreed not to touch you. I said I was a stranger to you, but that's a lie. I care what happens to you and if you're talking about contacting strange acquaintances, I want to help. I have connections too. There's no reason I can't —"

"I don't need your help," she said. "I'll do just fine on my own."

"Based on what evidence? To my knowledge this is the first time you've left Lynchwood without your sister or Tobias. A few days away from home doesn't change the fact that you're sheltered and inexperienced."

He didn't understand why she insisted on rebuffing his offer of help. It was illogical and irksome and just thinking of what could happen to her made Ewan's hands curl into fists. Confederate soldiers weren't the only danger to a woman like Marlie. The people who could hurt her without giving it a second thought were endless, and Ewan's entire body went taut with anger at the thought of it.

Marlie made a sound with her tongue against her teeth. "You didn't find me so sheltered and inexperienced that you didn't touch me. Or is it okay to take advantage of a woman like me when you're the one who benefits?"

Well. He had set himself up for that, he supposed.

"In case you haven't noticed, I've found our shelter and food, I've taken care of people, and I'm the one leading us to Tennessee! Stop acting like I'm just a lost little lamb!"

She marched off into the trees, and Ewan tried to gather his composure before resuming the conversation. She was right, but he wasn't wrong. There had to be some rational compromise they could make about allowing him to help her.

"Marlie." Her thrashing about in the underbrush abruptly stopped. The sound of cicadas and night birds filled in the silence she'd left behind. "Marlie?"

He sensed the gun against his back before he felt it, and reacted without thinking. He dropped to the ground, arm shooting up to grab the barrel and direct it away from him. Whoever was holding it pulled against the gun, digging their feet into the ground, and Ewan launched himself backward, knocking them down.

"Dammit," a male voice croaked out, and Ewan jumped and turned, hand pressing into the fragile windpipe and cutting off any further sound.

"Marlie!" he called out, panic rising in him. His head was pounding, his breath was coming in gasps.

He needed to know where she was.

A flash of dancing red and yellow caught his attention and he turned his head to see a group of men coming toward him through the trees. One of them held Marlie, his hand clasped over her mouth as she struggled. Ewan's gaze locked on her and he jumped to his feet, the gun he had taken from his assailant in his hand.

"Release her. Now," he said. His voice

came out as little more than a snarl.

"Looks like you're a little low in numbers to be making demands," said a shadowy figure from beside Marlie.

"Ouch!" the man holding her cried out, and then suddenly her voice rang out in the clearing.

"Show them the ribbon!"

Ewan had forgotten all about the red ribbon Penny had tied for him. He held up his wrist, as she'd commanded, revealing it.

"We are friends," she said. "In fact, we are running from the same man who hunts you."

"Anyone can wear a bit of red," one man called out.

"And anyone can set upon a woman in the middle of the dark woods," Ewan countered. "You call yourselves heroes?"

"Look at us!" Marlie said. "Do we look secesh to you?"

"Let her go," one of the men said.

She came stumbling out beside Ewan, and he took her hand without thinking. A rumble of laughter spread through the woods, revealing that far more men were watching than he had thought. Far too many to even consider fisticuffs.

"We got two lovers in flight, men," a man said. "Wouldn't be the first time."

"No," Marlie said from beside him. "You've got one member of the Loyal League and one representative of the Army of the Potomac who are here to assist you."

"Loyal League?" Ewan whispered. He'd known Marlie had mysterious depths, but she'd never mentioned they included spying. He had secrets of his own, but that didn't stop the indignant betrayal he felt. "What are you doing?"

"Taking my life into my own hands for once," she whispered back, harshly, then turned to the men. "Is anyone in need of medical attention?"

CHAPTER 22

Marlie refused to look at Ewan again. His expression was harsh, and frankly a bit frightening. She had once told him that she couldn't imagine him on a battlefield, but she'd been mistaken. The agility with which he'd taken down the skulker who attacked him, the way his hand had so confidently found the man's throat — that wasn't chance.

"War makes no man better, and most assuredly not me."

She thought back to all the times he'd hinted at what he'd done before being imprisoned, but she was only now realizing that he'd never told her outright. Not his regiment or what battles he'd fought in. Ewan never lied, but it seemed he was more than adept at hiding that which he didn't want her to know.

"I suppose I know why you had a Polybius square now," Ewan said stiffly.

"And that would be more than I know about you," Marlie snapped back. That wasn't entirely true. She knew so much about Ewan — but Ewan before the war. Ewan in her rooms. Now she could see the gaps in her knowledge, and how they aligned with the war. She could see Ewan flipping that man and pressing his palm to his throat, then looking wildly about.

For you. He was looking for you. She should have been frightened by that, and she was, but the part of her that had been lied to, abandoned, and forced from her home felt a surge of warmth.

"How could you believe this was a good idea?" he growled beside her.

"I didn't say it was a good idea, and I certainly didn't force you to come with me," she said. Warmth or not, she was still upset with him. With everything.

He emitted a low sound that conveyed how very frustrated he was with her, and one of the deserters marching alongside them gave him a narrow look.

"Do you think I'd leave you with a group of strange men known for pillaging the countryside?" he asked. A flash of lamplight passed over his face, revealing just how angry he truly was.

"These men fight against the Confederacy," she said.

"A common enemy does not mean they are friends to us," he said. "It does not keep you safe, and given their number, neither can I." He had been speaking in a low voice, but the last bit came out loud and harsh. Ewan's mouth slammed shut into a blanched white line, as if he'd just revealed confidential information. Given how closely he guarded his thoughts, perhaps he had.

"Your woman is safe here," the man holding the lantern interjected. "I'm Henry. If anyone gives you a problem, tell them you're a friend of Henry's. Won't be any more problems, maybe 'cept for them."

Marlie looked over at him; his skin was only slightly lighter than hers, but his hair was long, dark, and pin straight. She knew there were Tuscarora who piloted Union soldiers and fought with the skulkers, but she couldn't be sure of his tribe.

"Thank you, Henry. I'm Marlie and this is Ewan."

Henry nodded. "We've got rules like any army here, and unlike the Home Guard, we abide by 'em. No hurting women and children."

"Since you're here with the deserters, I assume that you have not served," Ewan said. "But surely you know what soldiers have done, soldiers on both sides, whether the rules allow it or no."

Henry stopped and faced Ewan. "Like I said. Tell 'em you're a friend of Henry's. These men know better, but if one of 'em don't, he knows better than to hurt a friend of mine. Your woman is safe."

Marlie was about to interject that she was no one's woman, but Ewan nodded and took her hand again. If she pulled away, it would create a scene, so she walked on, face heated. This would be the last time, though; Marlie was making decisions for herself from now on.

"Where are you taking us?" Ewan asked.

"To see our commander, who took ill after the last skirmish," Henry said. "We got a lot of sick men around here, and if you can doctor 'em, we'd be much obliged."

"How many men are you all together?" she asked. She had a few bottles of tonics, dried leaves for healing teas . . .

"About five hundred or so," he said. "Got everything from dysentery, headaches, diphtheria, festering wounds, blood sickness, fever — laying out ain't an easy life, miss."

Marlie was overwhelmed by the numbers, but she felt a kind of peace settle over her. She had been hoping for a way to help: She was no detective, no warrior, but she could help in this small way. And if she ingratiated herself with them on behalf of the Loyal League, she could offer the possibility of an alliance to LaValle, as he'd requested. With the right support, these men could do even more damage to the Confederacy, like a sickness that weakens from within, making a body susceptible to the least outside blow.

"I'll help as best I can," she said. They were heading up an incline, and Marlie understood they were in the mountains now. She had heard of skulkers in the caves in this region, and it appeared the reports were correct.

"And I'll assist you," Ewan said, interjecting again.

"I don't need your help," Marlie whispered, finally pulling her hand away. "I can do this myself. I know I'm one of your projects, but if you need to keep yourself occupied there are surely other ways to be of use."

Ewan's brows drew close together. "I understand that everything in your life has changed. But my feelings for you have not altered; I don't know what project you speak of, but I said I would protect you and help you and I intend to do it."

"Feelings for me? A few kisses in the dark do not connote feelings, Socrates. You need to understand something and understand it well — I am not in your control."

She stalked off ahead of him, shaking with a rage whose source she could not pinpoint. Ewan had done nothing to be the recipient of such a tongue lashing, but he was the most convenient target. She could understand this — logically, which he would appreciate — but she was just plain angry and the heat of it boiled her logic down to one molten spike, directed at whoever ventured nearest.

They walked on in silence until Henry led them behind a spray of kudzu that hid the entrance to a cave. It wasn't large enough to fit five hundred men, but a fair amount had crammed their way in, judging from the murmurs that echoed off the stone walls — and the stench.

Low fires were burning, more for light than to give off heat, and the trio picked their way around exhausted men lying stretched out on the floor. This wasn't so different from the prison: men down on their luck and lacking resources. But Tobias was not a few feet away, ready to step in if needed. No carriage waited outside the gates to bring her back to her life of luxury.

Ewan is here, some pesky inner voice reminded her, and she tried not to allow herself to feel heartened by that.

They reached a man laid out on a pallet, one pant leg cut off to reveal a sloppily bandaged wound. He was mixed race, with light brown skin that was flushed with fever. It was warm in the cave, but not so warm as to induce the sweat streaking through the dirt on his face. He was shivering, which wasn't a good sign.

"This woman is here to doctor ya, Colonel Bill," Henry said as Marlie knelt down beside him. The man turned his head stiffly, and startled a bit when he caught sight of her.

"Look at them eyes. You a witch woman?" he asked through chattering teeth.

Marlie debated what answer to give. Weeks ago, she would have taken offense at the question. But she thought about her mother's memoirs, of the work she had been taught that was passed down through generations.

"Something like that," she said gently, laying the back of her hand to his forehead. "I'm going to do my best to help you. And your men."

"My wife and kids is waiting for me," he said. "I told them I'd come home, so I'd

372

'preciate that." He struggled to smile and Marlie stood.

"I must go collect the items I'll need. Can you get plenty of water boiling?"

"Yes, ma'am," Henry said. "Do you need an escort?"

"For God's sake, I'll go foraging with you," Ewan said. The frustration in his tone was evident. Marlie rolled her eyes. Henry let out a chuckle.

"Day will break soon," she said, "meaning none of you should be out and about. We'll make the first trip, and if we need assistance, we'll come wrangle a few men."

Henry handed them a few burlap sacks and then they headed back out into the weak light of the impending dawn. Marlie didn't look at Ewan, not because she was angry but because she had pushed him away and didn't know what to do now.

They walked the path down the mountain in silence, and she thought that perhaps this was just how it would be between them now. That was what she wanted, wasn't it?

She spotted some young dandelions growing, the roots of which made a potent painkiller, and began to move toward them. Ewan took her by the arm, holding her in place.

"Marlie." He closed his eyes for a moment, nostrils flaring, and damned if it didn't remind her of the moment he'd found his release between her thighs. The thought of it sent a shock of desire through her, incompatible with her internal directive to avoid contact with him at all costs.

He lowered his mouth toward hers, slowly, giving her time to turn away, but she didn't. She waited for what seemed much too long and then his lips pressed firmly against hers. She marveled at how familiar — how right — his lips moving against hers, his tongue easing its entry, felt. He kissed her like a man without language, whose only method of conveying a message was this spectacular communion. She allowed herself a moment of that bliss, of desire racing through her recklessly, and then she pulled her head back.

"What are you doing? You agreed not to touch me again, quite easily I might add."

He made a sound of frustration. "Communication isn't easy for me. I don't always know what people mean, if I'm misunderstanding words and actions. But I don't understand what happened between our . . . encounter and today. Please explain yourself."

He stood waiting like a tutor who wanted to hear the multiplication tables recited.

"We established earlier that I owe you nothing," Marlie said. "Let me go, Ewan."

"Because you know nothing of me, is that right?" His brow bunched with trenches of contemplation. "Let me tell you. My name is Ewan Alexander McCall. My family worked the land of Helenburgh until we were driven from Scotland and arrived in the US, settling in Kentucky. I've told you of my childhood, but I suspect it's the war you wish to know about?"

Marlie nodded, pinned to the spot by the sheer emotion behind his words, by the intensity of his gaze, which seemed to freeze her in place — not with fear, but with curiosity.

"I enlisted and was seen as a mediocre soldier, and rightly so. But I rose quickly through the ranks once it was discovered that I was especially good at a particular form of information extraction that would benefit the Union in these dire times. For the first time, my attention to detail, my relentless questions and my . . ." He paused. "My lack of empathy, as I was told, were seen as beneficial."

Marlie wanted to pull away then because she felt a dread that she knew wasn't an omen, but common sense.

"Beneficial to what?" she asked.

"I was — am — a counterintelligence agent," he said. His shoulders slumped, but his grip didn't slacken. "When high-value enemy agents were caught, I was tasked with interrogating them. And if they didn't comply, if they didn't provide the information I knew they had . . ."

"You tortured them," she finished for him. She wished Ewan had never spoken, that she had let him just keep kissing her until the world came tumbling down. She pulled away and he did release her then. "And that's how you know Cahill."

Because you're cut from the same cloth.

He nodded. "You've seen his limp. I caused it, during an interrogation."

"Is that pride in your tone?"

"No, it is regret." His grip tightened on her arm, then relaxed. "The day I interrogated him was the day I began to question everything. It should have been clear: He committed an evil act, he had information, and I needed it to prevent more evil. But he brought out something in me . . . for the first time I took pleasure in hurting another person. For the first time, I hurt a man because I *wanted* to."

Those icy blue eyes of his were filled with a pain and confusion Marlie hadn't seen before. "I didn't kill Cahill because I feared becoming a monster. Instead I let one loose and he ended up on your doorstep."

She tried to reconcile the kind, helpful man she knew with one who could take on a man like Cahill and come out the victor. And she *could* see it, now that she really thought about it. How he did everything so precisely, and could justify anything. But it didn't make sense — when Ewan had hurt her with his words, he had suffered. What had it cost him to hurt men with his hands, to cause physical pain?

"Why are you telling me this?" she asked.

"Because I care for you, Marlie. I care for you in a way I've never cared for another person, that I never *wanted* to care for another person."

Two admissions in direct succession that pulled her heart in opposite directions. Marlie felt an actual pain and placed a hand at her chest as if keeping it from breaking into pieces.

"Ewan . . ."

"I won't lie to you. And I know this means that you will not have me. But I'd rather you hate me for the right reasons than for false assumptions."

He rubbed the bridge of his nose and squinted, as if he were in pain, then his icy gaze was on her once more. "You wish to paint me as a villain who would use you and toss you aside at his earliest convenience, like Stephen did to your mother. As a man who would value your mind and your body and your spirit so low that I could leave them behind at the Tennessee line without a second thought, and perhaps that would be best for both of us, but I would never throw you over, Marlie. You deserve better than a man like me, so the point is rendered moot."

He turned and walked into the woods, stooping to examine a bush a few feet away.

"Blackberry. You can use the leaves, berries, and bark, correct?"

Marlie stared at his hunched-over form, still reeling from his words. "Correct."

Ewan continued his acts of service and in that moment she understood them for what they were — not a pastime, not a distraction, but a form of devotion. But devotion from a man who would use violence to bend others to his will — even if he never lifted a finger against her — was a frightening thing.

Her thoughts were a dizzying jumble, but day was breaking and men were depending on her. She did not know what to say to Ewan, so she headed for the dandelions and began digging them up with shaking hands.

Chapter 23

Marlie sat beside Bill, lifting the cup of dandelion root tea to his lips as she had hours earlier, and for much of the previous night.

"Thank you," Bill said. "I wasn't sure what this Loyal League was about or if it was a trap or somethin', but if they got members like you, maybe we need to do some reconsidering."

"We'll talk more later," she said, though pride welled up in her.

With the help of Ewan, Henry, and some of the other men, she had set up a slapdash work space and had been mixing steadily since her arrival, with the exception of a few hours curled up beside her workbench in slumber.

In addition to the pain-relieving dandelion tea for Bill and the others, she'd made blackberry root and sweet gum tisane for those suffering from loose bowels and dysentery. The tonic of dogwood berries she was brewing would work as well as quinine for those men who were feverish. She'd made her rounds through dozens of men, figuring who needed what, applying the herbal astringent she'd made from a mélange of plants to clean cuts and open wounds.

Her fingers ached from stripping and crushing and macerating, and she was more tired than she had ever been in her life, but she kept moving. If she stopped, she would have to face Ewan, who trailed behind her, proffering up whatever tool or tonic she needed. She wasn't sure if he was playing at nurse or sentry, but she was too exhausted to decline his assistance.

She was angry with him, but that didn't mean much, because she was angry at everyone. He was now another person on a long list of those who had kept things from her. Why? To protect her?

But she hurt for him, too. He did not have her bedside manner, but she could see how he brightened when a man's pain was relieved. When he wasn't by her side, he was helping sick men get up and about, dashing out chamber pots and bringing clean water and strips of cloth to help the immobile wash themselves. These were projects, as she called them, but not the projects of a man without empathy, or a man who drew pleasure from the pain of others.

You should be frightened, she reminded herself. *You should be disgusted.*

It occurred to her that the men she was offering her services to now had done things she might consider evil in other circumstances: robbing secesh of livestock and crops, ambushing Rebels. They may have been the men who burned Cahill out of his lodgings. But could she judge them and tell them they were wrong as the Home Guard tortured their families and hunted them like dogs? She had thought the line between right and wrong was clear, but now it was hopelessly blurred.

She stumbled over a stretched-out skulker and Ewan's hand shot out to steady her even as she righted herself with her own flagging energy. Why did his touch, swift as if he'd been waiting to catch her, both irritate her and make her want to weep at the same time?

"Perhaps some rest would do you good," he said. "Someplace better than the stone floor where you dropped when you were too tired to work anymore." His voice was flat, neither harsh with anger nor tender.

Marlie nodded stiffly.

"Is there somewhere she can rest away from the men?" Ewan asked. Henry stepped out from a group and beckoned them. He led them out of the cave and up the mountain a bit, into the trees, where a smaller cave had been dug beneath the roots of an oak.

"No one should bother you two here." He clapped Ewan's shoulder, giving the words subtext that reminded Marlie of the last small space they'd been in and what had occurred. "We'll be moving out later tonight, getting provisions for a strike we've been planning. Come talk once the sun has gone down."

"Thank you. We will," Ewan said, and led her into the small space.

Marlie dropped onto the blanket that covered the hard ground, wincing as the gnarled roots and rocks pressing up through the hard earth jabbed at her. After a moment, she no longer cared about discomfort — she was just happy to lie still.

"You worked very hard," Ewan said, settling beside her. He left as wide a space as was possible between them, but his hand was stretched out in her direction.

"It felt good to be able to do something more for the war effort," she said. "I'm tired, but I also feel full of . . . I don't know.

It's like everyone I helped gave me a bit of their spirit maybe, and I can feel it. I used to feel the same after visiting the prison." She scoffed. "I'm sure you find that ridiculous."

It was strange how it still felt normal to sit and talk with him, even knowing what he had done. He had tortured people, but had a natural capacity for kindness. She saw it in all the little ways he'd helped her, both in her rooms and once they'd left Lynchwood. She couldn't ignore what he had done, but should she condemn him for it? Could she?

Ewan shifted a bit. "Do you know what I felt after I did my part in aiding the Union?"

Please don't say you felt anything good, Marlie hoped, as if it mattered. He was a torturer, no better than Cahill. But some stubborn part of her couldn't come to terms with that.

"Nothing," he answered when she didn't respond. "I guess I felt the satisfaction of a job well done, but I didn't feel sad or happy. I'd been given a task and I'd completed it. So if you can derive a sense of peace or fulfillment from your aid to the Cause, I won't judge that."

Marlie felt a press of tears at her eyes, the questions she'd been repressing since he'd told her finally bursting forth.

"Why did you do it?" she asked. "How did you even find yourself in such a position?"

Ewan seemed prepared; knowing him, he'd spent the time since he'd told her deciding what to say should she ask.

"A few months after I enlisted, I was sent reconnoitering by my commander and another soldier," he said. "He'd received word of a detachment of Confederates trying to relay messages across the Georgia border, to pass sensitive information into Virginia. Well, we came across a Rebel soldier, in the midst of an act that I'll only say was immoral in the extreme. And in that moment I reasoned that since he seemed to have no qualms about the use of pain, perhaps I wouldn't, either."

He picked up a pebble from the ground and tossed it from hand to hand.

"I thought I'd be reprimanded, that I had failed in the one thing I had sought for myself from military service: self-discipline. But my commander wasn't angry — he was enthused. The soldier I had beaten had revealed all the information we could have wanted. And when this was relayed to those up the chain of command . . . well, it seemed that what I considered the worst of me was to be an asset for the Federal Army."

"Do you still feel nothing?" she asked

"In regard to my missions, I feel nothing. I joined to help the Union and I did. For the first time in my life, everything that had been wrong about me was useful in doing something right. The only time I really felt something was with Cahill." He tossed the pebble across the cave. "He was the last man I tortured."

His gaze met hers, and she realized it wasn't cold; it was wary. It was the look of a boy who had been told he was strange and wrong his entire life, until some army officer had decided to use that strangeness as a tool.

The import of his last words sank in after a moment.

"You were captured for the first time after you lost your composure with Cahill?"

He nodded.

"How is it that someone so sensible kept finding himself in Confederate prisons?" she asked. She sat up, as something that had long struck her as uncharacteristic finally began to make sense. "So skilled at moving silently, at getting out of places that should have kept you confined. Yet you kept getting yourself captured."

"I wouldn't phrase it like that," he said, making a jerky movement with his shoulders before regaining his composure. "I just had a streak of bad luck."

Something in Marlie ached for him as he sat before her, unable to admit the truth of the matter to himself.

"You allowed yourself to be captured. Because you didn't want to keep hurting people," she said slowly.

"No." He gave his head a sharp shake. "I was given orders and I executed them. I wouldn't shirk my duties. That would be cowardly. Treasonous, even."

"That would be human, Ewan," Marlie said softly. "It's all right to admit you didn't like such work, even if you excelled at it."

"My brother is a detective," Ewan said, his voice thick with emotion. "He marches into Confederate lion dens on a regular basis to ensure that when the dust settles, the Union will be victorious. What kind of man would I be if I got squeamish over a few injured Rebs? What kind of man would I be if I hid from the simple duties assigned to me while other men fought and died on battlefields?"

"You tell me," Marlie said. "The Ewan McCall I know is attentive and kind. He assists me with my work and listens to everything I say as if it matters. He cleans houses destroyed by Rebs and rocks sick babies in slave quarters, and shows deserters how to repair their guns."

"I am the kind of man who left others weeping and slept fine afterward. I wish I could say I was something other than that."

Marlie knew that he was no longer discussing the war. That was fine, because neither was she.

"It is against your rules to wish for things that cannot be," she reminded him. "And perhaps you are exactly the kind of man you're supposed to be."

"The kind of man who breaks a man's finger to get what he wants?"

"What did you want?" she asked.

"The location of an arsenal of weapons being smuggled in by Northern secessionists, and their names."

"And by getting that information you saved lives and helped protect the Union."

"Don't," he ground out. He moved nearer to her, his angry expression visible in the weak light that filtered into their hiding spot. "Don't try to reimagine me, Marlie. I'm not some poisonous berry or plant that you can transmute into something better than it once was. I am not good."

"Isn't there something in your *Enchiridion* to the effect that if a man does something unjust because he believes it his duty, then he is the one hurt?"

He sucked in a breath, then his hand cupped her face, thumb passing over her cheek. She could smell the comforting scents of blackberry and pine and dogwood. "Would you say the same of a Rebel?" he asked. "A slave owner?"

"No! I don't give a damn about a Rebel or a slave owner!" She raised her hand to cup his face in kind. "Even you have admitted that there are limits to the application of logic, just as I can admit there are with science. I care about you for reasons I cannot explain and cannot seem to escape. I know that once we get to Tennessee, we'll part ways — maybe before then — but that doesn't stop me from wanting . . ."

She paused, shaken by the immensity of the feeling that welled up in her. "I don't have to transmute you into something good because you already are. I know it. I feel it the same way I can tell when a tonic is so well blended that it will have the utmost potency. You can call it silly superstition, or call me sheltered, but that won't change what I know."

He looked at her for a long moment, his icy gaze searching her face.

"Did you read to the end of *The Enchiridion*?" he asked.

Marlie nodded. A thrill went through her as his fingers grazed her neck.

" 'Whoever yields properly to fate is wise among men.' I consider myself wiser than most."

Ewan kissed her then. His lips moved over hers hard, but not ungently. His mouth clung to hers and his hands pulled her close until there was no space between them, as if the Fates had woven them together, binding them intractably.

Her whole body was warm with need, ready for more than the pull of his right hand against her bodice and the slide of his left hand into her hair. He eased her down to the ground, his body a delicious weight atop her.

Marlie ran her hands over his back, feeling the play of muscles as he dipped his hips, working them in a motion that mimicked what she knew could come to pass between them. What she *wanted* to come to pass between them.

Her hands left his back, dropping to her sides to pull up her skirts. The fabric was too much of a barrier between them. He pushed his weight up onto his arms to assist her, and then he settled himself on his knees between her thighs.

She held her skirt up at her waist, the

bunched fabric blocking his hands from view, but oh how she felt them. Each grasped an inner thigh, sliding slowly up the sensitive skin. Marlie made a low moan and bit her lip against the next — Ewan held down a thigh with one hand while the other notched against her sex, thumb pressing hard between the folds and rubbing her. Marlie trembled, her body unprepared for how quickly his touch brought her to the precipice of passion. And not just his touch; Ewan was staring down at her, that icy gaze gone heavy-lidded and hot. She sucked in a breath and his thumb rubbed more insistently, his gaze pinned her harder.

"So beautiful," he said. "I want to see you take your pleasure at my hand."

Marlie clenched against the unfamiliar pressure as he slid a finger inside of her, thrusting up while still rubbing her, then she was clenching around him as the friction sent shocks of sensation from her womb to her toes. Ewan was still watching, focused on nothing but giving her pleasure. Her back arched up as she pressed wantonly against his hand, her body demanding release.

"Yes. Like that."

She'd once miscalibrated her still and the steam had built up, too hot too fast, shattering an alembic to pieces. Marlie was fairly certain that the same thing was about to happen to her. She squeezed her eyes against the intense pleasure that concussed through her body, no longer moaning or gasping but held stock still in passion's invisible grip.

Ewan pulled his hand away and Marlie tried to absorb what had just happened. When she relaxed back to the ground and opened her eyes, she could see that Ewan's jaw was tense with strain, his trousers tented. A sense of certainty descended on her, but one that did not dissipate the shyness that came with asking what she was about to.

"I want . . . do you want . . ." She took a shuddering breath. "Make love to me, Ewan."

His eyes went wide and his nostrils flared.

"I want nothing more than that, but —"

"I know that I don't have much experience, but I choose to share this experience with you."

"It's just that —"

"I know you think I've been sheltered and I don't know what I want, but I do," Marlie said testily.

"I've never made love before," Ewan blurted out, and the shock of it knocked away Marlie's indignation.

"What?"

"I told you, I don't get along with others very well. I do have experience with women, but not that *particular* experience."

Marlie had been so sure that he'd use her virginity against her that she wasn't sure how to proceed.

"Oh. I understand. I suppose you're saving that for someone special." She turned her head aside, shame buffeting her from all sides.

"Marlie," he said. "Have you still not figured it out? I only have one criterion."

"Cognitive superiority," she said.

"Yes. Cognitive superiority, though I have added compassionate, spirited, and beautiful to that list, so I suppose I now have four criteria. Wait, no, just the one." His fingertips grazed her chin, turning her head so that their gazes met. "You. Marlie Lynch."

"That's very specific." Her heart beat wildly in her chest.

"I don't believe in superstition, but perhaps I was saving myself for someone. For you." He dropped forward onto his hands then, and this time his kiss was exceedingly soft, gentle brushes of his lips against her bruised ones. His hips rocked against her as they kissed, and she felt his member lengthen where his groin was nestled against her apex. Her hands went to his waist to undo his trousers and he stilled, except for the slight tremor that went through him at her touch. He was shaking . . . because of her.

When his pants were undone and his member warm and heavy in her hand, he nipped at her lips, drawing her attention. His gaze met hers as he pressed her down once more.

"If it hurts —"

"It can't hurt more than this root poking into my back," she said, drawing laughter from him. She laughed, too, and the tension between them eased a bit. He was still shaking as he positioned himself between her legs, and even as the thick head of his cock pressed into her slickness.

Marlie gasped and clutched at his back at the shocking sensation of fullness chased with incompleteness. His face nestled into her neck as he pushed into her, so slowly. His breath was a warm caress against her skin, and the small sounds of restraint he made paired with the hot friction of him moving within her was almost too much for her to take.

"Are you all right?" He stopped and raised his head to examine her face, concerned as he always was.

She ran a hand through his auburn locks and cupped him by the back of the head. "I'm always all right when I'm with you."

He thrust up more urgently, the thick length of him filling her, and she cried out at the unexpected pain.

"I'm sorry, love." He kissed her, caressed her face, for a long moment. Marlie suspected he was regaining his own bearings as well. Eventually, he began to move slowly, and she followed his lead. The pain didn't go away entirely, but it was crowded out by the alien pleasure of Ewan thrusting into her. Each stroke was a little more pleasure and a little less pain, until they had settled into a galloping pace, with him driving down and her rising to meet him. Their joining was ungainly, and they occasionally lost their tempo or banged teeth or foreheads, but that didn't detract from the fact that they were both drawing near to their release. He was moving faster now, his breath heaving in her ear, and she tightened around him as pinpricks of bliss ran through her.

"Marlie," he warned. He thrust hard a few times, then paused. "I imagine that stamina is something that comes with practice, but alas . . ."

Marlie undulated her hips, pushing him deeper into her. He resumed his thrusting, then a moment later cursed and withdrew, shuddering beneath her hands. A warm wetness splashed onto her thighs and then he collapsed beside her.

They lay still for a long moment, Ewan pulling Marlie onto his chest and running his hand over her back. They were both too tired to arrange their clothes, and she was content to rest just like that. She was sore, and was sure her hair was hopelessly tangled, but she felt a sense of calm happiness. Even war and injustice couldn't stop moments of joy in this world, she realized. It was moments like this they were fighting for.

"Back at Hattie's house, you told her about something that could stop a pregnancy."

Despair dried up Marlie's brief oasis of calm. Was that what he had been silently pondering? How to get rid of any possible evidence of their joining? Tears scalded her eyes and she wished she weren't so weak. Why did that one question hurt her more than anything had?

She sat up, feeling truly soiled. "Do not worry. I know how to prevent pregnancy.

You won't have to worry about an unwanted child."

Ewan's hand brushed over her hair and pulled her back down beside him. "No, that's not what I was thinking. Well, I did think 'What if I got Marlie with child?' What kind of man would I be if I didn't?" She regarded him warily, although she didn't move away from the soothing caress of his hand over her hair. "Then I remembered what I heard you say to Hattie, about the cotton root. And I thought about all of Vivienne's herbal mixtures. And I thought of you imagining your mother never wanted you."

He looked at her, as if some great understanding should have dawned on her.

"Marlie, your mother knew how to prevent pregnancy and how to terminate one. She did neither. Instead, she gave you everything she knew, and when that wasn't enough, she entrusted you to someone who could give you more."

Everything fell into place then, and the understanding of it hit Marlie like a blow. Not every woman in Vivienne's situation had a choice, but she had, and she had always chosen Marlie and what was best for her.

Marlie wiped at tears and Ewan assisted,

brushing away the warm droplets with his knuckles. "Do not ever think that you are easy to walk away from." His voice was pitched low and his expression was shrouded.

"We should rest," she said, forcing a smile. Just as in her rooms, the cave was a brief respite from reality. Thinking otherwise would only lead to pain. She would take what she could before they reached Tennessee, but she wouldn't allow herself a false security that could only lead to pain.

CHAPTER 24

He hadn't ever thought of his virginity as something sacred, despite holding on to it for longer than most of his compatriots. Men spoke of sexual relations in terms of conquering, claiming, owning, as if they were pillagers instead of lovers. Perhaps Ewan had done something wrong because *he* was the one who'd felt vulnerable, who had been left vanquished. At first he'd been focusing on their joining as if it were a problem to be solved, but Marlie's cries, her face, the squeeze of her around his penis — all of those had stripped his control away until he was a grunting, panting, sweating bundle of nerves. Marlie had been sated though, so perhaps he hadn't been so wrong after all. The problem was, without other reference points, he wasn't sure if the tenderness and calm he felt as he watched her sleep was normal or not. Or wanting to kiss her awake and slide into her again.

He wasn't entirely calm though; Marlie kept speaking of separating once they'd reached Tennessee. He had avoided thinking of the eventuality in depth before, when he'd decided there was no chance of anything further between them because of who he was and what he had done. She hadn't changed any idea Ewan had of himself — but if he maintained the belief that Marlie was intelligent and kind, but not foolhardy, he had to take her words into account. She thought him deserving of forgiveness. She thought it was all right that he had been hurt by what he'd had to do, instead of thinking him weak. Thus, any plans for them to go their separate ways was a problem, and like any problem Ewan was presented with, he needed to solve it.

He got up and ate a handful of blackberries and some of the sweet corn Henry had given them, letting Marlie sleep. It was a short walk to the larger cave, but he moved carefully in the waning sunlight, unsure if the Home Guard or wandering soldiers watched for signs of movement.

He paused when a shadow caught his eye, but it was only a group of the skulkers coming up the pass. More were stationed in front of the cave, some sitting and cleaning their weapons, others doing drills. Upon their first arrival, Ewan had thought the deserter camp like Randolph Prison in miniature, but now he could see it was more like his time spent with his battalion. This was not just some sad, starving group of men, but a trained militia.

He walked into the cave in a manner that showed deference, but not cowardice; that skill was learned in the army and prison both, and at home before that.

The scent of corn and pork and grains, most assuredly stolen from some of the local secessionists, emanated from several cook fires, and men queued up to gather their portions. Some men cleaned the mess that had accumulated overnight, and others were busy packing gunnysacks for a march.

Toward the back of the cave, Henry knelt beside Colonel Bill, who was still recovering. He was looking much better, though Ewan doubted he could get very far without assistance. Marlie's skills had their roots in mysticism, but she wasn't a sorceress.

Henry pointed something out on a map spread on Bill's lap, getting input from the semicircle of men crowded around them.

Ewan approached and paused a few feet away, and the men all stopped talking and looked up at him, marking him as an outsider.

"You and your lady getting back on the road? We might need more of her doctoring soon, depending on how the night goes," Bill said.

Ewan looked around at the deserters, watching their movements more closely. He could now see that what he had taken for the completion of daily tasks was more likely preparing to move out before a battle.

"That decision is up to Marlie," Ewan said. It was true, but he was also hedging. While he accepted that the skulkers had good reason for deserting, and found the men themselves to be as well acquitted as the Union soldiers he had fought beside, he wasn't sure where he stood with them. Marlie had wanted to help, and Ewan had wanted to help her. Now that the men were preparing to go into battle, he didn't know how to proceed. "What exactly will necessitate the need for her doctoring, if you don't mind my asking?"

"We're going after the Home Guard," Bill said. He leaned forward as if he would stand, then winced. "Well, not me. My men. We've suffered too many losses this last week, and we've got to send the message that they need to leave us be or face the consequences."

"I ain't slept in my bed in seven months,"

one man said. "Ain't sat at the table with my wife and kids, or plowed my land. I'm tired of living like this."

"And you think going after the Home Guard today will change things." It wasn't a question: Ewan was trying to figure out what exactly would drive these men to think this was the best course of action.

Henry shrugged. "Maybe. Maybe not. Won't bring my brother back, but if I can say I killed them that killed my brother, that's better than nothing."

When would tit-for-tat be enough? But he looked at the men with their hunched shoulders and weary eyes and understood that they were war, stripped of all the glory bestowed upon it by nation-states and government rhetoric. War was attacking or waiting to attack, seeking vengeance or freedom or, generally, some combination of both. It was both illogical and the most logical of human behaviors, and attempting to deter them would have been as useless as trying to stop Menelaus from laying siege to Troy.

"Indeed it is," he said. "I can tell you what I know of Cahill, if you think it would be of assistance."

"What do you know that we don't?" Bill asked.

"That he's a hard man to break. Physically and mentally. I won't call him evil, because that word makes him more than he is. At the base of it, he's just a man who sees no good in himself or in others, and he doesn't care who he hurts because of it."

Ewan felt a bit of something unclench inside of him as he spoke aloud thoughts that had long been shrouded by his estimation of himself. He'd been holding Cahill up as some malevolent force to measure himself against, but if he were truly like the man he wouldn't have cared what anyone, Marlie included, thought of his actions. He had done wrong, in a setting where right and wrong were muddled up with God and country; he wasn't offering himself deliverance, simply the acknowledgment that while he wasn't a good man, as Marlie believed, perhaps he could be. When this was over, the country would have to wash away the bloodstains and move forward. Why shouldn't Ewan have the same opportunity?

"That sounds personal," Bill said. "Maybe this fella has as good a reason to go to Lynchwood as we do."

"Lynchwood." Ewan didn't realize his demeanor had changed until the men in front of him stood, holding their rifles casually, but not as casually as one would if a

403

threat wasn't present. He took a deep breath, unclenched his fists.

"I think there might be a misunderstanding," he said. "Do you mean to say that you are preparing to head for Lynchwood, home of the Lynches of Randolph County?"

Ewan wasn't one for wishing, but in that moment everything in him pulled forward with the hope that perhaps he'd misheard, or there was another Lynchwood in Yalkin or Davidson.

"Yup," Bill said. "One of our scouts got word that the Home Guard is planning a big rout, aiming at flattening us once and for all. They come after us where we live and we go after 'em where they live, simple as that."

And it was simple, terrifyingly so. This was the war for the Union reduced from its grand scale to a few miles; would he have told Lincoln not to muster troops after Sumter? McClellan to pack it in after Gettysburg? There would be fighting until there was some unifying reason not to do so. There was no way to dissuade these skulkers with logic: Was there any more essential distillation of logic than "an eye for an eye"? And if Ewan told them the real reason why they should change their plan of attack, would that turn Marlie from a savior into a pawn?

Their eyes left his face and focused on something behind him, something that reduced the tension in the cave the slightest bit and had the semicircle of men easing up on their guns.

"Dammit," Ewan muttered before looking over his shoulder.

Marlie was taking in the scene as he had when he entered, and when her gaze settled on him, the self-conscious smile turned up her lips, reminding him of what they had shared hours before. She looked away quickly, though. His heart was full, but the horrible, maddening tickle began in his skull. Marlie had walked right into the middle of danger and his thoughts bounced frenetically about as he tried to figure out how to get her out of the situation. His skin was hot and his jaw was clenched tight. The cave suddenly felt as if it were closing in around him.

Marlie's smile faded as she approached. She put her hand on his sleeve, and the sensation both calmed him and focused the tumult in his mind into one objective: protect Marlie.

"Did you have a batch of bad berries again, Socrates?" she asked. Her silly question was like a pin to a boil, lancing the frantic thoughts that had been swirling in his mind just enough to allow him to think clearly.

"We have a slight problem." His voice came out strong and natural sounding, as if it had picked up on Marlie's calm and adjusted itself accordingly.

"Do we now?" Henry stepped forward. "It seems the only one with a problem here is you. Don't think just because you're an enlisted man you can come in here judging us for what we do and how we do it."

"Ewan?"

"This is a bit more complicated than berries, Marlie." He wanted to haul her up and run, to start swinging wildly to clear a path through the men. But he wasn't going to lie to her anymore, even by omission. "Bill and Henry have decided that their next target is Lynchwood."

He prepared himself for tears, or to catch her as she fainted away, but her hand left his arm as she whirled on Henry so fast that her skirts kicked up cave dust.

"Is this true?" There it was, hidden beneath her query, the quiet fury that welled up in her every now and again like the geysers out West. Ewan glanced at Henry and Bill, who didn't understand her sudden change in demeanor. Henry nodded resolutely.

"Lynchwood is my home," she said. "After all I've done to assist you, I believe it's within my rights to ask that you not attack my family."

"Maybe your family shouldn't be putting up Rebel pigs," a man said.

"Well, maybe your wives shouldn't let the Home Guard pillage your homes," she retorted sharply, causing an angry stir amongst the men. "Oh, is it not that simple? Can you not just tell the Home Guard to leave once they decide to take what's yours?"

"Marlie."

He knew she heard him, but she didn't even look his way.

"I understand your battle is with Cahill, but you cannot win by burning down the home of the very people who feed the wives and children who struggle to survive while you play this game of cat and mouse." She looked around at the men. "Do you think the Lynch farm is going to be quite as charitable if my family is killed in an attack by deserters?"

Ewan saw the moment the realization hit the men closest to them. Her initial tack, trying to get them to empathize, may have backfired, but getting them to realize they were attacking their own interest was a sure thing.

"Well, what are we supposed to do? Just let them get away with pushing us out of our homes and making us live like animals?"

"I didn't say that. I only wonder if you're going to burn down every house in three counties. Because he'll just move on to another if you burn down Lynchwood," Marlie said. Ewan heard that sinister tone in her voice, the same one he'd heard when she mentioned she could poison Cahill to get rid of him. "If you want to fight him, then fight him. I can tell you personally that he leaves Lynchwood every evening for reconnoitering, so if you go to burn it down this night I can only imagine it's only because you'd rather avoid a true confrontation."

Bill looked at Henry, and then back at Marlie.

A little of the anger went out of her then, and her gaze was pleading when it met his. "Cahill has already forced me out of my home. Knowing that it was destroyed because of him, that even the possibility of going back has been taken away, would be too much to bear. Please. Reconsider."

Bill sighed and then readjusted his

propped-up leg. "You know, we were on our way to Lynchwood when we ran into the Home Guard the other day and I got injured. We could have burned that house with you inside, you who came and tuckered yourself out doctoring us. The Lord works in funny ways, don't he?"

Ewan stepped forward. "I can help you, if it means leaving Lynchwood be. I can lure Cahill and his men to some place away from the house."

The perfection of the idea coalesced in his mind. How everything since he'd enlisted had been leading up to a confrontation between him and Cahill. He could help these men, and —

"No, that's all right," Henry said, abruptly interrupting the glorious showdown that had begun playing out in Ewan's head. "We can handle that on our own."

Ewan nodded, chastened. This was a militia, even if it wasn't sanctified by the state. He couldn't expect to just stroll into the cave and take over command — he freely admitted he hadn't been a good soldier, yet he had momentarily assumed this group of skulkers would have some need for him, as if they hadn't been waging war on their own for months. His hubris shamed him, and reminded him how easy it was for a man's ego to convince him he could be a savior when, in fact, no one was in need of saving.

"Right," Ewan said, nodding. "Marlie, what do you want to do?"

She stood twisting her hands. "Perhaps we should wait here with the wounded men. And that way when Henry and the others return, I can be of assistance. Before we get on our way."

And you can be sure that they kept their word and Lynchwood is safe.

"Just let me know what you need from me," he said.

"We can have a couple of our men guide you a ways toward Tennessee and connect you with some pilots who will take over," Bill said. "Our way of saying thanks."

"We'd appreciate that. The sooner I get to Tennessee the better," Marlie said with a nod, then turned and began making her rounds of the injured and ill men.

Ewan watched, feeling that heart-full sensation in his chest again, like he was balancing a cup that was filled to the brim and threatened to spill over with each step. The sooner the better?

Ewan tried to think of it logically, but there was none when it came to her. He couldn't force her to change her mind, but the thought of letting her go was unfathomable, a pain that was worse than the headaches he suffered. His brother, Malcolm, despite being a lady's man, had often spoken of love as if it were a plague that would only lead to one's undoing. He'd assumed Malcolm was wrong once he heard he'd taken a wife, but now, watching Marlie move through the men with her back to him, as if he were already out of her thoughts, Ewan realized just how erroneous he had been in straying from his ship. The problem was that the vessel he had clung desperately to for so long had now set sail. There was no going back and, if Marlie would not have him, no going forward, either.

He steeled himself against the pain of the realization and followed silently in her wake, ready to assist. If that was the only way to remain close to her for now, he'd take it.

CHAPTER 25

Marlie tried to still the tremors in her fingers as she changed bandages and applied poultices. The bravado that had seized her when she walked in on the skulkers' conversation had left her, and now she tried to focus on the work in front of her instead of the men gathering their weapons and bags and heading out of the cave. Instead of Ewan, who had been buried deep inside of her, who had driven her to madness with pleasure and restored her soul both in the span of a day.

How could she look at him again, when she was still sore from what they'd shared? She'd told herself it would mean nothing, that it was juvenile to think a physical act could change what must pass between them, but she hadn't anticipated how much she wanted to be wrong.

Taking is different from loving, she reminded herself, but hadn't Ewan given as well? It was too much to think on; she was on her own in the world, now, and stepping from Sarah's care into that of Ewan would only prove that she was truly as helpless as she thought herself to be. Once they got to Tennessee and separated, she would . . . would . . .

Henry walked over to her, the last of the men heading out on their mission.

"I just want you to know that I meant it. Your family is safe, from our hands at least."

She thought of Sarah sitting at home worried for her, and how close she had come to being harmed, and her throat went tight. She couldn't think it anything other than providence that she had been there to change the men's minds.

"Thank you," she choked out.

He nodded and marched out behind his men, pulling his long, dark hair back and tying it with a leather strap as he did. Marlie realized the move wasn't cosmetic, but a preparation for battle, and her stomach lurched.

What am I doing here?

She put a hand to her chest as the desire to follow after them and return to Lynchwood held her in its tantalizing grip. If Cahill was defeated, maybe there was a chance she could go back . . . but Melody would still be there. Even if she weren't, she had already made it clear to Marlie that neither her money nor intelligence nor family name would protect her. She would have to do that herself.

There was no going back.

"Marlie? Are you all right?"

Ewan was beside her again, reminding her of how quietly he moved. An image of them in a home, their home, and him sneaking up on her and giving her a fright before kissing it away flashed in her mind.

No. That's foolishness.

"I'm fine. I'm just relieved that Sarah will be safe."

"As am I, but I meant are you all right in a more corporeal sense." His cheeks went pink and she knew exactly what he was thinking of, then her face flushed, too.

"A bit sore," she said. "What about you?"

"Me? I'm wishing we could go back to that little hole in the ground and not think about Cahill or the war or Tennessee." His gaze shifted to her mouth and he took a step closer. She wanted to lean into him, but she took a step back instead.

"That book of yours warns against wishing for a reason. All the wishing in the world can't change reality."

"What reality precludes us being together

414

or guarantees our having to go our separate ways once we reach Union soil." And there it was; the truth that could not be avoided.

"The one in which I can be sold like a prize sow and you can't," Marlie said.

Ewan's eyes squeezed shut, and his nostrils flared. He brought his fingertips to his brow and pressed hard for a moment, before opening his eyes again.

"Marlie. I cannot understand how that must feel, but you are punishing me for things outside of my control. Again."

"What you see as punishment for things beyond your control is the only thing within mine." She tried to hold on to that, that this was the only way to keep herself safe from the world, and to keep her heart safe from Ewan.

"Did what passed between us mean nothing to you?" His face showed no anger, no upset, but Marlie had come to learn that Ewan kept the things he cared about most submerged beneath seas of rationality. She saw his emotion in the clench of his hand, and the way his Adam's apple worked in his throat.

"It meant everything," she admitted. Her throat had gone rough and the words barely choked out. "But what we do in the privacy of my rooms or some hidden cave has no bearing on the real world. Once you get back North, would you really risk your relationship with your family, your friendships, your standing in your community for me?"

She refused to cry. Not again. But her heart ached for what might have been between them.

"Yes," he said. His voice was impatient, as if he had tired of explaining a simple concept to her. His gaze bored into hers and his body fairly hummed with tension now. "I understand your reticence, but you make presumptions on what I would and wouldn't do without my consultation. That is called fantasy."

"No, that is called logic," she said softly. "I must see to the men."

She moved to walk past him and he let her, telling her everything she needed to know. He could pretend all he wished, but some part of Ewan had to understand that there was no future for them in a world where death and destruction plagued the land and men fought over whether people ike her would even deserve freedom.

was hours later when she finally sat down ide Bill, and Ewan, who was beside him. t of the men were fine, but she had checked and rechecked their progress and then set about to making some larger batches of general decoctions that might be of use when she had gone.

"How are you feeling?" she asked Bill.

"Ornery," he replied. "I hate not being able to go with the men. Henry is a fine leader, but I feel the same as when my kids first started heading off to the schoolhouse on their own." He chuckled. "Don't tell him I said so though. He'd never let me hear the end of it."

"Your secret is safe with me," Ewan said. Marlie glanced at him. His expression was neutral, carefully so. He did not look in her direction.

"I suppose you know what it's like, Ewan. I heard that when they came upon you, you almost took off old Larry's head when you thought they meant to harm your woman," Bill said. "Seeing you two makes me miss my wife something awful," he added quietly.

"Is she in Randolph?" Marlie asked, avoiding Bill's implication.

"No, she went to stay with some folks in Guilford. Other free blacks. We was the only ones round our way, and once I joined up with the Heroes she had no one to look out for her. I send her letters sometimes, but my writing ain't so great."

He looked askance and Marlie recognized the shame in him, one she had seen often in the slaves making their way North when they'd showed up in tatters and been received by Marlie in her fancy dress. It was the shame of knowing that being enslaved had denied him something vital. Marlie's heart ached for that misplaced emotion, but she couldn't tell him how to feel. She had never been in his place, and had been privileged enough to be able to run when threatened with such a fate.

"I'm sure she's just happy to hear from you," Marlie said.

"Well, I'll be happy when the Confederacy is sent to tarnation and we can be together again. That's the worst part of this skulking. Sometimes I wake up and expect her next to me, and there's nothing but Carl's hairy behind." He nodded toward a man a few feet away. Crinkles formed around his eyes as he laughed. "Don't tell anyone I said that, either."

Marlie understood Bill's words all too well; she'd felt a moment of panic when she'd awoken to find the light fading outside of the cave and Ewan gone instead of beside her, where she expected him to be. Just a few nights and it now seemed strange — wrong — to awaken without his warm, wiry figure beside her. That, and the tenderness at her apex, had been a much-needed reminder of how painful their parting of ways would be. She'd cauterized a few wounds for the skulkers as she assisted them, and she could cauterize her own heart if that meant surviving.

Is that what Maman did?

Her beautiful mother, who had rebuffed every man who'd shown her interest during Marlie's youth. Marlie had always thought it was because she had no need for a man, but perhaps the truth was more awful: She'd only ever loved one. And he'd taken advantage of her and deserted her.

Ewan rose from beside Bill, his expression tight.

"I'll return shortly," he said.

Bill and Marlie nodded and he stalked off.

"He's got a small bladder," Marlie said, when Bill turned a curious gaze at her.

"And a heart he wears on his sleeve," Bill replied. After that there was silence between them. Bill poked at the small fire with a stick, and the crackle and pop of wood mixed in with the murmurs of the injured men around them.

Marlie told herself it was the silence that made the time stretch on, that she was being silly, but then suddenly she was up on her feet and looking down at Bill. She didn't know where the urge came from, or why the words *Vas-toi!* echoed in her head, but she knew she had to go.

Bill picked up his rifle. Reached the long end of it out to poke Carl. He made a signal and soon all the remaining men who were capable were reaching for their arms.

"Did you hear something?" she asked.

"No, but when someone with eyes like yours jumps up like a haint whispered something in her ear, best to be ready for whatever's coming."

Carl crawled over. "The sentry should have been back ten minutes ago. I thought maybe he stopped to take a leak, but . . ."

"Ewan," Marlie said, and whirled to run but something gripped her skirt. She looked down and found Bill holding the fabric bunched in his hand.

"Running out and getting yourself killed ain't exactly what that man of yours would want."

Fear constricted her throat at the word *killed,* and her desire to get to Ewan pushed toward panic. But Bill was right. If this was something more than a hunch, she couldn't rush out blindly into the night.

Ancestors, help me.

Bill released her skirt and turned to confer

with Carl, and Marlie slipped away. There was a valley of difference between running wildly into the night and doing nothing, and the latter wasn't an option.

Chapter 26

The smile on Ewan's face was unnatural, unwanted, and yet he couldn't seem to form any other expression. Not in the instant when he first realized he was surrounded by Home Guardsmen as he fastened his trousers. Not when he was presented to Cahill, who held a lantern up to his face and stared coldly before saying, "So it *was* you."

Ewan had thought he'd feel rage or fear when he met Cahill face-to-face again, but he felt nothing. His mind logged the particulars of the situation: where the men with guns were, the angles of the shadows thrown by the lanterns, the fact that Cahill's moustache had been trimmed sloppily, one side higher than the other.

"Fan out and search for others," Cahill had ordered.

"What do you want us to do with him?" Roberts asked.

"Tie him to this tree."

Ah, so that's how it's going to be.

Ewan had considered fighting the men off, but given the number of men and weapons pointed at him that would have been asking for a quick death over a slow one; the slow one wouldn't be more pleasant, by any means, but he had a high tolerance for pain, and it meant there was a chance that he could escape and get to Marlie. He was no use to her dead, so slow it was.

He'd had to leave the cave, her blithe conversation with Bill driving him mad when all he wanted to do was demand she give him a chance to prove her wrong. But life didn't work that way. He could compel her no more than the North could the South or the Rebs could the skulkers. And so he'd walked away, leaving her safety to chance.

Now, with the Home Guardsmen dispatched to do his bidding, Cahill simply stood in front of Ewan. His back was to him; first he'd watched his men fan out to search for any skulkers in the woods, and now that they were all out of sight he stood as if waiting for something to emerge from the dark forest.

Ewan's arms had been tied back behind an old walnut tree, bound tightly at the wrists. He was still fully dressed, but his ventral side was completely exposed, like an animal prepped for vivisection. It was a morbid, but not inaccurate, comparison.

Ewan heard a shot in the distance and the shouts of men, and finally he felt something. He tugged at his restraints as rage and fear converted into energy. Marlie was out there, with only a group of injured and ill men to defend against the Home Guard attack. There didn't seem to be many of them; it was likely a detachment had broken off from the main squad with the intention of an ambush after the skulkers had headed toward Lynchwood. The Home Guard either had a man on the inside or Cahill had been prescient, but Ewan wasn't about to be the one to break the silence to ask which was correct.

Instead he inverted his hand and ran his fingertips over the rope knotted at his wrist. He could just graze the edges of it and tried to dig his fingernails in to pull it down closer.

His gaze was trained on Cahill as he worked, the hideous smile on his face a cover for his frustration as the tightly tied rope resisted the grip of his short nails.

Cahill's shoulders rose and fell in a sigh, then he turned and walked over toward Ewan. Five limping strides and then he raised his uninjured leg and kicked out at Ewan, his foot crushing Ewan's leg into the tree. Blinding pain rocketed through his leg and Ewan cried out — he wasn't super-human and some pain could not be toler-ated silently. Birds rose up from the tree branches, the sound of their startled depar-ture merging with the echo of his bellow. Any illusions he had about his tolerance to pain were shattered, along with his shin-bone. He tried to control himself but spittle flew through gritted teeth as he tried to put weight on his leg, and a pain unlike anything he'd ever known exploded where just a mo-ment before there had been none.

"Isn't as fun when you're on the receiving end," Cahill said. "You taught me that."

"It's never fun," Ewan said, his voice strangled by the effort to keep his compo-sure. He sucked in a deep breath and tried to breathe through the pain, slumping against the tree for support. He'd had a broken limb as a child — had broken his arm and didn't tell his family for days. He hadn't wanted to be a bother and the pain had faded to a dull ache that only flared up if he was careless. The doctor rebreaking the bone to set it when his mother had finally realized something was amiss had hurt far more, but that had also been manageable. This would be manageable, too, if he survived.

"That's because you were doing it wrong," Cahill said. "I remember you, all red-faced and worked up. I thought you were gonna cry, boy."

Cahill chuckled.

"The difference between us is that you cared," Cahill said. "You cared about those darkies getting what was coming to them, like you ain't never seen an animal put down before. You cared that you never got any information from me because you thought you had to break me, to teach me a lesson."

Cahill pulled a knife that looked designed to cut a man clean in half from a sheath at his side. Ewan shifted and bit his lip as pain flared up his entire leg.

"If you don't care, why are you here?" Ewan asked.

"Don't get me wrong, now. I *believe* in what I'm doing." Cahill pulled down an overhanging branch and sliced the knife clean through it, easy as if he were cutting through lard, and walked closer to Ewan. "I believe the North is full of cowardly men who deserve to die in their own filth. I believe these darkies are shit on the bottom of my shoe and that when the Confederacy wins they'll rue the day they fell for that abolitionist garbage. But I don't *care.* I'm here because I like doing this."

He was close to Ewan now, the knife's point pressing into the fabric at the thigh of the leg Ewan was using to support himself. His face was blank as he slowly pressed it through the material, sliding it into Ewan's flesh torturously slowly.

Ewan's eyes watered and his stomach turned, but Cahill was looking him in the eye and he refused to show how truly nausea-inducing the pain was. Instead he gritted against the pain, drew his head back until it hit the bark of the tree, then slammed his head forward, executing a technically perfect head-butt. He was going to die, but with the knowledge that he had mastered at least a few things in this life.

And that you stormed away from Marlie without telling her you love her.

That was a regret he couldn't think on. He focused on the small flash of pleasure he received when Cahill dropped the knife and grabbed his face, stumbling back. It was more of a reaction than he'd gotten from the man when he'd interrogated him.

Cahill looked up from between bloody fingers, then knelt and picked up the knife.

He walked slowly — he wanted Ewan to

have time to think about what was going to happen when he arrived, that was clear. Ewan sighed and leaned his head back against the tree. He wouldn't give the man the satisfaction. His fingers still scrambled against the knots at his wrist, the task slightly easier since he'd freed up the barest bit more space by loosening the rope. It wasn't enough though.

He thought of Marlie's smile in the dreary prison yard, of the curve of her bare shoulder when she'd walked into the shed with Tobias. Of her mouth against his as she took him inside of her, the sweetest pleasure he'd ever known. He opened his eyes, ready to face his death, and the nausea hit him again because there was Marlie, exactly where she shouldn't have been.

She was running up at Cahill from behind, a rock hefted over her head with two hands, her expression tied between fury and fear.

Ewan opened his mouth to bait Cahill, to distract him, but there was no time. Marlie moved fast, but not fast enough. Cahill noticed her just as she lunged, ducking out of the way so that the rock hit him, but only a glancing blow. Marlie stumbled but didn't fall, whirling and backing up as he advanced on her.

"Fancy," he said, and the relish in his

voice sent a chill down Ewan's spine. It was the first time Ewan had heard him emote, and the enjoyment in his tone was that of a cat that had stumbled upon a hapless rodent. "I didn't think I'd see you again, but God must be smiling down on me tonight."

Marlie didn't answer, just stared at him with chattering teeth. She moved from foot to foot, as if debating whether to run or attack.

"Run, Marlie," Ewan said. He regretted it instantly; when he saw the smirk that turned up Cahill's mouth he understood he'd just delivered Cahill his trump card.

The man lunged forward, a feint that worked perfectly. Marlie started and threw the rock in the direction he had lunged toward, but Cahill was already pivoting out of the way. The rock landed with a thud, leaving Marlie defenseless and Cahill straightened from his crouch, his wicked knife catching the scant moonlight.

He began his approach and Marlie turned to run, her panicked gaze skittering over Ewan as she did. The fear in her eyes sent a spike into his chest.

No.

Cahill tackled her from behind, buckling her at the knees and holding her legs tight as he pulled himself up the length of her body. Ewan growled in frustration, and leaned all his weight forward, ignoring the shooting pain in his legs. His gaze was pinned to Marlie and his mind was focused on his hands, slick with sweat and pulling slowly through the space he'd eked out in the knotted rope. He pulled and the rope caught at the meat of his palms. Ewan surged forward, using his leg as leverage so that he was nearly standing against the tree parallel to the ground, pushing himself forward and pulling his hands through the rope.

In front of him, Cahill had turned Marlie on her back and had one hand at her throat. "Told ya you wouldn't last five minutes," he said.

Marlie grasped at his hand, her feet kicking, mouth opening and closing as she fought for air.

No!

Ewan gave one last heave, felt the blood spurting at his thigh at the same time he felt his hands slip through the rope. For a moment he was in freefall, then he landed facedown, his injured legs slamming into the ground and shooting a pain through him that made him retch. But Marlie needed him. He pulled himself to a crouch and dragged himself toward them. The abandoned rock lay a few feet away from Marlie's kicking legs and he hoisted it up and drew his arm back.

"Cahill." The man looked up at him, his face a mask of excitement, and Ewan swung his fist forward with all his might, the rock facing outward. The blow caught Cahill in the temple with a horrifying smack and he flew off Marlie's prone form.

Ewan's arm shook from the force of the impact but he tightened his hold on the rock and advanced, ready to finish the job he had started so long ago. Ewan kneeled beside the bloody Cahill and held the rock up high over his head. Cahill's eyes fluttered open and their gazes locked, but then his eyes went unfocused and closed again. Behind him Ewan could hear Marlie coughing and by the time he glanced her way she had rolled to her side and was looking at him. She didn't say anything, likely couldn't, but she didn't give him any indication of what she wanted, either.

He would have to decide for himself.

"Perhaps you are exactly the kind of man you're supposed to be."

He held the rock high, breathing heavily, then let it drop. It landed beside Cahill's head and Ewan released a ragged breath.

Even that movement he could feel in his leg.

Marlie appeared beside him, breathing heavily, too. In one hand she held the long knife and in the other the length of rope that had bound him to the tree. Together, they hog-tied Cahill as best they could.

"What happened to Bill and the others?"

"I slipped out of the cave and into the trees, and then gunfire broke out behind me."

Ewan tried to stand and she came beside him, leaning down so he could hook his arm over her shoulder.

"Let's get away from this place, although Home Guard could be anywhere." Ewan tried to think but his legs pained him and his head was spinning.

"Come. You're losing blood and I have to tend to you," she said.

"You should leave me and go," Ewan said. The words were as painful to him as his wounds.

"Don't be ridiculous," she said. Was that anger in her tone?

"Marlie, be logical. You've already insisted that we must go our separate ways when we reach Tennessee. I don't agree with this, but I'll respect it. I'm injured; why wait for an arbitrary geographical line? Be reasonable."

She didn't say anything, just kept holding up his weight as they moved into the forest. She was dragging him more than carrying him, and Ewan knew they wouldn't get far.

"How is your leg?" she asked after they had made some progress.

"Manageable."

"I take it that means you need to rest now." She stopped and eased him back against a tree. "I can't see. Do you know what your injuries are?"

"One leg is broken, one is stabbed and bleeding heavily."

"Jesus, Ewan, why didn't you tell me you've been bleeding all this time?"

He heard the sound of ripping fabric and then her hand found his in the darkness. "Guide me to the wound," she said. He placed her hands over his thighs, but his arms felt heavy. He was feeling lethargic all around, in fact.

"I think I may have lost more blood than I realized," he said. "I feel like I need to sleep though I'm aware that I'm not tired."

"No, Ewan." Her hand was over the wound in his thigh and she pressed down on it, the sharp pain reviving him a bit. She worked as quickly as she could without much assistance from him, passing a strip of fabric round his thigh to stop the bleeding.

His eyes struggled to focus on her face in the darkness of the trees, and in his peripheral vision he saw a falling star streak through the night sky.

"I wish . . . that wishing could make things so," he said. He hadn't been entirely aware he was speaking aloud until Marlie responded.

"Why is that?" she asked. She was busy cutting through his other pants leg. He lifted her hand to his face.

"Because then I'd wish that you'd be safe once I die," he said. "Because I love you."

Her hands paused and one came to rest on his against her face.

"You're not going to die," she said. "If it's come to this, I advise you to save your wishes for something more useful, Socrates."

"Perhaps wishing that a beautiful woman with one green eye, one brown, would have me?"

He heard a hitch in her breath, then felt the back of her hand run gently along his jaw, the briefest of caresses. Then her hand was back on his leg, the graze of her thumb over his shin making him wince in pain.

"That's a better wish," she said. "But save it."

Disappointment made Ewan's head spin

for a moment, then she added, "I'm not sure you'll have me after I set this bone."

There, in the worst pain of his life, teetering on the brink of passing out, and short a pint or two of blood, Ewan smiled and made his wish.

CHAPTER 27

Marlie didn't know what to do when she heard the sound of boots approaching. Ewan was unconscious, though the bleeding had stopped. She held her hands pressed to the wound, mind running through different cures. The truth was, she wasn't sure he *could* be cured. That was an outcome she couldn't accept.

She turned and caught sight of a lantern, and the reflection off of a familiar wicked sharp knife. She was nearly sick with fear but swallowed against the bile and stood. She wouldn't let Cahill hurt Ewan. She wouldn't. . . .

The swinging lantern grew closer, and that was when she realized it moved smoothly — there was no limp in the gait of the person who carried it.

"Any sight of them?" a familiar voice called out.

"Henry! Henry, help, it's —"

"Quiet."

The voice came from behind her, and when she turned she saw a man bent down beside Ewan, his hand at Ewan's pale throat. The man was darker than her, a rough beard obscuring half his face. But when he looked up, his brown eyes fixed her with a hard stare that chilled her as much as Cahill's had. No, not hard: There was a frightening, liquid anger there, barely constrained. He pulled one of Ewan's arms around his neck as Henry approached.

"This who you were looking for?" Henry asked as he approached, lantern in one hand and Cahill's knife in the other. Marlie did not ask how he acquired it or what had become of its owner.

"If it's McCall it is," the man lifting Ewan said.

"Who are you?" she asked.

Henry took a step closer, hand gripping the hilt of Cahill's knife more tightly. "He said he was with that Loyal League group you mentioned and asked for the ginger. I thought he was a friend."

"I'm not a friend," he said. "I'm a man who doesn't leave a debt unpaid. And I owe this man's brother a debt." He nearly spat the words, but his anger didn't seem to be directed toward Ewan. "Help me get him to

437

shelter."

Henry and a few of the other skulkers helped carry Ewan to a nearby cave where a portion of the men had relocated after the attack. The skulkers had won in the skirmish against the Home Guard in Randolph, then doubled back to find their home base under attack.

Marlie dosed Ewan with the dandelion root sedative and set his broken bone as best she could. He came to for a moment, then receded back into sleep. He'd lost so much blood. . . .

Henry constructed a sturdy splint made from the strong branches of cherrywood while she tended to the other skulkers.

When she returned to Ewan's side the man who had come upon them in the woods, Daniel, sat staring at him. She took a seat on the ground beside him and waited for him to speak.

When he'd ignored her for far longer than was comfortable, she asked, "You're with the Loyal League, you say?"

He nodded. "I was very surprised to learn there was an operative already on the ground. Particularly one I had never had any contact with. Particularly a Lynch." He leaned back and regarded her, a derisive smirk on his face. "A rich, sheltered miss playing at war with her white soldier boy?"

Marlie resented the condescension in his tone. "You know nothing about me, sir, and whether my family has money or not is irrelevant to my utility. To the Cause."

"And what utility is that?"

"I care for people. I heal them. A man like you might look down on that, but my maman did, and my maman's maman before that. It's a gift, and some in the Loyal League seem happy to receive it."

"And what will you do when you tire of the war? Or he tires of you?" He inclined his head toward Ewan. Daniel's blunt words skewered her, but she wouldn't flinch away from questions she would ask of herself.

"Ewan isn't the type to handle another's feelings so casually. He doesn't lie. And if I decide to make a go of it with him, I won't regret it, no matter the outcome."

"People change," Daniel insisted. "Or sometimes they don't, but you never truly knew them."

"Do you speak from experience?" she asked. "Already forgotten your sweetheart and expect the same of every man?"

Daniel sucked in a breath, and Marlie reached a hand out instinctively, touching his shoulder. He had spoken from experience, she realized, but not the one she had assumed. "I'm sorry. I should not have lashed out at you."

Daniel shook his head. "I should not have baited you into it. It seems these McCalls have all the luck when it comes to love."

"I don't —" Marlie stopped. "I'm not even sure what love is."

"I watched you face off against an unknown man with nothing but your bare hands in order to protect this McCall," Daniel said. "If you don't know what love is, you're well on your way to finding out." He gave a bitter laugh. "May you have a better try at it than I did."

Ewan awoke with the bright spring sunshine warming his face. He didn't know where he was: There was a real bed, and daylight shining through a window. A Negro man stood beside the window, one arm braced against the frame.

Ewan's mouth was very dry, but he managed one brittle word. "Marlie."

The man turned to him. For a moment, his expression was gentle, but it flattened to something unreadable when he realized Ewan was awake, not talking in his sleep. "The prodigal son awakens," the man said.

"Where is Marlie?" Ewan said, sitting up. His head swam, but the last thing he remembered was sitting with Marlie under a tree. Had she run when she had the chance? Had she been captured? His heart began thudding painfully and he reached a hand to his head.

"In Tennessee, as are you. She's making you some tisane and bone broth, as she has been for the duration of this trip," the man said. "I'm Daniel. Your brother and . . . sister-in-law had asked that we detectives keep an eye out for you, and they'd had word of a man fitting your description wanted for a prison break in the area."

"Is the Loyal League in the habit of using resources to hunt down missing family members?" Ewan asked irritably. He wanted to see Marlie. He couldn't trust the word of a strange man.

"No, but if an opportunity arises while on a mission, I'm not one to turn it down," the man said. "And the opportunity to draw even with your brother is not one I could pass up."

"Do you owe him so large a debt?" Ewan asked, confused. He knew Malcolm was charming, but the intensity in this man's face was at odds with his words.

"I begrudge him that debt. I begrudge him his wife. But he saved me and I cannot live with him holding that over me too."

441

The door opened and Marlie walked in carrying a tray. She was thinner than she had been, and her hair frizzed messily around her face, but the smile she gave him when she saw him sitting up was radiant.

"You're awake," she said, placing the tray on the table next to his bed.

"I certainly hope so. If this is a dream and I awaken in yet another Confederate prison, I'm going to be sorely disappointed."

She laughed, and the sound soothed away his aches and worries.

"Daniel is going to accompany you to Kentucky," she said.

Ewan glanced at the man. "Paying the debt still?"

Daniel nodded, then strode out of the room.

"There was a letter. From my aunt." She ladled up a spoonful of broth and fed it to him. Ewan savored the rich flavors, but his gaze was on Marlie's closed-off expression.

"She apologized. Said she loves me. Asked me to come back because Melody left soon after news of Cahill's death."

Ewan swallowed hard.

"Do you want to go back?" he asked.

Marlie inclined her head to the side. "I miss Sarah. I want to go home. But I don't think Lynchwood is my home any longer.

I'll have to search for a new one."

Ewan opened his mouth to speak, but found his lips wrapped around the spoon.

"My contact with the Loyal League has asked if I would accompany you and Daniel," Marlie said. "He says there are places along the way where my work can be useful, and he'd like me to teach some of their operatives."

Ewan felt both pride and worry, but pushed away the latter.

"That's wonderful, Marlie," he said. "And once I make it home?"

She spooned up some broth for him, her smile faltering.

"We'll see, Socrates. Open up."

"Don't forget we still have to finish the translation," he said before closing his mouth around the spoon. It seemed he wasn't above manipulation.

Epilogue

Kentucky, two months later

"Are you sure this is the proper placement?"

Marlie looked up from where she was tightening a bolt on the still she and Ewan had been constructing over the last two weeks and stared at him. He nodded abruptly, and cleared his throat.

"Right. It's your design so you would know if it wasn't."

"Correct," she said, bending over to resume her work.

He took a step closer to her, leaned his cane against the worktable in the spare room of his small home, and rested both of his hands on the flare of her waist. "In fact, I think perhaps you only asked me to assist you because you were tired of weeks of my bothersome behavior while I convalesced."

"Whatever do you mean?" she asked, standing and turning to face him. His fingertips remained in place as she turned, tracing the circumference of her waist through the gingham dress she wore and then locking behind her back when her nose was a few inches from his. His eyes were warm with mirth, closer to sky blue.

"My need for distraction in the weeks after we finished translating your mother's book was obvious. Did you or did you not threaten to break my other leg if I didn't stop trying to get up and walk about?"

"That was not a threat, it was a sound medical recommendation, seconded by your doctor and your mother, I might add," she said. "Sometimes a patient must be coerced into health."

"And sometimes a patient is very amenable to coercion, depending on the person doing the coercing," he said, pulling her closer into his embrace and nuzzling against her neck. "You can only blame yourself for giving me a good reason to recover more quickly."

And there it was. Ewan *was* recovering quickly, which meant it was time to bring up the topic he had been steadfastly avoiding.

"The still is almost in working order, too. It should survive its impending move with no problem," she said.

His arms pressed into her waist and then

released, as if he had realized he was tightening his hold on her.

"I thought we agreed this was the best room for it," he said. The mirth had left his eyes.

"In this house, yes," she said. "But I noticed a room for rent in town that will rent to Negroes, above the pharmacy, actually, and I think now that you're fully mobile perhaps I should relocate."

She couldn't look at him as she said it. She enjoyed their daily meals, and waking up beside him in bed — even the time passed with his mother when she came by to check on her boy. But she had also enjoyed her life with Sarah, and that didn't change the fact that she had been living, and loved, under false pretenses.

"I don't understand. I thought that you would stay here with me," he said. "Malcolm will be here in a few days with his wife. I want you here to meet them."

"I can come by for dinner," she said. She picked up a wrench and began tightening bolts, but Ewan placed his hand over hers, staying the motion.

"No. I want you *here*," he said.

"Why?" she asked.

"Because we get along well," he said. "And I'm used to having you here."

"We can get along well even if I don't live with you," she said, trying to hide her disappointment. "And being used to someone is not the same as —"

She stopped herself before saying too much.

"Marlie." His expression pinched. "Do you not like being with me? I know I'm difficult and I won't lie and say I'll change completely, but I can modify my behavior if necessary."

"You're fine as you are," she said. *I love you as you are.*

"Then why do you insist on leaving?"

Marlie wasn't quite sure herself. Perhaps because she had no idea what she was to Ewan, though she didn't doubt he cared. Because she was frightened of never being able to move on once he decided to hurt her, as everyone in her life had.

"Well, I feel foolish," he said. He dug into the pocket of his jacket. "Am I to assume you have no interest in this?"

Marlie's heart stopped at the sight of the shining band in his hand.

"What is that?" she asked.

"It's a gold ring, used to signify the desire to spend the rest of one's life with another human."

"Why?" she asked.

"Well, primarily because one has found the sole person who makes them feel at peace and whom they can't imagine spending a single day without."

"Ewan," she said.

"Marlie?" He raised his brows.

"Tell me why."

"Because I love you, which you are aware of but continue to operate under the false assumption that this is some lark. I thought perhaps wearing this ring might serve as a reminder of my commitment to you. And hopefully yours to me, if that's what you wish."

She was staring at the ring, her happiness warring with her fear.

"But . . ."

"If you want me to get on one knee that's not possible right now, but I'll help you onto the table beside the still if that makes this more romantic for you."

She stuttered out something between laughter and a sob.

"I need time," she said. If he was disappointed he hid it well, but that wouldn't be out of the ordinary for Ewan.

"Of course," he said. "I'll just remind you I was planning to ask before you announced you were leaving, so don't think this is in reaction to anything other than my desire to be with you."

His cheeks went pink and he cleared his throat before grabbing his cane and making his way toward the door.

Marlie stood holding her wrench. She thought of the last pages of her mother's book, and the hopes and wishes she'd shared for Marlie.

"I know that you will find great love in this world, as well as success, not because of that science you now hold so dear but because I have seen it in my dreams and I have felt it in my bones. I only hope you understand what you deserve better than I did. When the time comes, close your eyes and listen to your heart, which may lead you astray but will always guide you to the path you were meant to take."

Marlie closed her eyes and clutched the wrench in her hand.

"Ewan?"

There was the sound of his cane thudding against the floor, and then silence. "Yes?"

"Yes."

"Is that your answer? Already?"

"Have you changed your mind?" She opened her eyes and began walking to him.

"Well, no. I had just begun to form a plan to make you change *your* mind, and now I've got to scrap it."

She walked into his embrace and sighed as his lips brushed her cheek. "You know, I've come to enjoy debating with you. Feel free to convince me at your leisure."

He kissed her then, as was only logical.

ACKNOWLEDGMENTS

First and foremost, I'd like to thank the Kensington Publishing team for their unerring support and guidance with the Loyal League series. Meeting and working with everyone at Kensington has been a pleasure.

I'd also like to thank Bree, Courtney, Alisha, and Rebekah for having my back when the going gets tough; Lena for being a great partner in crime; Julia for always helping put things in perspective; and the many other authors who form an awesome support network.

Lastly, I'd like to thank the readers who make writing these books worthwhile. Every tweet, email, and message help me immeasurably.

AUTHOR'S NOTE

One of the reasons I enjoy writing about the Civil War is the research. (This is paradoxical because the research is also the hardest part.) Because the pop culture narrative has been flattened into a few two-dimensional stories — Southern belles, brothers versus brothers, etc. — finding a rich and varying American history in my research, and being able to use this history in my books, have been wonderful.

In *A Hope Divided,* I feature Southerners who, for a variety of reasons, fought back against the Confederacy on their own soil. This is fascinating to me, viewed through the lens of Southern pride's near erasure of these narratives. Some of these people were Quakers or abolitionists, others simply did not agree with the secession, but all provide a more nuanced view than has been provided in most studies of Northern and Southern citizens during the war. There were also Unionists, like Sarah Lynch (based on Richmond, Virginia's Elizabeth van Lew), all over the South, engaged in the work of subverting the Confederacy.

I've listed some reading materials, but more and more research is coming out about this, after years of Lost Cause revisionism, and I hope this helps Americans see that even when we seem the most divided, there are always, *always,* people fighting for freedom in places we are told there are none. That should not be forgotten.

SELECTED BIBLIOGRAPHY

The following is a selection of the books used to research this novel:

Abbott, Karen. *Liar, Temptress, Soldier, Spy: Four Women Undercover in the Civil War.* New York: HarperCollins, 2014.

Auman, William T. *Civil War in the North Carolina Quaker Belt: The Confederate Campaign Against Peace Agitators, Deserters, and Draft Dodgers.* Jefferson, NC: McFarland & Company, Inc., Publishers, 2014.

Bynum, Victoria E. *The Long Shadow of the Civil War: Southern Dissent and Its Legacies.* Chapel Hill, NC: University of North Carolina Press, 2010.

Cooper, Alonzo. *In and Out of Rebel Prisons.* Oswego, NY: R. J. Oliphant, 1888.

Jordan, Robert Paul. *The Civil War.* Washington, DC: National Geographic Society, 1969.

Lause, Mark A. *A Secret Society History of the Civil War.* Champaign, IL: University of Illinois Press, 2011.

McPherson, James M. *Battle Cry of Freedom.* New York: Oxford University Press, 2003.

Pratt, Fletcher. *The Civil War in Pictures.* Garden City, NY: Garden City Books, 1955.

Sprague, Homer B. *Lights and Shadows in a Confederate Prison.* New York: The Knickerbocker Press, 1915.

Van Doren Stern, Philip. *Secret Missions of the Civil War.* Westport, CT: Praeger, 1959.

■ ■ ■ ■

READING GROUP GUIDE: A HOPE DIVIDED

ALYSSA COLE

■ ■ ■ ■

ABOUT THIS GUIDE

The suggested questions are included to enhance your group's reading of Alyssa Cole's *A Hope Divided.*

DISCUSSION QUESTIONS

1. Marlie is living with her father's side of the family, the Lynches, when she encounters Ewan. The Lynches are Unionists, people who supported the Union while living in the South. Did you know anything about Unionists and their attempts to aid the North during the war?

2. Many of the men imprisoned with Ewan are "deserters" and "skulkers," men who refuse to fight for the Confederacy and have taken up arms. Skulkers often lived in the forests near their homes, and fought guerrilla-style warfare against the soldiers and militia men tasked with catching draft dodgers. What were some of the reasons these men (and women) gave for resisting the Confederacy?

3. With the men either drafted or fighting Confederate soldiers, the wives and fami-

lies of the deserters often suffered, particularly because they were shunned by their secessionist neighbors and families. What were some of the challenges they faced?

4. Marlie attempts to move past the spiritual roots of her work with medicinal plants and focus on science. How does this help her survive? And what makes her change her mind?

5. Marlie makes a disturbing discovery about her lineage. Why does this affect her feelings for Ewan, and how does she overcome this?

6. Ewan's work for the Union cause made him feel unworthy of affection. How does he come to terms with his past, and his future? Did you agree with this?

ABOUT THE AUTHOR

Alyssa Cole is a science editor, pop culture nerd, and romance junkie who recently moved to the Caribbean and occasionally returns to her fast-paced NYC life. Her writing has been featured in publications including *Vulture* (*New York Magazine*'s entertainment blog), *Heroes and Heartbreakers,* and *The Toast.* When she's not busy writing, traveling, and learning French, she can be found watching anime with her real life romance hero or tending to her herd of pets.